MW00928599

THE
NIGHTHOUSE
KEEPER

THE NIGHT KEE

Also by Lora Senf

The Clackity

HOUSE
PER

A Blight Harbor Novel

LORA SENF

Illustrated by
ALFREDO CÁCERES

 ATHENEUM BOOKS FOR YOUNG READERS
New York London Toronto Sydney New Delhi

ATHENEUM BOOKS FOR YOUNG READERS

An imprint of Simon & Schuster Children's Publishing Division
1230 Avenue of the Americas, New York, New York 10020

This book is a work of fiction. Any references to historical events, real people,
or real places are used fictitiously. Other names, characters, places, and events
are products of the author's imagination, and any resemblance to actual
events or places or persons, living or dead, is entirely coincidental.

Text © 2023 by Lora Senf
Jacket illustration © 2023 by Alfredo Cáceres
Jacket design by Karyn Lee © 2023 by Simon & Schuster, Inc.
Interior illustration © 2023 by Alfredo Cáceres
All rights reserved, including the right of reproduction in whole or in part in any form.

ATHENEUM BOOKS FOR YOUNG READERS is a registered trademark of
Simon & Schuster, Inc. Atheneum logo is a trademark of Simon & Schuster, Inc.
For information about special discounts for bulk purchases, please contact Simon & Schuster
Special Sales at 1-866-506-1949 or business@simonandschuster.com.
The Simon & Schuster Speakers Bureau can bring authors to your live event. For more
information or to book an event, contact the Simon & Schuster Speakers Bureau at
1-866-248-3049 or visit our website at www.simonspeakers.com.
Interior design by Karyn Lee
The text for this book was set in Celeste OT.
The illustrations for this book were rendered digitally.
Manufactured in the United States of America
0923 BVG
First Edition
2 4 6 8 10 9 7 5 3 1
Library of Congress Cataloging-in-Publication Data
Names: Senf, Lora, author. | Cáceres, Alfredo, 1983– illustrator.
Title: The nighthouse keeper : a Blight Harbor novel / Lora Senf ; illustrated by Alfredo Cáceres.
Description: First edition. | New York : Atheneum Books for Young Readers, 2023. | Series:
Blight Harbor ; 2 | Audience: Ages 10–12. | Audience: Grades 4–6. | Summary: When Evie Von
Rathe discovers that the ghosts in Blight Harbor are disappearing, she teams up with a young
ghost named Lark and ventures into the Dark Sun Side, where she unravels a personal mystery
and battles with shadow creatures to reach the Nighthouse and release the trapped souls.
Identifiers: LCCN 2023009876 (print) | LCCN 2023009877 (ebook) |
ISBN 9781665934633 (hardcover) | ISBN 9781665934596 (ebook)
Subjects: CYAC: Ghosts—Fiction. | Mystery and detective stories. |
LCGFT: Thrillers (Fiction) | Novels.
Classification: LCC PZ7.1.S45 Ni 2023 (print) | LCC PZ7.1.S45 (ebook) | DDC [Fic]—dc23
LC record available at https://lccn.loc.gov/2023009876
LC ebook record available at https://lccn.loc.gov/2023009877

To Miriam
and Martin.

Because you are kind
and brave
and all the proof I need
that magic is real.

♥

THE
NIGHTHOUSE
KEEPER

THE BLIGHT HARBOR HERALD

July 15

Dear Desdemona,

My family needs your help. Our beloved house ghost, August, has disappeared. We've always treated him like part of the family, and he was present for every celebration and holiday. We even kept a room for him (except, of course, when we had houseguests). We've looked everywhere. Even the basement, which he <u>hated</u>.

I guess we did something to upset him. We would do anything to make it right.

What can we do to get our friend back?

Sincerely,

Brokenhearted in Blight Harbor

Dearest Brokenhearted,

First, my condolences. It is always hard to lose a loved one, even when that loved one is long departed. It sounds as though your dear August has moved on. This is a perfectly natural part of the afterlife and happens to every specter. Where your August has moved on to is one of the great mysteries of both this world and the next. I suggest you have a celebration of the afterlife for your August and spend time remembering the things about him that made him special to your family.

Allow me to add one more thought: the otherworldly have very little to fear. If August was reluctant to enter your basement, you may well have a concern. For the safety of you and your loved ones, I suggest you vacate the house immediately until you have the space thoroughly spiritually cleansed. An exorcism may be in order.

I hope this brings you peace.

Kindest regards,

Desdemona Von Rathe

PART ONE

Welcome Back

"I'm sorry, Evie. She's gone." Mr. Seong's words and the sadness in his kind eyes made my heart drop like a rock right into my stomach.

"Gone where?" I asked, but I was afraid I already knew. Florence—the ghost that lived in my best friend, Maggie's, house—had moved on. To where, I wasn't sure, but it had happened. It was *supposed* to happen. Ghosts weren't meant to stay forever. Eventually, they all left.

"Off to wherever they go, I suppose." Mr. Seong looked deflated. He stood in the doorway, with only an empty and quiet house behind him. I'd been concerned about Florence being lonely while Maggie and her mom were away for the summer, but I'd never once considered that Maggie's poor dad might have been lonely too.

"When?" I'd planned to stop by and visit Florence every few days while my friend was on her trip. And I did. At first. But since my "adventure" with The Clackity and Pope in the strange neighborhood with the purple sky, I hadn't really gone out much (Des was keeping me pretty close). So, after weeks of meaning to, I'd finally gotten around to visiting Florence, only to discover that I was too late.

As sad as I was, I was even more surprised that Florence hadn't waited for Maggie before she left for good. Maggie had always been the ghost's favorite, and the idea that Florence would go without saying goodbye felt wrong.

"I wish I knew. Last night, maybe? Early this morning?" He ran a hand through his dark hair and stared down at his slippered feet.

"She didn't even say goodbye to *you*? What did her note say?" Blight Harbor's house ghosts generally found a way to communicate with the people they lived with. They couldn't talk (at least, not in a way that most people could hear), but they could type, or write, or draw pictures. Florence usually used the big chalkboard in the Seongs' kitchen if she wanted to say something.

When Mr. Seong looked back up at me, there were tears in his eyes. "No note. Nothing. Do me a favor and don't tell Maggie, okay? It'll ruin her trip, and there's nothing to be done about it, anyway."

Now there were tears in my eyes too. Florence had been part of the Seong family since before Maggie was even born. I'd been friends with Maggie for so long that the ghost had been like family to me, too. She'd been there for birthdays and holidays and even those hard days when you'd just needed someone to listen. Ghosts were generally good listeners—better than people, for sure—and sometimes I had a lot that I needed to say. "I don't understand how she could just leave like that."

"I know, Evie." Mr. Seong came out onto the porch and gave me an awkward side hug. It was a pretty big gesture for him. "If it was her time, it was her time. Maybe . . . maybe saying goodbye was just too hard?"

"Maybe," I managed. But I didn't believe it. Despite the cold and heavy sadness, there was still a bright, hot little spot in the middle of me that said something wasn't right. Bird settled into his favorite place on my collarbone and nudged me with his tiny head. The little black tattoo sparrow had been with me for just a few weeks, but we already understood one another. I knew my buddy was trying to comfort me.

I turned away so that my best friend's dad (and the elementary school principal) wouldn't see my tears. Mr. Seong had seen me cry plenty of times, but he didn't need to today. He was sad enough already. I made my way down the porch steps and to my bike.

From behind me, Mr. Seong called softly, "Please, Evie. Don't tell Maggie. She'll be home soon enough."

"I promise," I said over my shoulder.

And I meant it. I wouldn't tell Maggie. But I was absolutely going to tell my aunt Desdemona.

To my surprise, Des was on the front porch, sitting on the stairs with her knees bouncing as restlessly as mine often did. She waved with one hand while picking something out of her tangle of dark curls with the other. I'd expected her to be at her weekly community meeting. I had no idea what she met *about,* or even who she met *with,* but she never missed a week.

"Meeting get canceled?" I called as I parked my bike in the driveway and crossed the lawn.

Des shook her head. "Not canceled. We took a break. I came here to get you, and then we're going back." She pulled at her hair again and this time found what she was looking for. A small silhouette of a sparrow not much larger than a fat honeybee came free of her thick hair. Pinching the dark shape of the bird gently between two fingers, Des held it in front of her. "Go back to where you belong," she said, releasing the tiny shadow creature.

The sparrow fluttered back to the wall of our enclosed porch and joined the rest of the flock that had followed us home from the abattoir where we'd first met them. I had a shadow creature of my very own—Bird, the little living tattoo who'd been with me since that awful, surreal day I'd met The Clackity.

Bird fluttered his wings as if to say hi to his friends, but he stayed put on my skin.

"What? Why?" The sounds that came from my mouth probably sounded more like whines than questions. I'd never attended one of Aunt D's boring Friends of Blight Harbor meetings, and I wasn't interested in changing that fact—especially right then. I was sad and worried, and I didn't want to listen to a bunch of old people argue about street signs or the community garden or whatever it was they did. "Maybe next time."

"Nope. You're coming," Des said. She didn't use that responsible-adult-in-charge voice often, but when she did, there was no use arguing with her. I tried anyway.

"Des, I'll be fine. Seriously. Nothing's going to happen to me between the kitchen and the couch." Aunt D normally didn't have a problem leaving me alone for a few hours, but ever since my—*our*—recent adventure, she'd kept a closer watch on me.

She shook her head again. "It's not that. We need you there today."

"You do?" What could they possibly need me for? I had zero opinion on the shrubs lining the sidewalks or the paint color of the post office.

"We do. Get in the car. I'll explain on the way." She was already up and heading toward her SUV.

There was no arguing with Des when she was set on something, and she seemed to be set on this. Besides, I was a little curious to find out why a bunch of adults needed a twelve-year-old at the meeting. "Fine. I have something to tell you, too."

"I'll drive slow," she said.

I went first, telling Aunt D about Florence.

I hadn't noticed the dark circles that had formed under Desdemona's eyes until they narrowed in grim concern. She listened quietly and then said, "It's worse than we thought."

"'We' who?" I asked.

It didn't take me long to find out.

What I learned on the short car ride between our house and the meeting hall was that Aunt Desdemona did, in fact, belong to a community group. But it was *not* a group that met to discuss parks and stop signs and other things a "normal" citizen group might be interested in. Instead, this group focused on otherworldly issues that cropped up in Blight Harbor from time to time. Not little stuff like the problems Des wrote about in her advice column. This group discussed bigger problems that affected the whole town, like an unexpected rise in the poltergeist population or spells-turned-curses cast by people who had no business (or experience) casting them. They were like a neighborhood watch, but way cooler and a lot weirder.

I wasn't exactly surprised that Blight Harbor had a group like that. More than anything, I was irritated and a little hurt that I hadn't known my aunt was part of it. I sulked on purpose, scooting as far from Des as I could and resting my head on the window. "You lied. We don't lie to each other."

"I most certainly did not lie," Des said, glancing over at me. "You never asked."

"Shouldn't have to."

"You're a child, Evelyn. You can't be involved in everything."

"I. Am not. A child," I said more loudly than was necessary, since we were in the same car. I could feel my face burning. I was almost as tall as Des and nearly thirteen. Plus, I'd been on an epic journey to save *her* from certain doom less than a month ago. It wasn't fair for Des to play the you're-only-a-kid card.

"We'll discuss this later," Des said in that tone I was starting to get used to—the one that said not to argue too much. "You'll learn a lot at the meeting."

"I still don't know why you need me," I said, trying to sound less annoyed than I felt.

"Because," Des said as she parked the black SUV in front of Irv's Clays and Glazes, a store I'd never been in, "we think another door has opened. And you were the last person to go through one."

I had no idea what to say to that.

"Well, to go through and come back," Desdemona added.

I sat, frozen.

Des was quiet, waiting for me to process.

Finally, "What do you mean another door has opened?"

"A door," Aunt D repeated as she turned to face me, "like the one you went through in the abattoir."

"But . . . but you went through too."

"I did, but you came back."

I shook my head. It felt like my brain was full of bees and tree sap as I remembered the vile fog from that otherworld that had made all my worst memories come flooding back. The fog I'd walked through not once but twice. "But you came back too."

"Not on my own, I didn't. You brought me. You carried me."

"But I . . ."

"Let's go inside." Des's voice was gentle but firm. "There's a lot you're about to learn. Questions later."

My hand was shaking when I went to open the car

door. It hadn't done that in a while. I'd thought I was done with doors to weird places. I'd thought that whole . . . adventure . . . was behind me. Suddenly I wasn't so sure. Des put her hand on my arm. Sometimes my nerves made me feel like I'd float right up and away like a helium balloon. The gentle pressure from Des's touch was reassuring. My feet stayed on the ground.

We were the only people inside Irv's Clays and Glazes—there were no customers or even a shopkeeper to be seen. The air was thick with ceramic grit, and the sun fought its way through windows that looked like they'd been washed with a paper towel covered in grease. The light that made its way in shone (sort of) on dusty counters and dustier shelves. Bottles and jars and boxes were strewn about, each covered in a thin layer of silt.

Along another wall stood three tables that looked like they'd come from the piles of free stuff people left out on their lawn after a yard sale. The tables were cluttered with cups and bowls and vases and a few objects so misshapen, I couldn't tell what they were supposed to be. The pottery in the shop made my terrible art class projects look like masterpieces.

Judging by the coat of dust on everything, if anyone ever bought anything from Irv's, it didn't happen very often. For all I knew, no one ever shopped there. The more I thought about it, the surer I was that I'd never seen anyone come in or out of the store. In fact, if there even was an Irv, I couldn't remember having ever met him, which was odd—in a small town like Blight Harbor, shop owners were known by just about everyone.

Even weirder than all that was the fact that I couldn't even remember having noticed the *shop* before, despite it being right next to Mrs. Bradbury's Sweets and Teas, which was basically the best place on the planet. (Mrs. Bradbury kept special candy behind the counter, and for fifty cents and the promise of one good deed, you could have a bright gem of hard candy, guaranteed to taste like whatever it was you most wanted. Baklava? Your grandmother's pumpkin pie? Sunshine? Mrs. Bradbury had it all.)

"Where is everyone, and why are we . . . ?" I began to ask.

"Questions later," Des reminded me.

We walked behind the grimy front counter and made our way to a door I hadn't noticed before. As Des put her hand on the doorknob, I asked, "Are you sure? That I'm supposed to be here, I mean."

Des nodded. "We all agreed."

We walked into a spacious room that couldn't have been more different from the rest of the shop. Bright sun streamed through pristine windows, and everything shone in the warm light. The smell of lemony furniture polish filled the air. Like the first room, the walls here were lined with shelves, but the bottles and jars on them were neatly organized and filled with colorful liquids and powders and dried plants and flowers. And books—there were so many books, it was hard to imagine there was space for even one more. I liked this room immediately.

Couches and chairs were arranged in a big circle, and

on those seats were blankets and throws in more colors than I could count, each clearly handmade—knitted or crocheted or something. In the middle of all that was a large wooden table, round and low to the ground. On it was what appeared to be an in-progress Scrabble game and different decks of tarot cards, all mixed together. Some cards were in piles, while others were laid out, waiting to be read.

The room was bright and warm and interesting, but not as interesting as the people in it.

It was Lily I saw first—dressed in her usual multiple shades of brown and wearing her inch-thick glasses—and I was glad for it. She smiled from a small, overstuffed couch and gave me a wave. Lily was Blight Harbor's head librarian, the first real witch I'd ever met, and my second-best person (after Aunt Des). I wondered who was working at the library with both of us here and hoped for their sake they remembered to dust—nothing spun Lily up like a dusty library.

On the couch across from Lily sat the Blight Harbor chief of police, Mary McCreary. She wasn't in uniform and she didn't look very official except for her expression, which was serious and stern. Only her brown hands, twisting and untwisting a turquoise-colored blanket, indicated that she might have been nervous about something.

Chief Mary was talking quietly with a man I immediately recognized as Steve Hammond, the mayor's husband. While Mayor Mordelle-Hammond was thought to have some vampire lineage in her family tree, her husband had always seemed as regular as a person could be. He was a nice guy with a big farm-boy smile and light, perpetually sunburned skin. Only there was no smile today. Steve (he hated being called Mr. Hammond) wore a worried look that I'd never seen on him before.

In the chair next to Steve was a man I didn't recognize. He was . . . well, I can't remember exactly what he looked like. He was the least interesting person I'd ever seen. That sounds mean, but it isn't supposed to be; it's just that there was nothing at all about him that made any sort of impression. As soon as I shifted my eyes from him, I forgot what he looked like. Blink, and when I opened my eyes, it was like seeing him for the first time. It almost made me dizzy.

The unrememberable man wasn't talking to anyone or doing anything, just looking out the window. At least, I thought that was what he was doing. The only memorable thing about him was the bright orange baseball cap on his head. On the cap was an odd enamel pin, a solid and shiny black circle about the size of a fifty-cent piece. In a way, I guess he was both the least and the most interesting person I'd ever seen.

On the other side of the room, Pastor Mike Sanchez listened intently to the conversation between Steve and Chief Mary. He didn't look as much like a pastor as he did a dad going to a baseball game, which he might have been, since his three boys all played ball.

All five people turned in our direction as we walked into the room.

"Evelyn, good to have you with us today," Pastor Mike

said cheerily. It felt like I was being welcomed into his congregation.

I muttered a thanks as Des sat on the same couch as Lily, leaving enough room for me to fit between them. Sitting, I scooted as far back into the couch as I could go.

"Does she know why she's here?" asked Lily. She gave my arm a squeeze that said, *Glad you joined us. Stop worrying so much. This is fine.*

"Just the basics," said Des, as serious as I'd ever heard her. "That a door has likely opened, and that she knows more about doors, and about getting through them, than the rest of us."

"More than anyone," said Steve.

"Almost," said a soft voice from the other side of the room. It took me a second to register that the voice came from the man in the orange cap. I'd forgotten all about him.

"Yes," agreed Steve, sounding embarrassed. "Almost."

"Can someone please tell me what's going on?" I asked, trying to sound as polite as possible despite the twitchy, nervous feeling in my hands and feet.

"Des, I think that's your call," said Chief Mary softly.

Aunt D sat quietly for a moment, her hands in her lap and her eyes turned up toward the ceiling. I'd seen that pose before: she was making a decision. Finally she turned to me. "Evie, do you know where Blight Harbor gets its name?"

I didn't, so I shook my head.

Des took my hand as she began. It was a little embarrassing, but I didn't pull away. "As you know, this town is full of wonders—unusual and otherworldly. What we consider a part of our community—neighbors, if you will—others consider curses. Or bad omens. Or *blights*." She let go of my hand so she could gesture with hers. "Have you ever heard a ghost being called a blight?"

I shook my head no again, but it kind of made sense—*if* you were the sort of person who thought that ghosts were bad—to call them that. With a couple of *very* notable exceptions, most of the ghosts I'd met were perfectly nice people. *Blight* felt like an offensive word to use.

Des went on. "Well, this place is a safe place for those spirits. A *harbor*. So, Blight Harbor." She raised an eyebrow, asking me if I was following her.

I nodded.

"Otherworldly beings aren't here by accident. Blight Harbor is built on thin ground, and the borders between here and elsewhere are very . . ." She paused, looking for the right word.

"Porous," said the strange man. I'd nearly forgotten him again, but his orange cap helped, almost like a pin keeping him in place in my mind.

"Yes," Aunt D agreed, "the borders are porous."

"When you say 'elsewhere,' do you mean the place where I—we—went last month? The place through the door in the abattoir?"

"I do," Des said. "It doesn't have a name, at least not one that we know of, but it's been called the Dark Sun Side for as long as anyone can remember."

The name was as good as any I could think of for

that otherworld with the purple sky and bright black sun. "I know that it's a real place. I mean, Lily's cousins live there. But I thought when The"—I didn't even want to say its name out loud; it tasted bitter in my mouth, like speaking its name might summon it—"The Clackity . . . went away, the door did too."

"It did," Lily answered. "But that wasn't the only door. Evie, how do you think my cousins got here the night you came back?"

I could feel my face heating up because right then I felt really, really foolish. It had never occurred to me to ask how Jane, Martha, and Grey had traveled from their world to ours that night when they helped me undo the awful magic Pope had inflicted on my aunt.

"And that's the primary purpose of this little group," said Des, gesturing around the room. "To keep an eye on those doors and make sure they stay safely shut. We do our best to keep anyone or anything from coming or going without our knowing about it. And we watch for signs that doors are closing. Or, very rarely, we watch for signs that new ones are opening."

"It used to be rare," said Steve.

I had a million questions, but the first one that came out of my mouth was, "So why am I really here?"

The room was so quiet, I swear you could hear the sun shining. Des had worried eyes, and Lily wouldn't look at me. Steve looked down at his hands, Pastor Mike looked sick to his stomach, and Chief Mary stared out the window. I had no idea what the man in the orange cap was looking at.

Finally Des spoke up. "Honey, going in the doors is simple. You just . . . walk through. Coming back out . . . is much more complicated."

"Almost impossible. Doors stay in place in this world, but on the other side, they move. Or close. Or disappear," Chief Mary said quietly. There was an edge of sadness to her voice.

It seemed to me like maybe they were wrong, and I could clear that up for them pretty easily. "I came back just fine. And my door was exactly where I left it."

"Someone needs to tell her the rest," said the almost-invisible man.

I couldn't take it any longer. "Who *are* you?" I asked in what I'm sure was not my nicest or most patient voice.

"I'm Irv," he replied. "We've met before. Often, in fact. It's okay that you don't remember. Most people don't."

So *this* was Irv of Irv's Clays and Glazes. *Weird.* He was his very own mystery, but one that would have to wait for later. Not much later, though. His impermanence made me nervous. But just below my Irv-nervousness was something else. Something that had the sewn-up eye and sharp fingers of the panic I associated with the Dark Sun Side. Maybe I wasn't as finished with that place as I had hoped.

"You said there's more." I looked directly at Irv. Or, more accurately, at his cap. Trying to focus on his face was giving me a headache. "So tell me. What's going on?"

"Oh, if he tells you, you probably won't remember. No

offense, Irv," said Lily. She spoke a little too loudly, but that wasn't unusual.

"None taken," he replied.

This was getting us nowhere. I'd always wondered why adults spent so much time talking, and so little time doing. "Would someone please—" I started, but Chief Mary cut me off.

"Okay, Evie. Here's the deal. We have a situation in Blight Harbor. There have been reports of doors opening, doors we've never seen before. Only they're not staying open for long. It seems as soon as a door shows up, it's gone again. At the same time, a number of the town's ghosts have gone missing, with more gone each day." My heart skipped a beat as I thought about Florence. "It would be nice to believe it was just a case of choosing to move on at the same time—"

"To heaven," Pastor Mike interrupted. "Or—"

Chief Mary jumped in. "Sure. Maybe, but that's too much of a coincidence. We think there's a connection. Based on the timing, it appears the ghosts are going through the doors for some reason. Or being taken." For the first time since I'd entered the room, Mary actually sounded like the chief of police—assured and in charge. I was grateful, because it meant someone was finally telling me something.

"Evie," said Des, "tell them what you told me. About Florence."

So I did.

The room full of adults listened to me, and I could tell they were paying attention to every word. When I finished, they were quiet for what felt like a long time.

Finally Pastor Mike said, "That's enough to convince me. We have to do something to stop this."

"Honey," Aunt Desdemona said to me, "if they're going through the doors on their own, that's not a good thing, because we want them to someday move on. And if they get lost on the Dark Sun Side—if they can't find their doors back home—they'll never get to wherever it is they're supposed to end up. There's no moving on from the Dark Sun Side—it's like a spiderweb you get tangled up in, especially for our dearly departed neighbors. If they're being taken, well, that's worse, isn't it?"

Chief Mary continued, "You went in and came back without a problem. . . ."

"Oh, I had problems," I assured her. I'd had The Clackity and Pope and Mother Witch and seven impossible houses, and that was just the start of my list.

"Acknowledged. That was a scary, brave thing you did. But the fact is, when it was time for you to come back, you came back without *that* part being a problem. We need to figure out how, and why, because we've got to send a search party in after the ghosts. They're citizens as much as you and me, and we need to make sure they're safe."

I liked the way Mary talked to me, directly and without trying to soften things. She didn't treat me like I was too young or weak to understand.

"That's going to be dangerous," Steve said. "How can we be absolutely sure they're not leaving on their own?"

I didn't think he was asking for my opinion, but I was

the one who answered. "Because Florence wouldn't leave like that—without saying goodbye or leaving a note or anything. Without waiting for Maggie."

Desdemona took my fidgeting hand in hers. "Maybe she's fine. Maybe not. Either way, we need to find out. We're not much of a harbor for Florence or the rest of our spirit friends if we don't do our best to take care of them."

"And you want me to be part of the search party?" I was surprised to find that not only was I willing to go back to the Dark Sun Side, but I was kind of excited about it. Especially if it meant not having to go alone.

Des squeezed my hand hard enough to hurt a little. "Absolutely not."

The sharp, painful peck to my collarbone told me Bird agreed with her.

"Absolutely not," Des repeated firmly.

We were back in the car, and I was back to sulking. The meeting had ended when Chief Mary received a text. Another worried community member had reported a missing house ghost, and the chief wanted to personally look into every report.

"Then how am I supposed to help?" I was frustrated. What was the point of inviting me into the Dark Sun Society (at least, that was what I was already calling the group in my head) and not letting me actually *do* anything?

"They're going to want to hear your story when we meet next week. Not just the coming in and getting out, but all the parts in between. There might be something you say that shows us how you did it."

A thought occurred to me, and it made my hands sweat. "Des. When you went through that door in the abattoir, how were you planning to get out? If you knew all that stuff, you had to have thought about that, right?"

Silence from the seat next to me.

"*Right?*" I asked again, wiping my hands on my jeans to dry them off.

"I had a plan," Des said. There was something in her tone I didn't like.. I knew she wouldn't lie to me, but I also wasn't convinced that *she* was convinced her plan had been a good one. I filed the thought away to grill her about later.

Instead I said, "Next Saturday is too late. What if more ghosts go missing? What if they need our help right now?"

"We can't help them if we're not safe ourselves, if we don't know what we're doing. We'll make a plan—a safe, well-thought-out plan—and then we'll go back."

"We?"

"Not you."

"You?"

Des sighed. "Maybe, honey. I don't know."

There wasn't a chance I'd let her go back there without me. Either we were both going or neither of us were, but I knew I needed a solid argument before I tried to convince her. And I knew my aunt well enough to know that now wasn't the time.

We were both quiet for a minute, and then she said, "Evie, look at me."

I didn't want to, but I did. Des still had dark circles under her storm-grey eyes (eyes that had been brown before our time in the strange neighborhood), but now they didn't just look tired. They looked worried, too. And maybe a little scared.

"You have to promise me," she continued, "that you won't go through one of those doors. Not to look for Florence, and not to look for anyone else. If I'm with you, *maybe*. But never, ever alone. Never again."

I took a deep breath. "I promise." It wasn't a promise I liked making while a million *Yeah, but what ifs?* filled my mind, but it was one I would keep. Because we didn't lie to each other, me and Des.

After a late lunch of leftover vegetable curry and rice, I helped Des clean up. We were both quieter than usual, each of us afraid to say the wrong thing and reignite our disagreement, I think. We didn't argue often—not *real* arguments—and I knew for a fact that neither of us enjoyed it when we did.

"Hey," I said, dish towel and plate in hand, "I'm sorry about today. I'm sorry if I acted like a jerk. I just . . . want to help, I guess."

Des turned to me from the sink. "I know you do. And you will. But of all my jobs, keeping you safe is the most important. You understand that, right?"

"Yeah," I said. "It just seems like you and the rest of the DSS could use as much help as you can get."

"The DSS?" Des knit her dark eyebrows in confusion.

I blushed a little. "The Dark Sun Society. That's what I named your group. In my head, anyway."

Aunt D's eyes sparkled. "I like it. I bet the others will too. I'll let you tell them next week."

I put the last plate away. "That actually sounds really embarrassing, so probably not."

"You make me crazy, you know," she said with a smile.

"You make me crazy too," I told her. But I hugged her as I said it. Things felt okay between us again, and I was glad.

I went to my room to grab my backpack before I left the house for the afternoon. It was heavier than it had been a few weeks ago, but I'd recently learned a lot about the kinds of things that were smart to carry with you. Just in case. Before leaving, I pulled my red hair up in a messy bun (and not just because I wanted to show off my undercut). I put on my black eyeliner—I was getting better at it—and the silver necklace Des gave me the same night she'd shaved my hair. Real silver, to protect against all sorts of otherworldly threats. Along with dark tank tops, dark jeans, and my black All Stars, the necklace and eyeliner had sort of become my uniform for the summer.

On my way out the door, I gave Des one more hug. "Love you," I told her.

"Love you, too, sweet girl. I'll see you at Lily's? Just be there before dark, okay?"

"Promise," I told her as I headed into what was left of the summer day.

The ride to Maggie's was a pretty short one, even on a full stomach. As I made my way through the summer-bright neighborhood, I couldn't help but wonder how many houses now held sad and worried families who were missing their ghosts.

Was Malcolm sitting in the turret of the lavender

Victorian, sifting through the pages of the novel he'd never finished?

Were the Barkers still trying to get their new puppy to stop harassing poor Emilia?

Had the Washingtons—the newest family in town—finally gotten used to having a house ghost, or were they still sort of freaked out?

In just a few minutes, I was at the front door of Maggie's small, neat house, ringing the doorbell for the second time that day. Thinking about our town's ghosts had gotten my stomach tied up in a jumble.

Mr. Seong answered the door, and he didn't look all that surprised to see me. He shook his head. "She's not here, Evie. I was hoping maybe, but . . . she's still gone."

I hadn't really expected Florence to have returned, but I'd be lying if I said the idea hadn't planted a little seed of hope in my brain. "Yeah, I didn't think so. I actually wanted to know if I could borrow a book from Maggie?"

It wasn't a weird request—Maggie and I borrowed stuff from each other all the time—and Mr. Seong didn't hesitate. "Go for it. You know where they are."

I did. Maggie had shelves in her room full of the kinds of books we both liked, mostly spooky stuff and old fables and fairy tales (the real ones, not the sparkly, happily-ever-after kind). But the book I was after wouldn't be on Maggie's shelf. It would be on her bed.

Florence *usually* used the chalkboard in the Seongs' kitchen to communicate with the family, but not always. If she had something she wanted to say just to Maggie,

Florence would leave little notes or drawings in the margins of whatever book Maggie was reading at the time. It started when Maggie was little, and she'd kept it a secret from everyone. Everyone but me, that is. Not that the notes were ever dangerous or bad—they were just a special thing between two friends, and Maggie liked having that little secret between them. Over time, Maggie got in the habit of leaving a pencil on her nightstand and a book facedown on her bed, opened to whatever page she'd left off on.

As I headed down the hall to Maggie's room, I hoped she'd left a book out for Florence. More important, I hoped that with Maggie gone, Florence had left a note for me. Something that might tell me where she'd gone. Or why.

Maggie's room was neater than usual—her parents had probably made her clean it before she left for the summer. On her bed was a well-read copy of *Coraline*. It was open and facedown.

My heart thudded in my throat, and that was when I realized I was nervous. Nervous that Florence had left a note. Equally nervous that she hadn't. I picked up the book with only slightly clammy hands and turned it over.

Florence *had* left a note on the bottom of page 59 in her neat, old-fashioned handwriting. The note didn't make much sense. Not at first, anyway.

This is what it said:

Taking the Child to school. Home soon.

I had no idea what that meant. What Child? I sat on the foot of Maggie's bed to think about it. Maggie was the only child in the Seong house, and school had been out for weeks, except . . .

Except.

Before Florence became the Seong family's house ghost, she had been a person. And people had things like families and hobbies and jobs. And Florence once had a job. She'd been a teacher.

I wasn't exactly sure when Florence had lived—or died—but I knew she'd been a teacher back when Blight Harbor had just one school building for the whole town. That school, Blight Harbor Primary, still stood not too far from the shiny new elementary school. The buildings were separated by a wide green playground and a chain-link fence, but you could see one from the other.

The Old School—that was what everyone called it—wasn't used for anything, but it was maintained by the same people who took care of the parks. Lily often talked about how it might someday be a museum, and, given how much Blight Harbor loved its history, I figured there was a good chance that would happen eventually.

So I was pretty sure that Florence didn't mean to be gone for good, since she'd written, *Home soon.* And I was pretty sure I knew which school Florence had gone to. What I didn't know was who the Child was that she was taking there. Or why. But I was going to find out.

On the wall above Maggie's nightstand, a messy collage of unframed pictures were pinned so that their corners and edges overlapped one another.

Like always, the collage made me feel warm and sad at the same time. Feelings are messy things, and that collage gave me some of the messiest feelings of all. Words like *bittersweet* and *nostalgic* and *melancholy* all sort of fit, but there was more to it than even those. The pictures themselves were happy, and I was even in a bunch of them, smiling or laughing or giving Maggie the side-eye while she was probably saying something totally inappropriate in a voice so quiet only I could hear.

What made the collage complicated—for me, anyway—were all the photos of Maggie and her parents. Family vacations, holidays, and even a couple from when Maggie was little that looked like they'd been taken in a department store studio. The three Seongs, a whole and normal family, with pictures to prove it. Little milestones and big events, all there in one ordinary, extraordinary collection. There was even a photo from the last day of school just a few weeks earlier, the three of them celebrating as summer started.

There was no collage on my bedroom wall, no new photos of me and my parents to add to a growing collection.

When my house burned to the ground and my parents disappeared, I was just eight, so that was when the photos stopped. The only reason I had any pictures at all was because my mom and Aunt Des had been friends as well as sisters-in-law. My mom had sent Des a few printed photos every Christmas, and Aunt D had kept them all. After I moved to Blight Harbor, Des had taken the extra step and printed everything she could find from my parents' social media. All those photos—all but one, which I kept with me at all times—lived in a shoebox under my bed. I wasn't ready to put them up around the house I shared with Des or tack them to my bedroom wall, but I liked knowing they were there.

So I was thinking lots of mixed-up thoughts when I unpinned one of Maggie's photos and slid it like a bookmark into the pages of *Coraline*. The shot was of me, Maggie, and Florence (along with a few people I didn't know in the background) from Maggie's last birthday. In it, Maggie and I had our arms around each other in the Seongs' backyard. Florence stood just to the side, beaming at her favorite girl. As always, Florence wore her greyblue dress and had a pencil stuck in her honey-colored bun. I'd never seen her without that pencil and figured it was something she'd done during her teaching days.

In the photo, Maggie and I cast long shadows, but Florence didn't have one at all. Bright sun glimmered through her edges, giving her a warm glow that was totally appropriate for the kind ghost I knew her to be.

I liked the picture; it made me happy. But that wasn't why I took it. When you're searching for someone, it makes sense to carry a photo of them.

I almost ran down the hall and was nearly out the Seongs' front door.

Maggie's dad, sitting in his favorite chair and watching television, stopped me in my tracks when he called, "Did you find what you were looking for?"

I had. So it wasn't a lie when I said, "Yes, thank you!" and waved *Coraline* at him.

"You girls must have that one memorized by now," Mr. Seong said with a half grin.

"I mean, yeah. But you know how every time you reread a book you find something new?" Again, I wasn't lying. Florence's note hadn't been there the last time I'd read that book.

"Indeed. Well, enjoy."

"Thanks again, Mr. Seong!" I dropped the book into my backpack as I left.

I started toward the Old School, but I didn't make it very far before I hit my brakes in the middle of the street. Something other than Bird was nagging at me. I wondered if I was being too hasty, if maybe I should wait for the DSS to make their decisions before I jumped in on my own and tried to do something. I needed someone smart to help me decide what to do.

There was only one person I could ask.

I turned my bike around and started pedaling in the other direction. It wasn't much of a ride from the Seongs' house. Down a hill, through a nice-but-nothing-fancy neighborhood, and I was there.

Lily's medium-brown house was unassuming. I parked my bike in front of the slightly-darker-brown garage door, and before I could get to the similar-but-slightly-different-brown front door, I was greeted by the smell of baked goods wafting out the open window. Only the front yard, wild with herbs and flowers, had any other hue. Like Lily's wardrobe, her house was made up of various shades of her favorite color, but both the paint and the wardrobe were misleading. Lily and her house were both full of the best, *brightest* kind of magic.

I didn't even get a chance to knock—most of the time, Lily opened the door before I had a chance to rap on it. Today was no exception. Before I'd made it all the way across the drive, Lily was waiting for me.

Witches, I thought affectionately.

"Evelyn," Lily said, with what looked like flour and powdered sugar in her hair and on her tan apron (which was exactly the same shade as her summer-bronzed skin). "You're early! I wasn't expecting you and Des for a few hours. I'm baking for our game night." She reached out and squeezed my arm, which meant, *You surprised me. I'm happy to see you. Good, you can help me bake.*

I had no intention of helping her bake—there was no time for that—but that didn't mean I didn't want to eat whatever delicious thing she was making. I sniffed the sugary air. "I can tell! Butterscotch cookies?"

Lily shook her head. "Pecan caramel blondies."

On a regular day, that would have been enough to keep me from going anywhere. Lily's baking was legendary. But I had things to do.

"Come on in," she said, stepping aside so I could get through the doorway.

"Can't," I told her. "I just have a question. Maybe two."

Lily pushed her thick glasses up a bit and gave me a thoughtful look. "Hm. Not coming in—even for blondies. You must be on a mission. Or about to get into trouble."

"Sort of the first but not the second," I said.

Lily looked unconvinced. "Ask away. I have baking, and you have . . . something suspicious . . . to do."

I rolled my eyes (because I was exasperated, but also because I wanted to avoid eye contact with Lily—I kind of *was* up to something, and I knew she could read me like a book). "How bad do you think it is? The missing ghost thing, I mean?"

Lily took no time responding. "Bad. I think it's bad."

"How much time do you think we have?"

"Probably not as much as we need. Certainly not as much as we'd like. It always seems good things come slowly, but the bad things, well, they never take their time, do they?"

That was all I needed to hear.

"Thanks, Lily." I gave her a half hug and turned to go.

Before I could take a step, Lily had me by the arm. This squeeze said, *Stop right there. I think you're up to something dangerous.*

"Evelyn Von Rathe, you're not up to something dangerous, are you?"

Nailed it.

"No. I promise. I'm just worried, and I want to find Florence. I mean, I want to find them all, but especially Florence."

Lily's face softened. "I know you do. You want to take care of people, to keep them safe. You're just like Des, you know. In the best ways."

I nodded, blushing a little at the compliment. "See you tonight," I said.

"See you tonight. I'll have more blondies than even *you* can eat."

I smiled. It was a challenge I was willing to accept.

"Oh. Hang on. One more thing." Lily disappeared into her house. I was disappointed when she didn't return with a few blondies for the road (they were still cooling), but my disappointment quickly turned into puzzled interest as she filled the doorframe with a clutched fist. "Here," she said, handing me a small metal object.

I took it from her and realized it was Irv's odd enamel pin—the black circle he had been wearing on his orange cap. I was surprised to remember any sort of detail about Irv, but especially something as plain as this.

"Why?" I asked, genuinely perplexed.

"No idea. I was going to give it to you tonight, but now's as good a time as any."

"Um, thanks?" It was sort of a weird gift, but also sort of cool. Plus, it *was* my favorite color. I pinned it onto my backpack so I wouldn't lose it.

"You can thank Irv next week. He'll be the one in the orange cap." Lily smiled as she said it.

I gave her a *haha, very funny* look and one more half hug for good measure.

With a wave and a goodbye, I was back on my bike and headed to the Old School.

Bird was perched right in the middle of my back where I couldn't see him, and he didn't give his usual little wave when we left Lily's house. That could have meant a thousand things or nothing at all, but I assumed he was being judgmental (or maybe it was my own guilty conscience that was nagging at me).

"I know," I said to him. "I could have told Lily where we're going. But why make her worry? And she would, you know."

Bird shook his tiny head but didn't reply.

A narrow, one-lane road snaked around Blight Harbor Elementary, behind the playground, and stopped right at the front of the Old School. The road sort of petered out into a makeshift parking lot that was nothing more than a patch of gravel.

The lawn around the older building was neat and clipped, and the school itself stood primly in the late afternoon sun. It was painted a dark red, and the windows were trimmed white with a front door to match. The building was a small rectangle, and just one story, but the roof pitched up high like a capital letter A. On top of that pitched roof was a small belfry with a brass bell gone green with age. It was the most interesting thing about the building.

Or so I thought.

I expected the front door to be locked and was surprised when it opened easily. The hinges didn't even squeak. For some reason this bothered Bird, and he gave a nervous little ruffle of his feathers, almost like he'd shivered. I realized then that there were goose bumps on my arms, and I shivered a little too.

"Stop it," I told Bird (and myself). "There's nothing to be nervous about."

But I wasn't sure I totally believed that, because if Florence had been here but never made it back home, there might've actually *been* something to be nervous about.

I'd been in the Old School before and knew there wasn't much to it: a main classroom, a storage room, and a small room that didn't seem to have much purpose other than as a place to pull the rope to ring the school bell.

The main room smelled dusty and warm. Afternoon sun came through the windows and illuminated everything enough to see just fine. Old desks were neatly lined in four rows of four. In front of the desks, on the farthest wall from me, was a well-worn chalkboard. A wood-burning stove stood to one side of it, while on the other side sat a larger desk meant for the teacher.

While the unlocked door probably should have been my first clue that this was a bad idea, it was the chalkboard that told me maybe I needed to get in and out of there . . . fast. Someone had written a large capital *R* in the center of the slate, but the bottom of the *R* trailed off into a squiggly line, like the writer had been inter- rupted. After the letter, and across the rest of the chalk- board, were four lines, clean on the dusty surface. They looked very much like four fingers dragged through the dust, like maybe the owner of the fingers had been pulled away. It was only one letter, but that *R* looked just like Florence's handwriting.

My heart was thumping in my chest and Bird was turning worried circles on my back. I froze, not because I was having a panic attack, but because I was trying to be very still and very quiet. I was just steps away from the front door. I listened for sounds, any sounds at all, ready to bolt back into the sunshine if I heard anything.

Nothing.

The school was absolutely, perfectly silent.

What I *could* hear were the occasional cars passing on the main road and the sounds of children playing in their summertime yards. They were all totally normal, those sounds, and they were so close. It made me a little braver.

That was when I noticed something glinting in the sunlight. On the dusty floor near the teacher's desk was a coin. I picked it up to find that not only was it a perfectly shiny penny, but it was from the year I was born.

"Lucky penny," I told Bird as I slipped it into my jeans pocket. It crossed my mind that Clackity called me that very thing not so long ago, but I pushed the thought aside. This penny was *good* luck. I was sure of it.

Slowly, and as quietly as I could, I walked my sneakered feet across the hardwood floor of the classroom toward the two rooms in the back. I ignored Bird's pacing as I went.

I almost called for Florence but thought better of it. If she were there, I'd find her soon enough. And, honestly, I didn't want to hear my own voice echo in all that quiet.

The storage room was empty aside from some random junk on the shelves that lined the walls. With only one small window, it was darker than in the classroom, but I could still see well enough to tell that Florence wasn't there.

The other room was mostly empty as well, except for a faded couch probably meant for tired teachers, and the dangling, frayed rope leading up through a small hole in the ceiling to the belfry.

There was more light in this room than in the storage room, but I still nearly missed the door on the back wall. It was the same-color wood as the walls around it, and there was no handle. Instead, there was a notch—a half circle carved into the wood—to slide your fingers under and pull the door open.

Which was what I did.

Bird was having a conniption on my shoulder. I swatted at him lightly. For an otherworldly protector, he could be a serious scaredy-cat.

The door popped open with a tug. The space behind it was empty, save for a rod that probably once held hangers, and a couple of hooks on the walls. It was a coat closet, and an empty one at that.

"See, it's nothing," I whispered. My words might have been sure, but my heart was beating triple time, and I couldn't shake the spidery, crawly feeling on the back of my neck.

I closed the door.

I was relieved but also disappointed. Wherever Florence was, she wasn't here. I was almost out of the room and back in the classroom and out the front door when I heard a noise coming from the other side of the door.

The door to the empty closet.

The door I'd just closed.

It was a shifting, scraping sound, like heavy wood being moved.

My first thought was that the old schoolhouse was settling so much, it was going to collapse, which was silly because even though the building was over a hundred years old, it was sturdy.

My second thought was mice. Or maybe raccoons.

I didn't have a third thought, because right then I yanked open the door to surprise whatever four-legged creature was making itself at home in the coat closet.

Nothing.

There was still nothing in the closet.

Except.

Except there was.

In the back of the closet, there was another door where there hadn't been a door a minute before.

With a shaking hand, I patted Bird. He was pecking at me now, and I needed him to stop so I could focus. So I could think.

The door was a faded, ugly black color, and the wood

showed through where the paint was worn away. The door was short, maybe four feet tall, the kind of door that would open into a crawl space instead of a full-size room. It was cracked in places and didn't hang quite right in the doorframe, like it had been broken and fixed more than once. I could feel cold air seeping through those cracks, chilling the inside of the closet and cooling the sweat now running down my forehead. I could smell that air, too. It smelled like a cave, deep down inside, where there's never been any light. It smelled like a place where you weren't supposed to go.

I knew that smell.

The last thing I should have done was open that door.

I did it anyway.

Maybe because it was a mystery, like something straight out of the scary books and movies I couldn't get enough of. Or maybe I opened it because, when a strange door shows up out of nowhere, you sort of just *have* to. Those reasons were part of it, but really I opened that door because I wanted to find Florence. Opening doors wasn't the same as going through doors. I wanted to bring her home and make that sad, worried look in Mr. Seong's eyes go away.

Still, I should have known better.

The door handle was black—iron, maybe. Long and narrow and just big enough for me to slide my hand under to grip it. That metal handle was cold—flagpole-in-December cold. In only a couple of seconds, my fingers started to cramp and tighten. I pulled the handle, but the door didn't budge.

The smart, scared part of my brain said, *Great—it's locked, so we don't have to worry about it. Nothing to see here. Let's go home and make a sandwich.*

But the foolish, braver part of my brain knew I just hadn't pulled hard enough.

Against my better judgment, and despite Bird now pecking my shoulder so hard that I knew I was bleeding a little, I gripped the handle tighter. Then I pulled again, hard this time. The door stuck like it was warped in its frame, but it gave just a little.

The next two things happened at the same time:

Bird got very quiet and still, like he knew I was going to try to open that door whether he liked it or not, and

I took a deep breath and really put my weight into it, yanking the door handle as hard as I could.

The door flew open, and before I fully knew what I was seeing, I screamed a pretty serious swear word. Behind the door was a long hallway, way too long to make sense inside the small schoolhouse, and what little light there was left showed me there were even more doors along each wall, but I didn't have time to think about that because a lot happened at once.

Cold air poured into the closet from that hallway that shouldn't have been there. It might have been summer outside, but inside the coat closet it was the dead of winter.

More important than the cold air between me and the dark hallway was a girl. She sat on the floor, cowering like she expected me to hit her. Her long, ratty hair hung down her face, hiding one of her eyes. Her visible eye was in shadow. She reached for me, and I almost fell over backward as I backpedaled out of reach.

I was still screaming as I slammed the door in her face.

All at once, I knew what Florence had been trying to write on the chalkboard. She'd only managed the one letter *R*, and there was no way for me to know for sure, but I did. I knew she'd been trying to write *RUN*.

I made a break for it, dashing out of the closet, through the bell rope room, and into the classroom. I was headed straight for the front door, praying I could outrun whatever was in the schoolhouse with me. Though, for all I knew, she might not even have chased me.

Turned out, she didn't have to.

Because now, silhouetted by the open front door, the girl appeared. Her stringy hair still hung in her face, but now I could see both of her eyes. And they were black and empty. Everything else about her was washed out, like one of those old photographs—the kind that are brown instead of black and white.

Part of my brain was clear enough to recognize that the light didn't stream through her edges, because she didn't have thin edges. She wasn't a ghost. She was *something*, but not a ghost.

I couldn't move, and Bird seemed to be frozen too. While I stood in the middle of the classroom and turned into an almost-peeing-myself statue, she shook her head back and forth slowly. She raised one thin hand, not reaching for me this time, but with her palm out like she was trying to stop me.

The not-a-ghost girl looked over her shoulder at the open front door, then back to me. When she spoke, she sounded like a girl, but also as if she was very far away. "Please. I need your help."

The figure standing between me and the passing cars and the living children playing in their yards was little. I don't mean young—she looked about my age—but she was small, like she'd never once had enough to eat. Her dress hung on her like she'd borrowed it from a bigger, taller person.

She's hungry. It was a weird thing to think, and it made my stomach clench up in a hard ball, but I was also certain it was true. I had a million other thoughts colliding in my brain, but none of them would turn into words in my mouth, which had completely dried up. I tried to swallow, but that just made it worse. Bird was perched on my collarbone, red-hot and tense, which confirmed for me that this was not a great situation.

Finally I said the first thing that made any sense: "What do you want?"

"Out." Her voice was just the echo of a voice, like she wasn't actually in the room but down in a well. The sound of it gave me the full-body creeps.

"Um. So, yeah. That's okay with me."

The not-girl-not-ghost acted like she hadn't heard me. She wrapped her skinny arms around her chest. "I've been in-between for a very long time. I'd like to get out now. I'd like to *be* again."

I had no idea what she was talking about. "If you mean from the hole in the closet, you *are* out. Maybe . . . your eyes haven't adjusted yet?" I immediately felt awkward for saying something about her ink-pool eyes. I mean, she might have been embarrassed about them, and I didn't want to make her feel bad. I also really didn't want to make her angry. Hungry and mad seemed like a bad combination in this particular situation.

Her expression didn't change, but I threw my hands up in front of my face, because in the time it took for me to blink, she'd moved. The girl wasn't in front of the door anymore. She was two feet in front of me, staring at my face with those glassy black eyes.

"I'm sorry," I said. I meant that I was sorry for the comment about her eyes, but she didn't take it that way.

"Don't be sorry. I'm not your fault." She reached a hand up and put it on the side of my face, like a nice grandma might do if you told her something sad. That hand was real, and somehow felt strong, and it was as cold as the iron handle on the black door she'd been hiding behind.

I tried to back away, but I was already up against the teacher's desk. There was nowhere for me to go unless I wanted to fall backward and lose whatever advantage I had by staying on my feet. As a rule, ghosts didn't scare me, but she was no ghost, and if I'd learned anything from The Clackity, it was to be careful about trusting otherworldly strangers.

We stood there, her cold hand on my sweaty cheek, and she leaned closer to me, her face lifted up to mine, and kept talking. "It's not your fault at all, but you can help me. I need you to come with me. Please come with me." As she spoke, some of the inky black in her eyes started to leak out and drip down her face like tears made of oil. And worse, *so much worse*, a black mist spilled out of her mouth as her lips parted. The mist sank a little, then rose into the air between us like fog.

Her face was so close to my face, and I knew I'd have no choice but to breathe in whatever she was breathing out. I did my best to hold my breath, but that's hard to do when you're basically hyperventilating. I couldn't help it, and I inhaled, a quick and shallow breath. But it was enough.

When I breathed in the mist, my mouth and throat and even my lungs filled with that cold cave—*grave*—air I'd smelled coming from behind the door. That smell I knew so well. The smell of a place with a purple sky and black sun.

My eyes clouded up, and I had to blink a bunch of times to clear them. When they sort of refocused, I took another deep breath. This time it was from surprise.

The girl was still small and still wore clothes that were way too big for her.

But she had . . . changed.

Her hair was a rich chocolate brown, smoothed away from her face like she'd just brushed it. And her eyes weren't black pools after all; they were warm and brown, just a little lighter than her hair. Around her neck was something I hadn't noticed before, a necklace with a rectangular pendant half the size of a playing card, hanging just below her collar. The chain looked like brass, and the pendant was some kind of a shiny black stone. It was simple, not especially pretty, and had the look of something old and valuable.

She wasn't terrifying anymore. She was just a girl. I mean, she was a something-other-than-a-ghost girl, but a girl all the same.

"Please come with me? Please help?" Her voice was different too. It didn't sound like it was coming from the bottom of a well anymore. It was soft and sad and sounded like a regular voice coming from a regular distance away.

My head was still scrambled, and my eyes weren't working quite right, but despite all that, I *knew* I'd been wrong about her. She *was* nice. She was scared and alone and nice. I felt silly for having been afraid of her. In fact, I was having a hard time remembering what I'd been so scared of in the first place.

Something on my shoulder itched and burned a little. I scratched at it, then ignored it.

"Sure. Of course I'll help." I vaguely remembered I'd come here, to the Old School, for a reason. Looking for something, maybe? But this girl really, really needed my help. Now I didn't just feel silly, I felt embarrassed and a little guilty that I'd even considered not helping her.

She smiled, and it was a big, sweet, slightly gap-toothed smile. "Thank you. I just know you'll be the one who can help me."

She took me by the hand and started leading me to the coat closet and the door inside it.

I pulled away from her. There was something I was forgetting, but my brain was so muddy that I couldn't find it. "How long is this going to take? I think . . . I think there's something I'm supposed to be doing."

She seemed to think about it. "That depends. Maybe not long. Maybe a little longer. It's hard to say until you get there."

I started to ask her where *there* was, but then I forgot why it mattered. Then I forgot the question entirely.

"What's your name?" It hadn't occurred to me to ask until just then.

"How about Margaret? Or Sally? No"—she smiled like she'd thought of something amusing—"call me Portia."

This all should have struck me as strange, the girl not being sure what her name was. But it didn't. "Okay." I smiled and meant it when I said, "Portia's a nice name."

Portia took my hand again and led me toward the door in the back of the closet. The cold air still poured out of it.

"Should I put on my hoodie or something? I mean, it's freezing."

"Not at all. The cold is temporary. When we get down the hall and through the in-door you'll be fine. A jacket will be too warm when we arrive."

"What's the 'in-door'?"

"You'll see. It is . . . remarkable."

I hesitated. There was a spot on my shoulder that felt like it was on fire, and just for a moment I wasn't 100 percent sure I wanted to step through a door that hadn't been there a few minutes before.

Portia put a hand on my arm. It surprised me enough that I looked down. Her fingers were longer than I'd remembered, and I hadn't noticed before that her nails were painted black. "I know you're unsure, but I need you to trust me. You do trust me, don't you?" Her voice was cloying, like too-sweet vanilla frosting.

Of course I trusted her. Why wouldn't I? So I followed her through the door.

I hitched my backpack up and didn't ask any more questions as we went through the short door into the long hallway. There, the air smelled of old wood and fresh dirt, which wasn't a terrible combination. The hallway wasn't bright, but there was enough light to see by. Where that light was coming from, I had no idea. The hallway was very cold and very windy. I hunched over a little, wrapping my arms around me like the girl—Portia—had done just a few minutes before, wishing I'd put my hoodie on after all.

Portia walked in front of me, taking the lead. She wasn't as short as I'd thought. In fact, she was at least as tall as me. And it turned out her hair was black after all, and a whole lot longer than I remembered.

We made our way down the hall, and even though I was huddled over from the cold, I couldn't help noticing the many doors to either side of us and the art hanging on the walls between them. The art was random and a little creepy, if I was being totally honest. The paintings were all big, nearly as big as the door we'd just come through. The only thing the paintings had in common was their complete and total weirdness. I didn't get a good look at all of them, but one painting was of a path through what looked like dark woods. One was of an old-fashioned train. One was just a storm brewing in a dark sky. One was of a dark hole in the side of a hill. One was of a bunch of spiders. One looked like the surface of the moon, and another was completely black—no, not completely. It had what looked like a moon-pale face in the lower right-hand corner. That face had one staring eye and a very wide, broken-toothed grin. The last painting was of a tower, standing tall and night-dark and alone in a ragged landscape.

I almost asked about the paintings, but the question drifted from my mind like it had never been there at all, and I focused as best I could on following Portia.

"Almost there," she said as we reached the end of the hallway. Her voice was deeper, older than it had been before. At least, that was how I remembered it, but my mind seemed less and less trustworthy by the minute. I felt silly all over again. Silly for making mistakes, and silly for confusing such simple things as someone's height or the color of their hair.

"You might have been quite a problem, mightn't you?" Portia asked. It wasn't really a question, and she said it more to herself than to me.

We reached the end of the hall and found ourselves in front of another door. This one was ugly and black just like the first, but it was a normal size. I looked up at Portia to ask her what was on the other side, but her face was hidden by her long black hair, and while I couldn't read her expression, I could tell how tense her shoulders were in her snug-fitting dress.

She reached her long, bony hands to the door and pressed them against it, not like she was trying to open the entrance, but as if she was feeling for something behind it.

She was quiet, listening. Finally, "*You* have to open it," she said. "If something is waiting, I'd prefer it sees you first."

That should have been the moment I said, *Yeah, no, I don't think so*, but my foggy brain thought, *Yes. Of course I will.*

So I pushed on the door (there was no iron handle on this one). When it didn't budge, I put my shoulder into it and shoved. The door flew open, and I stumbled through it. Three things happened as I went across the threshold.

First, my head cleared. The fog lifted, and suddenly I was seeing and thinking like I should.

Second, one look at Portia told me she was not the same little girl I'd met just a few minutes before.

Third, Bird completely freaked out.

PART TWO

The Dark Sun Side

Bird was spinning in erratic circles on my shoulder. When I instinctively patted him, he nearly burned my hand. I glanced back to check on him, which was when I got a good look at Portia.

The person who followed behind me was a middle-aged woman, not a little girl. She walked cautiously, poking her head across the opening and staring for a long while, first one way, then the other. She took her time, carefully scanning the world beyond the long hallway and strange door. Portia was clearly looking for someone, or something, and when she was finally satisfied it wasn't there, she stepped through.

After she'd fully emerged, her hair and dress moved in a wind I couldn't feel, and her weird pendant glinted against her dress. Her eyes were black again, but now she wasn't crying oily tears. She was smiling a nasty smile, like she'd just cheated at a game and won, and that smile went all the way to her eyes. She was seriously happy with herself.

"Very well done, child. Nothing was expecting you, so nothing was waiting."

I started to respond, but my words got caught up in a deep, hacking cough. I doubled over and, out of habit, covered my mouth with my hand. When I pulled it away, my palm was caked in cold, ropy black slime that quickly turned to fog and disappeared into the air. Bird didn't move much, other than to brush my back with his soft wing as he tried to comfort me. I wiped at my face in case any of that black stuff was still clinging to me. I found a tiny bit at the corner of my mouth, and it evaporated from my fingertips.

"What did you do to me? Was that poison? Was that a *spell*?" I could feel my eyes get huge in their sockets as my hands clenched into sweaty fists. I wasn't scared—that would come soon enough—but I was angry. Angry at whatever it was Portia had done to me. Angry at being tricked into losing a game I didn't even know we were playing.

She shrugged her shoulders. "Poison, spell, sometimes there's very little difference, isn't there?"

I pointed at her and yelled, "You're a *bad* witch!" I coughed again and spit on the ground, trying to get the last of the cold out of my mouth. The witches I knew would never have done something like this, but I couldn't think of what else she might be.

Portia made a face like she'd smelled something gross. "A witch? Of course not. Witches are useless unless you want a mediocre love potion or a second-rate indoor herb garden. I'm a Keeper. A Keeper of the Radix. And a Keeper of the Nighthouse that serves it." She gestured behind me, and I turned to look for the first time at where I'd ended up.

We were in some kind of wild and rocky place. A warm place. Not hot like the summer day I'd left behind only a few minutes ago, but warm enough that I was fine in my jeans and tank top. The ground was mostly dirt and stones, and what little grass there was grew long and scraggly and so dark green, it was almost black. The air carried that cave smell I'd noticed in the closet, but it also smelled a little like old perfume. Or gasoline. Or both. It was a smell I knew well—the smell of a world that had its own rules and where impossible things happened on a regular basis.

Off in the distance, I could see the tree line of what looked to be a dense forest.

In the opposite direction, the ground became a shore-line, but there was no lake or sea lapping at its edges. Only black. It was the deepest, blackest black I'd ever seen, and I knew for a fact that it went down and down and never stopped. I had hoped never to see this black nothing again, and instead I was looking at an entire ocean of it.

Down the shore, a flashing light shone high above the ground. I squinted and saw that its source was a lighthouse, black and narrow and looking an awful lot like a stalagmite growing from the ground. The beam of light radiating from the lighthouse was dull and yellow. The sky above it was purple, the purple of violets or ripe plums. In that purple sky hung a black sun. That sun was both bright and dark at the same time, and seeing it made my anger bubble up and threaten to overflow like a pot boiling on a too-hot stove. Anger at being back in this world with its bruised sky and black sun without meaning to. Without *wanting* to.

"What is a raydis? And what is a night house? And why the heck did you bring me here?" My entire body was so tense, it felt like my bones might crack.

"The *Radix*." Portia gestured toward the black expanse. "The Radix is the root, the source, of everything that matters. Of power and magic and everything wonderful you're too stupid to comprehend."

"I'm not stupid." Even Bird puffed up at the insult.

She raised a dark eyebrow. This time, her smile belonged to a bully. "You did follow me down the hall. You *did* open the door. I'd say you're not the smartest child I've ever encountered." I wanted to say something, but she was kind of right and I couldn't come up with a good comeback, so she kept talking. "The Nighthouse should be obvious, even to you." She pointed down the coastline toward the lighthouse . . . the Nighthouse. Which I guess made as much sense as anything else in a place like this.

That was when it hit me: I hadn't just walked down a hall and through a door. I'd gone through one of Blight Harbor's thin places, something I'd promised Des I wouldn't do. Because it was dangerous. Because it was easy to get lost. Because those doors usually didn't stay where they were supposed to.

I was finally getting scared, and that made me angrier. "I'm done here. I'm going back." I stood as straight and

tall as I could, squaring my shoulders in a way that I hoped looked very brave and determined. On my collarbone I could feel Bird doing the same thing.

"And how do you suppose you'll do that?" Portia pulled her thin lips into a smirk and gestured over her shoulder to where the door was.

To where the door had been.

Now there was nothing there but more coastline and black and purple sky. The door, my way in and my way back out, was gone.

My heart kicked into high gear, and I could feel myself wanting to hyperventilate. Tears crept into my eyes, and there wasn't a thing I could do to stop them. I was going to cry in front of this . . . whatever she was.

She ignored all that and kept talking. "Besides, you agreed to help me. And when you've done a simple task for me, you can go home. I suppose it's possible that a less-than-bright child like you might do something inane and die along the way, but if not, you're free to go."

I ignored her insult. If there was a way out, I wanted it. And if that meant I had to do some sort of job for her, I wanted to get going. So I pulled myself together. Sort of. "What? What do I have to do?"

"Simple enough." She held up three skeletal fingers. "One, go to the Nighthouse. Two, retrieve the soul light from the center of the lantern. Three, return it to me."

"A 'soul light'? What do you mean? How exactly am I supposed to do that?"

"The *light*, girl." She pointed to the sickly yellow beam of light flashing from the top of the Nighthouse.

"The beacon, of course. *Retrieve* means 'to get and bring back.' It's a pity you aren't brighter." She narrowed her dark eyes and leaned in like she was trying to decide if I'd understood.

I huffed. "Isn't it a flame? How am I supposed to carry a flame? Is there a superspecial magic flame basket or something?" Even in this horrific situation, I couldn't stop the sarcasm from leaving my mouth.

Portia looked up into the sky like Aunt Des sometimes did when I was being especially exhausting. When she looked back down at me, her smile was gone. She was all business. "You can't mistake the soul light. You'll know it when you find it. And you'll find it there, in the Nighthouse. That awful creature on your skin may even be helpful."

"Bird isn't awful, he's my friend. And if you know what the soul light looks like and you know where it is, why don't you go get it yourself?"

The Nighthouse really wasn't *that* far away. If I could walk there, so could she.

A storm gathered in Portia's eyes, and when I looked into them, they were wild and scary. She took a deep breath and tried to sound calm, but there was no way to hide the rage in her voice. "Don't you think I've tried? For decades, I've sent scores of souls to fetch it, but it has never been returned to me. But ghosts are worthless, so perhaps it will be you, a living soul, who can bring back what is mine."

"Is that where all the ghosts have gone? You've brought them here?" I jabbed my finger toward the foreboding Nighthouse. "You sent my friend *there*?" There was no doubt in my mind that Portia had appeared to Florence looking like a child in trouble and, of course, Florence had tried to help her. Her note—*Taking the Child to school. Home soon*—made perfect sense now.

Portia shrugged and said, "Perhaps. I can't remember one from the others. So here we are, me needing my light and you needing to go home. Seems we both have a riddle to solve, and the Nighthouse is the answer."

"But what happened to . . ." That was all I said, because the look on her face stopped me cold. She was staring down at our feet. And she was terrified.

When I saw what she saw, I realized why. The black from the coast had silently crept up, and now it had reached us, puddling around my feet like the tide was coming in. It swirled around my ankles, and long, thin tendrils of it reached toward Portia's feet. It didn't hurt. It didn't feel like anything at all. But I absolutely didn't want it on me. I knew from experience that this blackness was stronger, *more* than it appeared. I lifted one foot, then the other, trying to shake the dark off. Weightless, it clung on.

Portia backed away quickly, stumbling and falling once, but she was up on her feet again in a flash. Always moving, moving away from the creeping black tide. That terrified look never left her eyes. She started talking, blubbering really, but not to me. She was talking to the black tide, or to whatever was controlling it. "No, you'll get what you're owed. I swear it. Give me time. Just a little more time."

The black surged toward her, but I think it was just a threat. If that stuff wanted to reach her, it would have.

With that, Portia's arms and legs grew long, twice as long as they had been before. They stretched thin and sharp, like the limbs of some kind of awful bug. Her hands and feet grew, the fingers and toes elongating to end in claws. Talons, maybe. She crouched down on all fours and actually snarled, then spun around and ran (if you could call it that), skittering away from the black tide and away from me. I watched in shock as she went, faster than I could have imagined, until she disappeared into the dark woods that stood opposite the coast.

The black tide didn't follow her. Instead it receded and joined the rest of the void it had come from. There was nothing left of it on my legs or my feet, like it had never been there at all.

And just like that, everything was still. The void—the Radix—seemed static at first, but as I watched, I saw it swirling and shifting, more shades of black than you could even imagine. It made no sound at all, but it didn't have to. Its depth, its foreverness, said plenty. I didn't know what the Radix really was, but I'd learned enough to be scared of it—enough to know that you could get lost in it. Or swallowed by it.

I found a relatively flat spot on the rocky ground and sat down, leaning against my backpack and resting my head on my bent knees. I knew I needed to get myself together as a cold flood of panic threatened to sweep me away. I closed my eyes, trying as best I could to come up with my next step. But the more I thought about it, the more jumbled it all got. My door back home was gone, Portia was about as trustworthy as The Clackity, the Nighthouse looked like the last place I wanted to go, and I was worse than alone because Portia was out

there, somewhere, creeping around in the woods.

I decided there was only one thing I could do.

I could pull myself together and find Florence and then a door to take us back to Blight Harbor. I had no idea where to start, but starting was the only thing I

could do. If I was here, I could at least try to bring our ghost friends home to Blight Harbor.

I looked around me in every direction. Nothing but shore, the Radix, the forest where Portia had scuttled off to, and in the distance, the Nighthouse. I wasn't sure that I would actually go *into* the tower—I certainly didn't trust that Portia would send me somewhere safe—but that was where the ghosts had gone, and at least it was a direction to go (and, if I was being honest, the tower was calling to me in a way I couldn't deny). Bird and I would figure out the rest as we went.

I took a deep breath, trying to fill myself with all the confidence and determination I could muster. I'd made it home from the Dark Sun Side once before, and I could do it again.

That was when a voice behind me said, "It's not safe here. You should get moving. And I'm going with you."

6

I whipped around so fast that my neck cracked.

A kid stood behind me. A boy dressed in old-fashioned clothes. His white shirt was tucked into baggy pants, with suspenders holding them in place. He was small but in a wiry, strong sort of way that said he could fight his way out of a bad situation (and probably had). His dark, wavy hair was cut short, and freckles were scattered across his light brown nose and cheeks. His clothes and hair had the same old-fashioned look as Portia—like an antique photograph come to life.

I was *not* about to be fooled again.

"No way. You're a trick, just like she was. Get out of here, before I . . ."

"Before you what? Kill a ghost? You're about a century too late." The kid laughed, showing a small chip on a front tooth. That laugh—the way it sounded and the way the kid's face changed when they smiled—told me I'd been wrong about one thing at least. She was a girl, not a boy. The clothes and the short hair had thrown me off. But it didn't matter to me if she was a kid or a grown-up or a unicorn or a houseplant. No way was I trusting her.

Bird, it seemed, felt differently. He danced around my back, making it clear that he not only trusted the new kid but was thrilled to have her with us. I smacked at him harder than was strictly necessary.

"Lark." Her voice was louder now, like she was trying to get me to pay attention to her rather than swat at Bird.

"What?" I asked.

"The name's Lark. And now that you know that, you've got the upper hand. Make you feel any better?" It did, a little. Names were powerful things on the Dark Sun Side, and this girl had just given hers freely.

"If that really *is* your name," I said.

The girl sighed. "It's not like I have it tattooed on me or anything, so I'm not sure how to prove it to you. Speaking of tattoos, that's a good one you've got there."

Bird spun happy circles at her compliment.

I rolled my eyes.

"Okay, how about this? My whole name is Loretta. Loretta Sue McCreary. But nobody calls me that unless they want a fight. I go by Lark."

It sounded true. Clearly Bird, who was a good judge of character, trusted her. And the knot in my stomach and the fluttering in my chest both told me I wanted it to be true too. Because I didn't want her to be a liar or another monster. But mostly, because I didn't want to be alone.

"It's a good name," I told her. Thanks to my Lily

Lessons (which is what I called the sort-of-witchy nature stuff Lily taught me), I knew a bit about birds, and what I knew about larks was that they aren't very social. "A good name for someone who's alone. And you're alone, aren't you?"

Lark nodded and her eyes got hard, like she was daring me to feel sorry for her. I'd been on the receiving end of pitying looks way too many times and knew how lousy it felt. I wasn't about to give this tough girl one of those looks.

"So unless she wants to do this solo, it looks like she's stuck with two birds," Lark said, not to me but to Bird, who was perched on my collarbone. To my total irritation, Lark smiled and Bird ruffled his feathers in what felt like laughter. They were sharing a joke. Which was me. I was the joke.

"I'm right here," I said. I was kind of angry at both of them. If I'm being honest, I didn't like how much Bird liked the new kid. How much he seemed to trust her. It didn't help that I was still mad at myself (and embarrassed) for being tricked by Portia and breaking my promise to Des. My insides felt like they were on fire, or on the verge of collapsing, or both.

Bird read my mind. I felt the soft brush of a comforting wing. A voice in my head that sounded like mine said words that weren't: *Lark knows a lot about this place. More than you and I have time to learn.*

Lark looked hard at Bird, and I could feel him looking back at her. She nodded, and then, so did he. Something had passed between them, something silent but important. Maybe it was an otherworldly thing. Or maybe they did it just to get on my nerves. Either way, I didn't understand it, and I didn't like it. But that didn't mean I didn't trust my little buddy, even when he was annoying.

I stared at my feet, thinking, trying to cool down, trying to see reason. I could feel Lark's eyes on me, but I wasn't ready to meet them yet. Bird trusted her, and that wasn't nothing. But I'd already been fooled once that day, and I wasn't excited about making another bad choice.

"You got a name?" Lark asked after a quiet minute.

I hesitated.

Bird nudged me with his little head. *Tell her. It's okay.*

"Evie," I said, still not looking up. I took a deep breath. "Evelyn Von Rathe. But everyone mostly calls me Evie. Unless they want a fight," I added with what I hoped was a smile, even if it was a weak one. I was trying here.

Lark looked thoughtful. "You're lucky, then. That's a good name." I nodded, waiting for her to explain what she meant, but she didn't. She stood with her hands in the pockets of her baggy pants, looking relaxed, like this kind of thing happened to her every day. The weird sun made her edges glow, and she looked almost gold in all that black and purple surrounding us.

"Bird trusts you, but that doesn't mean I do." I frowned then, because I had questions. "Why do you even want to help me? And how do I know you're not like *her*? Portia looked like a kid at first too."

Lark looked amused and maybe a little offended.

"Portia? Is that what she called herself? Well, Portia it is, then. I'm *nothing* like her." Clearly, she had dealt with Portia before.

"How do I know that?" It was a real question. I wasn't being a jerk. I really needed to decide if I could trust her or not.

Lark sighed. Then she walked to the edge of the shore and squatted down. She reached into the black tide with cupped hands. When they came out, they were full of that dark liquid fog. It drifted through her fingers, fell slowly to the ground, then ran down the shore and back into the rest of the black ocean. She wasn't scared of it, and it didn't try to grab her. That convinced me. I wasn't sure what she *was*, but she wasn't like Portia.

"How old are you?"

She shrugged. "Eleven? A hundred and eleven? What does it matter?"

It was a weird answer, but it also made sense. "You've been . . . here . . . a long time, huh?"

"Uh-huh. That's a true story."

"And you know how to get to the Nighthouse? Because I'm going to find my friend—all of my friends, hopefully—and a door home, and that's the direction I'm heading."

"Pretty sure."

That stopped me. "Pretty sure? You mean you've never been there?"

"Nope."

"But it's the only thing out here for miles. Why

haven't you been there? Why haven't you tried?"

"Didn't say I haven't tried. Just said I haven't been there. I'll explain it as best I can, but for now you need to make up your mind. Are you going to trust me? Are we going to try to get you home?"

"What's in it for you?"

Lark seemed to think about it. "Maybe I'll get home too. If not home, at least I'll be somewhere that's not here. And maybe we'll beat Portia at her own game. If not, and this all goes sideways, at least I'll have some company for a while. This place gets lonely."

You know what? I believed her.

"Okay, what's first?" I asked. Something heavy lifted inside me, not much, but enough that I noticed. I guess what I was feeling was relief. It would be nice to have someone else with me and Bird.

Lark stared at the black tide for a minute. I could tell she was making up her mind about something by the way she chewed on the insides of her cheeks. "First, I need to show you something. Come here. Carefully." She walked to the edge of the shore, and after hesitating a little, I followed her.

When she got close to the tide, Lark held her hand out toward me, silently telling me to stop. "Whatever you do, don't fall in. I don't want to go in after you—not that it would do much good." She crouched down again, and this time she gestured for me to join her.

"What are we doing? I know a little bit about this stuff. I've . . . I've seen it before."

Lark cocked an eyebrow, curious. "You've seen the Radix?"

"Yeah. I've been to this . . . side before. It was different, but the sky and the sun were the same. And I didn't know what the Radix was called or that it even had a name. I just called it the black nothing."

"You understand it, then?"

"Mostly. I think."

"That isn't good enough," said Lark. "You asked what comes first, and this is it. A lesson. The most important one."

I was scared to get too close to all that black, but I was also curious. I crouched down on my knees, maybe a foot away from the edge of the shoreline. The black tide didn't move at all.

"Watch." Lark reached down into the darkness. It should have just been a few inches deep where the tide met the shore, but she kept reaching down until her arm was in all the way to her shoulder. It disappeared into the black.

"So it just drops off a little? Okay. Why is that a big deal?"

Lark didn't answer my question. At least, that was what I thought at first.

"Lie down on your stomach and scoot as close as you can to the edge."

"This is weird," I said. But I did what she told me, because now I was super curious. I put my backpack down and slithered on my belly until my face was just inches from the end of the shore. For the first time, I realized that this, the Radix, was the source of the cave smell. It smelled cold and empty and . . . old.

Up close, I could see all sorts of swirls in the tide. It didn't make any sound at all. There was something about that swirling, something that made me want to keep staring at it. But I had fallen for that trick once before and wasn't about to again. I closed my eyes to block out the hypnotic churn.

"Evie, are you listening?"

"Yeah," I said, and I was, but even with my eyes closed, part of my brain was still focused on all that shifting black.

"Put your arm in. Like I did. *Carefully.*"

And I did, because Lark said so but also because I wanted to. But first I said to Bird, "Buddy, you know what to do. If I get lost, you bring me back, okay? A little blood is worth it." Just a few weeks before, Bird had saved me from stepping into this same black nothing by pecking me out of the spell the void had cast. The pain had brought me to my senses. It had worked once, so I hoped it would work again.

Bird fluttered in agreement.

When my arm was all the way in the Radix, I realized I could keep going. My fingers still hadn't touched the bottom. And the tide wasn't wet or cold or warm or anything. It was like touching the idea of a cloud.

"Now," Lark said, "reach back under the edge, like you're lying on a bed and grabbing something below it."

That snapped me out of my daze a little, because it didn't make any sense. That wasn't how shores worked. Shores weren't hollow—they didn't have an *underneath*.

"Reach under." She didn't sound impatient; she sounded like she understood what I was thinking.

So I did. I reached back under the shore. And my arm reached all the way under, just like she said, and went as far as it could. I didn't touch anything at all. The tide kept going, right beneath us. Something in my stomach shifted in a not-very-pleasant way. I twisted my arm a little and patted up, toward the bottom of the shore. There couldn't have been more than six inches of land between us and the Radix below.

That was enough for me, and Bird didn't have to do a thing, because all of a sudden, I was freaked out. I jerked my arm out of the black and scooted away from the edge. I sat up and almost yelled at Lark, "What was that? What kind of beach *is* this?"

Lark sat by my side. We both looked out into the weird, swirling black.

"Not a beach. A cliff. A cliff floating right at the edge of the world. You couldn't feel the bottom 'cause, best I understand it, there isn't one. If you fall into the Radix, you just keep falling."

"Yeah, I know. I fell into it once. Was pushed, actually." My skin crawled and my hands and feet started sweating as my body remembered what Pope's shove to my shoulders, and all that falling, had felt like.

"You *what*?" asked Lark.

"Bird saved me," I said, like it explained everything.

It must have explained enough, because Lark nodded. "He's a good one, aren't you, friend?"

Bird puffed up until I thought he would burst, which made my own heart swell a bit. He really was the best little buddy.

"Portia said the Radix is a . . . a source?"

"Think of it as a well, I suppose. But also, maybe, a small universe."

I shook my head. Lark was making things more confusing. "But what *is* it?"

She squinted, staring out at the ocean that wasn't an ocean. "It's power. Just a whole lot of power. And it can be turned into a tool if you know how. Or a weapon. It's not evil, but it *is* dangerous. Mostly, I think, because it's hungry. Not hungry. Selfish. And it won't come after you, but it will gladly let you come to it."

I thought about how there had been a time in the strange neighborhood when I'd lost myself just by looking into the Radix, and how much I had wanted to get closer to it. "Was it trying to hypnotize me?"

"I don't think it tries, I think it just *is*."

And right then two things came together in my head like a pair of cymbals crashing. "Portia tricked me. Hypnotized me, I think. And it happened after I breathed in some black fog that she breathed out. Was that . . ."

"Uh-huh. Portia's been stealing from the Radix for a long time. Remember how I said it can be a weapon? That's what Portia's been doing. She stole as much power as she could and made it into a weapon. Made *herself* into a weapon."

"It doesn't like to be stolen from." I thought of iron chains and John Jeffrey Pope with a shiver.

"You're catching on. The Radix doesn't want to be separated from itself. She took some, and it wants its little bit back."

"How much power does she have?"

"Compared to all this?" Lark waved her hand toward the black expanse. "Not a lot. Compared to us . . . plenty. But every time she uses that power, the Radix notices, and she digs herself a little deeper in debt to it."

"How do you know so much?"

Lark stood up and brushed her hands on her pants. "Been here a while." I knew there was more to it, but her tone said she was done talking.

I wasn't ready to give up. "Yeah, but—"

She interrupted. "Let's see what's in that knapsack of yours. If we're lucky, you brought something useful along."

Lark made her way up the shore—the cliff—and away from the Radix. I grabbed my backpack and hurried after her. She led me toward a big, flat rock maybe a hundred feet from where we'd been. It was as good a place as any to sit for a minute and go through my stuff. I'd become pretty thoughtful about what I kept packed at all times, especially after my last trip to the Dark Sun Side.

I hoisted myself up on the rock next to Lark and

put my backpack between us. I shielded my eyes with my fingers and looked up. "Hey, what's with the black sun? The purple sky I can handle, but the sun weirds me out."

"I just told you there's an endless source of powerful magic that you can touch with your hands, and you want to know about the sun?"

"Well, yeah."

"Honestly," she said, "I have no idea."

I shrugged. That made two of us.

I opened my backpack and started to take things out. I had:

My favorite lightweight black hoodie

My phone (which wouldn't turn off or on—the screen had turned a silvery grey like passing clouds)

A flashlight

A Swiss Army knife

Three granola bars

Two bottles of water

Two pairs each of socks and underwear (which I hoped Lark wouldn't notice)

A box of matches

A vial of oil

A vial of salt

A vial of holy water

Black eyeliner

Coraline with the photo of me and Maggie and Florence tucked inside

That was it.

(Well, almost. There was one other thing, but I wasn't ready to share that, so I left it inside.)

Lark looked everything over. She was especially interested in the flashlight after I showed her how to turn it on and off. She tilted her head to one side and looked at me. "You planning to run away from home?"

"No!" I almost yelled. "I never would. I like to be ready just in case."

Lark nodded. I expected her to grill me about it, but she didn't. Instead she said, "I ran away once. Didn't get me anywhere good."

I almost asked her where it got her, then swallowed my words back down. It was obvious. Running away from home got her right where we were.

I changed the subject as I packed my stuff back into my bag. "How far away is the Nighthouse? How long will it take to walk?"

She shook her head. "That's the wrong question. It's not about how long it will take, 'cause that's not how it works here. It's about what we—you—have to do to get there. And we won't know until we start."

All I wanted were some straight answers that would help me get home, but it didn't seem like they were coming anytime soon. Right at that moment, my situation finally sank in, and when it did, it made me ache in my bones.

Soon, all across Blight Harbor, lights would be winking on as the regular sun—the yellow sun—set in the regular sky. Bikes would be making gunk marks on driveways as kids rushed home from swimming or playing ball or building forts in the woods (while the more nocturnal families would be getting ready to start their days). The house ghosts that were left would be joining their people for dinner (even though they couldn't eat it). Windows would be opened to let in the breeze. . . .

It wouldn't be long until I was late getting to Lily's house, if I wasn't already, and Des would realize something was wrong. They'd find my bike at the Old School soon enough—I hadn't exactly hidden it. But what they wouldn't find was the little door that Portia had led me through. I was pretty sure that door showed up only when Portia wanted it to. Which meant it would look like I'd disappeared into thin air. Worse, Des might've thought I *had* found a door and, despite my promise, gone through without her. Which I had, I guess, but that hadn't been my fault.

It made my stomach hurt to think that Des would believe I'd lied to her, that I hadn't kept my promise.

It made my heart hurt to think of her, sad and alone and worried sick about me.

My hands were shaking and my breathing was shallow.

I took a deep breath and let it out. I also closed my eyes and counted to ten. It wouldn't do me any good to have a panic attack. I wasn't sure I liked Lark yet, but I didn't want to freak out and have her leave.

Once I trusted that my voice would be steady, I tried again. "When can we get moving?"

"Up to you, Von Rathe," Lark said. "This is your quest."

I shook my head. That wasn't helpful. It struck me as a little weird that she had called me by my last name—and hadn't messed it up the first time like most people did—but not weird enough to distract me. I was going to have to make some decisions. "All right." I hopped off the rock. "Let's go to the Nighthouse."

Turned out, I might have had some magic of my own, and those words might have been a spell. Because as soon as I said them, everything changed.

The ground shifted under my feet. Not just a little—enough to make me almost lose my balance. It felt like the world was sliding away beneath me.

Which, it turned out, was exactly what was happening.

I leaned forward and threw my arms out to keep my balance. My body understood that something was going very wrong and did its best to compensate, but my brain wasn't keeping up so well.

Lark didn't have that problem—she knew exactly what was happening. She stared over my shoulder, back toward the cliff's edge. Her eyes were enormous.

When I looked back and saw what she saw, my entire body went numb and tingly and heavy all at the same time. I was completely frozen in place, but that didn't matter, because we were sliding toward the precipice and the Radix beyond. It was like the world was on a table-cloth, and giant hands were pulling it off a table, along with us and everything else.

I remembered the foreverness of the Radix.

I thought about the thin six inches of ground between us and it.

My heart turned into a rock and lodged in my throat. I probably stared for two seconds, but it felt like forever as I watched rubble and grass and the entire ground tumble into the void. And I was moving along with it all.

An enormous rumbling filled the air as rocks and sticks and dirt bounced against each other. A low cloud of dust from the dry, falling earth floated around, mixing in with all that black. The land was flat, and there was no snow, but it was an avalanche.

"What . . ."

"Run." Lark's voice was low and afraid.

Her fear, and the thought that Florence had tried to write the very same word back in the schoolhouse, unfroze me.

So I ran.

It was like running on a treadmill or up a descending escalator. I ran as hard and as fast as I could, Lark in front of me urging me on and Bird beating his wings frantically on my back like he could make me go faster. It was hard to gain any ground—twice the effort to go half the distance. Ahead of us, the tree line of the forest—which had once seemed so far away—was getting closer by the second. Some tiny part of my brain that was still thinking reminded me that Portia had disappeared into those woods like a giant insect, which meant we'd be running from her, too, if we managed to escape the Radix's pull. Or running *with* her, maybe.

I was doing okay, nearly keeping up with Lark, when I made a mistake.

I looked back.

I looked just in time to see the big slab of rock we'd been sitting on only a minute before reach the edge of the cliff. It balanced on the precipice long enough for it to look suspended in midair before toppling over and down into the abyss.

Nothing in any science class I'd ever mostly day-dreamed through had prepared me for what it felt like to watch thousands of pounds of rock get knocked off the edge of the world like a vase of flowers.

I lost track of what I was supposed to be doing, which meant I also lost my footing.

I hit the ground hard and felt the skin on my knees open up when they slammed against the earth. I was slid-ing back toward the Radix on my hands and knees. Lark pulled farther ahead of me, now that she was going one way and I was being pulled the other. She hadn't noticed I'd fallen, and I couldn't find my voice to scream and tell her. I dug the toes of my sneakers in as hard as I could and scrambled with my hands, but there was no way to get traction.

I couldn't help it. I looked back again.

The void was maybe twenty feet away, and there was now so much dust in the air that my eyes stung, and I couldn't tell if I was crying or if my eyes were watering from the irritation. Honestly, I think a little of both. I took a huge breath, ready to try to scream again. But all I got were two lungs full of air that was mostly dust. I coughed so hard, I almost threw up.

Some things you just know. And I knew that I was maybe ten seconds away from dying—or from falling forever, which maybe would have been worse. It wouldn't be my first tumble into an abyss, and while Bird had saved me the last time, I didn't think he could again. He'd told me I had to be the one to move forward, had to take my own steps, but taking steps forward was my biggest problem at the moment.

Bird flapped his wings frantically, urging me to keep trying, when cold hands wrapped around my left wrist and pulled.

I squinted my watering eyes to see Lark, both hands around my forearm, pulling as hard as she could. She was strong, but being a ghost, she was also light, so she wasn't about to pull me up on her own. I had to help save myself. I didn't know if it was Lark's pulling or the fact that she was risking herself to save me, but whatever it was, it was enough for me to get my feet working again.

I got my right foot steady under me, and when I lifted my left to do the same, I swear to you I could feel it hover over the precipice. I didn't look back this time, but I didn't need to. I knew how close I was to falling off the edge of the world.

At this point, I had adrenaline where my blood should have been. I ran, Lark right in front of me with a death grip on my hand. I had a new reason not to look back, because now the tree line was coming at us in a hurry.

We crossed into the forest, or I guess the forest crossed into us. We didn't let go of each other, even though that might have made more sense. We dodged trees and hurdled roots. The speed of the earth made it hard to be sure where to step next other than to make sure it was forward.

My rational brain knew we were slowing down—there were so many obstacles that we had to avoid—and we were either going to lose all the ground we'd made or run into a tree and get carried into the Radix with it.

Then I saw something that gave me a little hope.

Ahead of us was a clearing. I put my head down, trusting Lark to guide us, and ran with everything I had left in me. If we made it there, at least we'd have fewer obstacles to deal with. I didn't know how long we'd have to run—it was the Dark Sun Side, so for all I knew maybe the Radix would keep pulling forever—but the running would be easier in a wide-open place.

We reached the clearing, and maybe a dozen steps in, we stepped onto a dirt trail. As soon as my feet met that trail, everything stopped moving. The change was so sudden that Lark and I both pitched forward past the path and onto the forest floor. I lost my balance again, but Lark managed to stay upright.

I didn't bother trying to get up, because I was shaking too hard. Instead, I collapsed face-first onto the black grass that grew next to the path. Nothing had ever felt as amazing as lying flat on my face on the not-moving ground. Trying to catch my breath, I drew in the gasoline perfume of the grass and the damp earth scent of the forest floor. It smelled wonderful. My scraped-up knees stung, but it wasn't any worse than road rash from falling off my bike. The knees of my jeans were only a little shredded and the blood was already drying. Around us, the sounds of birds filled the air.

It was almost normal.

Lark sat on the grass next to me. I could sense her there, waiting. She didn't seem ready to spring up and run again, which gave me hope that the nightmare landslide might be over.

Finally I was pretty sure I could talk without coughing or puking. "What. Was. That?"

"S'pose it was the beginning. Like I tried to tell you before you got upset, getting to the Nighthouse isn't about distance. Or time. It's not about how far you have to go; it's about what you have to do to get there."

I was glad my face was buried in the grass and dirt, because it meant Lark couldn't see that I was blushing. I didn't think she'd noticed that I'd almost had a panic attack before the ground started moving. I had a sick feeling in the pit of my stomach, the feeling I always got after I messed up and acted like a jerk or freaked out.

We stayed like that for a minute, her patient and me embarrassed. Quiet.

When I did look up, long pieces of dark grass stuck to my sweaty face, and I had to peel them off. I thought about apologizing (even though Des liked to remind me that panic attacks aren't something you have to apologize for). And then I thought of something important to ask, but a movement caught my eye and stopped me from speaking.

A grey spider the size of a little kid's hand was creeping over Lark's right arm. Horrified, I stared as it made its way to her shoulder and stopped there. It was so big that I could see it lower its plump body onto her, almost like it was getting comfortable. The monster spider perched on Lark like a pirate's parrot.

"Don't move," I whispered. Frantic and still half lying on the ground, I searched the forest floor for a stick or rock or something else to beat the thing to death with. Saying I didn't like spiders would be an understatement, and this was the biggest and grossest one I'd ever seen.

"Von Rathe . . ."

"Shh . . ." I didn't want Lark to spook it. Didn't want it to scamper away, where it would disappear and hide and then I'd never know where it was until it decided to drop out of a tree and into my hair.

"Evie, stop. It's okay. This is Clyde."

It took a second for her words to make sense. When I looked back in her direction, she was absentmindedly petting the spider with her left hand. I swear the thing was purring.

"It's . . . Clyde?"

"He's been with me a long time. Haven't you, Clyde?" In response, the spider brushed up against her lower jaw, nuzzling her.

I had no words.

"He's harmless. And he's my friend. And he's useful. And you're not going to lay one finger on him. Not that it would matter—Clyde's been dead a long time. Haven't you, friend?"

"A ghost spider." I said. It wasn't a question so much as an acknowledgment of one more impossible thing on a day that had already been full of them. Bird peeked over my shoulder, curious.

"Of course. You don't think I'd let a *live* spider crawl on me?" Lark shuddered a little.

I closed my eyes and rubbed my forehead. The spider could wait. It didn't seem like he was going anywhere except back into Lark's shirt pocket (where I assumed he'd been up until now). So I got back to what I'd been planning to ask. "You could have run faster without me, huh?"

"Much."

"You didn't have to come back for me."

"I did."

I didn't know if she meant that yes, she had come back or that she had *had* to.

"Will that happen again—the avalanche thing?"

"No idea."

That was not the most reassuring answer.

"What's next?" I asked, hoping for something more decisive from Lark.

"Up to you. What do you think?"

That was decidedly *not* decisive.

I sat up. When I did, my head swam and I was nauseous all over again. My throat felt like I'd eaten a bowl full of gravel. I found a bottle of water in my bag and drank nearly half of it. I could have finished it, along with the second bottle, but I wasn't sure when I'd see water again, so I made myself stop. I kept glancing over at Clyde, making sure he was staying put. The spider seemed perfectly content half-tucked in Lark's pocket. In fact, he might have been napping.

Around us, the forest was quiet. A breeze rustled the leaves, which blocked out enough of the black sun and purple sky that everything felt almost normal. Almost right.

"The path," I said. "Everything stopped . . . sliding . . . when we reached the path. So maybe we're supposed to take it?"

"Is that a question or a decision?"

"A decision," I snapped, and thought, *One of us had to make one.*

"Good enough. Let's get moving."

Bird nudged my back with his little head. He was as eager to get moving as Lark was.

I, on the other hand, wasn't actually sure if I was ready to go. My body wouldn't stop trembling, and my heart was quivering in my throat rather than beating in my chest where it belonged. My brain knew I'd almost fallen again into the black nothing—the Radix—but my body seemed to still be catching up.

"Wait. Before we do anything, one question: Why are you here?" I was stalling, but I was also curious.

Lark seemed to think for a minute. Then, "I made a mistake. I thought I could make something—someone— better. But I couldn't, and then I got stuck here. Why are *you* here?"

"Long story," I said. "I was looking for someone, a ghost, actually. But I was too late. I ran into Portia, and . . ."

I gestured around, hoping Lark would understand that I meant, *And then all this happened.*

"A ghost, huh? You're from Blight Harbor, then." It wasn't a question.

I sat up straighter. "Yeah! I am. You know Blight Harbor?"

Lark nodded. "Born and raised. Most haunted place I've ever seen."

"Still is," I said, and a thought occurred to me. I dug through my backpack until I found *Coraline.* I took out the photo and showed it to Lark. "You haven't seen her around lately?" I asked, pointing to Florence.

Lark took the picture from me and ran her fingers over it, stopping on the image of Florence. She looked from the photo to me, then back again.

Finally, quietly, "That's Miss Dwyer."

"Who, Florence? You *know* her?" It was pretty much the last thing I expected Lark to say.

"She was my teacher once. Nicest I ever had. And smartest, too. How do *you* know Miss Dwyer?" Lark took another long look and added softly, "She's still really young. To be a ghost, I mean. Doesn't seem right."

That's a lot, coming from a ghost who barely made it to double digits, I thought, which made me feel a little embarrassed and ashamed. The fact that Lark had died when she was eleven was horrible, no matter what had happened to her. Plus, Florence *was* young for a ghost. Younger than Aunt D, for sure. Maybe not a whole lot older than a teenager.

"Maybe she got sick?" I said, because I felt like I had to say something.

"Or maybe she shouldn't have been mixed up with the Pope boys," Lark said darkly. "Her fiancé was stand-up enough, but he had a brother who was real trouble."

I didn't think the day could have surprised me more than it already had, but the news that Florence—and Lark, for that matter—had known the Pope family made my stomach hurt. I couldn't get out of the poisoned shadow of that murderer, and it seemed impossible that Florence dying young and knowing John Jeffrey Pope was a coincidence.

I kept all that to myself as Lark handed the picture back to me, even though it seemed like she'd rather keep it. I glanced down at the image one more time and immediately dropped it in the tall grass as a scream caught in my throat.

I'd only snatched a glimpse of the picture, but it was enough. In the crowd of strangers standing behind me and my friends, one figure stood out. It was impossibly tall and had a moon-pale face that was too long and too wide by half, and that face was split by a broken-toothed grin. Its one good eye stared right at me.

"What?" Lark asked.

I didn't respond as I snatched the photo off the ground and looked at it again. Yes, there was a tall figure in the crowd, maybe even unusually tall, but it was just a smiling man. It was not—despite what my overactive imagination had conjured up—The Clackity, come back to haunt me.

"Sorry," I said. My mouth was sawdust dry. "I saw something that wasn't there and it freaked me out."

"Whatever it was spooked you good."

I stared at the man in the picture, searching for a trace of anything other than human. My brain was spinning. Clackity had found ways to spy on me during my last trip to the Dark Sun Side. Was it doing it again now?

"You didn't see anything weird about this picture, did you?" I willed my hands to stop shaking before Lark noticed.

Lark shook her head. "Other than all the colors? Nope. What—"

"I'm good," I interrupted, wanting to change the subject. I'd only just met Lark. I didn't need her thinking I was losing it already. The Clackity was long gone, and it certainly wasn't in the picture I was holding.

Slowing my breath, I put the photo back into the book and explained how I knew Florence and what was happening to the ghosts in town. Then I told Lark all about the schoolhouse and getting tricked by Portia. I was embarrassed about the getting tricked part, but it seemed Lark knew Portia well enough that she'd understand.

Lark listened and nodded occasionally, but she never interrupted.

When I was done, she said, "You really are a Von Rathe."

"What does *that* mean?"

"Back . . . before . . . my best friend was a Von Rathe. Mae. I was always coming up with adventures and getting us in trouble—not real trouble, the fun kind. Mostly. And Mae was always right there with me. I miss her." She reached out and touched the sterling silver chain I wore around my throat with her fingertips. "Mae wore real silver too. Her momma insisted. I used to tease her about that necklace." Lark looked away, but I was pretty sure there were tears in her eyes.

Lots of things happened in my brain at once. I wanted to stop everything and ask more about Mae, but grilling a crying person about someone they would never see again seemed insensitive. Also, I wanted to take Lark's hand, or put my arm around her, but I didn't know if that would be okay or not. It was awkward.

"What are the chances that you know Florence and one of my relatives?" It wasn't really a question I expected an answer to, just one I thought out loud.

"Blight Harbor wasn't that big," Lark said. "We all knew each other. And everyone knew everyone's business."

"It's still kind of that way," I said.

Lark stared at me long enough to make me look away. Finally she said, "Von Rathe, what year is it?"

I told her. And then she was quiet again for a while.

"It really has been a hundred years," she said, and her voice was so sad, I wanted to cry too.

I needed to say something, anything, that might make her feel a little better. Then I remembered, "McCreary, right? Your last name?"

Lark nodded.

"That's our police chief's last name. Mary McCreary. She's great. I mean, she's intense, but great."

"A lady police chief." Lark smiled a little. "That's something."

The conversation was slowing down. I had so many questions for Lark, but it still didn't seem like the right time to ask any of them.

Instead I stood up. My knees still felt wobbly, but I wasn't shaking anymore. It was time to get back to the plan and make our way to the Nighthouse.

"You ready?" I asked, holding out my hand to help her up.

Lark took it and rose to her feet. "Yup. Let's do this."

We both stepped onto the path—all four of us, I guess, if Bird and the dead spider counted. I caught myself holding my breath and gave a sigh of relief when the ground stayed put like it was supposed to.

I shifted my backpack and checked on Clyde. He was dozing on her shoulder, but the look on Lark's face made me stop and stare at her. She was at least a little afraid, that was pretty clear, but mostly she seemed to be in awe. She was staring down at the rough dirt trail and didn't look up at me when she spoke. "It's never shown up for me."

"The path?"

"Mm-hmm."

"What does that mean?"

She looked me in the eyes then, and I realized that hers were more than brown. They had flecks of gold and green dancing through them. "We have to work together to get to the Nighthouse. We go together and we get there together."

"Yeah, okay." It seemed obvious to me we'd be going together, but if she needed to hear it, I'd say it.

That was when something crashed in the forest. It sounded like an animal tearing through the trees. And it was moving toward us, fast. All the chittering birds stopped talking and the rest of the forest went dead quiet.

If there had been fear in Lark's eyes before, it was full-on panic now. "Evie, do we have a deal? We go together?"

"Sure." I could have been agreeing to anything. I was honestly more concerned about whatever was making that noise than answering Lark's question.

Lark looked around in every direction, searching for something, then back to me. "No, you have to *say* it: 'Lark, we have a deal.'"

I glanced around nervously, trying to find the source of the racket in the otherwise silent woods and wondering why *now* was the time for this particular conversation. "Lark, we have a deal." It wasn't that long ago I made a deal with Clackity, but I already trusted Lark a hundred times more than that awful creature. The image of Clackity that my brain had conjured up in the photograph flashed through my mind, and I shook my head to clear it.

The crashing sound was coming closer. I wanted to

run again. I had no idea where I should go, but it seemed like a smart thing to do.

Lark didn't move.

"Shake on it," she said, and shoved her hand toward me.

"Fine." I grabbed her hand with mine.

That was the moment Portia crashed through the trees and into the middle of the dirt path.

Her arms and legs were still sharp and bug-like, and her skin was flaking away in thin strips like she was molting. Which maybe she was. Her face had changed too. It was longer and narrower than before, her eyes bigger and rounder but just as black. She was beginning to look a whole lot like a giant, pale praying mantis. Somehow it was all made even more horrific by the fact that her dress and necklace and lank black hair still hung on her contorted frame.

Portia was the monster that hides in your closet, the thing under your bed.

When Portia spoke, sharp, wet teeth glinted in her mouth. She was looking at Lark. "What have you done?" she asked, her voice hoarse and angry. A thread of grey saliva dripped from the corner of her mouth, and I couldn't take my eyes off it.

Neither of us answered. We stood there in shock. Our handshake had turned into a vise, and we held on tight.

"WHAT HAVE YOU DONE?" This time she screamed the words, and I swear the whole forest shook. Clyde scampered down and back into Lark's pocket to hide.

The monster towered over Lark, who had to tip her head back to look Portia in the face. I took a half step back, wiping my sweaty hands on my shirt. In fact, my whole body was covered in cold sweat.

Lark let go of my hand and stood up as tall as she could, which wasn't very tall at all. "We made a deal. With our names. And we shook on it." Her voice hardly wavered at all.

Portia, on the other hand, was trembling with anger. Even her dark hair seemed furious. It twisted and writhed like greasy snakes. "Stupid, worthless, insolent girl. I cannot undo what has been set into motion. This changes nothing for you."

Lark nodded like she understood. I was glad one of us did.

Portia kept talking. Her voice was dangerous. "She might have been there already. This might have been finished. If she dies before she's done, before she reaches the Nighthouse and brings me my soul light, I will find you. I will find you and you will wish you'd never been so arrogant. You don't win, girl. Not against *me*. Not ever."

"If you want your 'soul light' so badly, get out of our way and let us pass. Although, I'm sure if you wait long enough, the Radix might come find you and then you won't need it." I didn't know if Lark's bravery was real or fake, but it was impressive. Bird seemed to agree—he was literally clapping his wings together.

Portia bared her pointed teeth at Lark and a growl like rusted metal came from her throat. Her chin was shiny with slick grey drool. Then she turned her eyes to me. It was all I could do not to cower behind Lark.

"You, child. This changes nothing for you, either. You

get to the Nighthouse, find what is mine, and bring it back to me."

Like Lark, I nodded. Unlike her, I didn't have any brave, calm words to go with the nod.

Portia twisted her head to the side, like she was trying to see me from a different angle. "And if you manage to get to the Nighthouse and she is still with you, may I suggest you toss her from the top and let the Radix decide what to do with her? She is not your friend."

"It would help if we knew what was waiting for us," Lark said, and thankfully, Portia took her terrible eyes off me and turned them back to the smaller girl.

Portia snarled, but it was also a smile. "So many things. So many things, I can't remember them all. But it will depend on her"—she jutted her chin toward me—"and the path she chooses."

"You could make it easier for us," Lark said. This time she was quiet. It was almost a plea.

"I cannot undo what has been set into motion. If she dies, girl, it is on your head."

And that was the last thing she said to us.

Portia whipped around, skittered on all fours, and climbed up the nearest tree. She was fast, and I lost sight of her in no time. There was a heavy rustling, and leaves began to rain down, right above us at first, then farther away. Somehow, she was making her way from one tree to another. I didn't care how—I was just glad that she was going. I took a ragged breath and listened to the sounds of her moving through the trees until I couldn't hear them anymore.

Lark and I stood like that for a minute, listening and not talking. Soon the birds and whatever other little things lived in the forest started making their noises again. I ran the confrontation with Portia over in my head, trying to make sense of it.

"For real," I said when it felt like talking was safe again, "what did you do to make her so mad?"

Lark stared off in the direction Portia had gone. "I got in her way. Back when I thought there was still a chance to stop her—to save her—I tried."

"But why? Who is she? To you, I mean."

Lark patted Clyde absently. She didn't look at me when she answered, "My aunt. My momma's sister."

"Your aunt? But she's . . . she's a monster. Like, literally a monster."

"She wasn't always. Or she was, I guess, in the way people can be inside. She wasn't an actual monster until she'd been here a while. But by then it was too late for her, anyway. I don't really want to talk about it right now." Lark was looking at something far away, farther than the trees around us and maybe farther than the Nighthouse beyond.

I thought of my own aunt, Des, who protected me with a fierce sort of love and who cared for me with the gentlest sort. I couldn't imagine having that monster for an aunt instead. It made me sad thinking about it, and I could only start to imagine how it made Lark feel.

"Is she going to keep showing up like that?" The question came out a whole lot braver than I felt.

"Maybe," Lark said. "But I don't think she'll show

herself often. Won't want to give away her position."

I laughed a sharp, ugly bark of a laugh. "What are we going to do to her?"

"Not us." Lark stroked Clyde, who'd climbed back up on her shoulder. "She's hiding from the Radix. That's what she's worried about."

Her and me both, I thought. Instead I said, "What was all that talk back there about how nothing changes?"

"Later," said Lark. "Let's move on to whatever's next."

I wanted more of an answer than that, but I also wanted to get moving. Besides, it seemed that Lark and I were going to be together for a while. There would be time for more questions.

The dense forest blocked out everything but random patches of purple sky. I had no idea where the Nighthouse was. "How do we know which way to go?"

"The path showed up for you. You said we should take it. So we do."

It wasn't much of a plan, but I had nothing better to suggest. Trusting my gut had mostly worked out the last time I was on the Dark Sun Side, and I hoped it would work now.

We started walking, me carrying my backpack and Lark carrying Clyde (Bird didn't count, since he was basically a part of me and didn't weigh anything, anyway). My feet kicked up puffs of dust when I walked, but Lark's didn't disturb a thing. Her shadow, long and thin, seemed to amble jerkily behind her in the weird light, not quite in step with her quick, even stride. Where I'd come from, ghosts didn't have shadows, but then again, they didn't talk, either. It was just another reminder that things were different on this side.

It might seem like it should have been strange, having a ghost and her dead spider as traveling companions, but thanks to years in Blight Harbor, I was perfectly okay with the idea.

Thinking about Blight Harbor was a mistake, because it made me think about Des again. I missed my aunt, and right then I wanted her near as much as I'd ever wanted anything. But there was no turning around, no backtracking and running home. The only way back to Aunt Des and the rest of my life was to reach the Nighthouse and do whatever it was I'd have to do.

It seemed neither of us had much to say. What I did have were a thousand questions, but Lark clearly wasn't in the mood. She radiated something that felt a whole lot like anger, and I was familiar enough with that to know better than to push her. Lark hadn't lost her temper with me yet, and I wasn't anxious to see what happened when she did. She was little, but she was tough.

The walking was easy. It wasn't uphill or anything, and the day wasn't too hot. The trees were mostly pines and maples, and the path wound through them gently—it was like any trail through any forest anywhere. It was calm, but it was boring. Lark was walking fast—sort of stomping, really—and had put a little distance between us, but not enough to worry about.

I stopped to grab a handful of rocks off the path

and chucked the first one at a nearby tree, just because. It hit with a satisfying *thunk*, but I lost track of where it landed.

The next rock missed the tree by a mile, and I was glad Lark hadn't been watching me throw it as it disappeared into the forest.

The third throw went high and up into the branches of a tree weighed down with thick greenish-black leaves. It took me a second to figure out what felt weird about that. Then my brain put it together: it never fell out of the tree. I'd never gotten a rock stuck in a tree before, and I almost told Lark about it before I remembered her scowl and changed my mind.

My fourth throw was perfect. It sailed toward the center of a thick trunk. But the rock never struck, because before it could hit the tree, the leaves of a low branch wrapped around it like a catcher's mitt, grabbing the stone out of midair.

I stopped and watched, waiting for the rock to fall. Waiting to realize that my eyes had played a trick on me. It didn't. They hadn't.

"Hey, come here," I called. Lark was a few yards ahead of me.

"What now?" she asked. Her mood really was foul.

"Come here, watch this."

She sighed a deep, irritated sigh, but she came my way. By the time she reached me, I had a new collection of throwing rocks.

"Watch," I repeated as I tossed a rock underhand

toward the tree. Once again, leaves caught it mid-flight. But this time, the branch lowered itself just a little to make the catch.

Before I could say anything, a grinding sound came from the leaves, and tiny bits of dust—dust that used to be a rock—sifted from the leaves and down to the ground. The branch returned to its previous position.

"Did you . . ."

"Yeah," Lark said. "Do it again."

So I did. Another rock, another catch, another stone crumbled to dust.

"What does it mean?"

Lark crouched low on the side of the path and stared out into the woods. After a minute, "Drop one here." She pointed to a clump of grass near her feet.

I dropped a smallish rock into the grass. This time, the grass wrapped itself around the rock. I was close enough that I could see the individual blades working as they pulverized the stone into nothing.

Clyde climbed up as high as he could and perched on Lark's head like a hat. Maybe to get a better view. Maybe to get as far away from that grass as he could. Bird was halfway up the side of my neck, watching warily.

My heart was pounding in my ears. I was scared for sure, but I was excited, too. Because if Portia had gotten caught up in this killer forest, it might've meant that we were done with her after all.

I found a thin stick on the path and tossed it into a nearby shrub covered in spiky red berries. The bush pulled the stick into its branches, and seconds later, there was a grinding sound followed by a faint puff of what looked and smelled like sawdust.

Lark and I stared at each other. Clyde was still crouched in her short hair. It turned out spiders could look nervous.

"I s'pose," she said, "this means we're staying on the path."

A creaking wooden sound followed by a crash came from the forest behind us. We both whipped around to find that a tree had fallen across the path where we had stood just a few minutes before. The tree was massive, and its branches and dark leaves were draped across the dirt trail.

"That was almost us." I started toward the tree to get a better look at what might have knocked it over.

"Be careful," Lark called after me.

I waved her off. I could handle a fallen tree.

A soft breeze I hadn't noticed before rustled the leaves. Well, more than rustled. The closer I got, the more they moved. By the time I reached the tree, the leaves shook in a strong wind I couldn't feel.

The rest of the forest was still.

"Von Rathe, let's go." Lark was at my heels. "I don't like this. It doesn't feel like an accident."

The path around the downed tree was littered with twigs and leaves. I nudged a stick with the toe of my sneaker. It didn't move, and the leaves that clung to it didn't try to crush my toe.

"Maybe they die once they fall off?" It wasn't a question I really expected an answer to. I picked up the branch and, quick as I could, jabbed my finger at a leaf and pulled it away. The leaf didn't try to grab my finger, but I made a surprised noise all the same. The tree on the ground was still quaking in what was beginning to seem a lot like rage.

"What?" Lark asked, startling me. She was right behind me again and I hadn't heard her coming. Ghosts were sneaky like that.

"It's like . . . metal," I said, pressing the leaf gently between my fingers. But that wasn't it exactly. The leaf was unnaturally hard, and I had no doubt that if I ran my finger along its edges, it would cut me like a razor. Still, metal wasn't quite the right word. It was something I'd never felt before. It was something that didn't exist outside this place. That much I was sure of.

"Let's go," Lark said. There was worry in her voice.

"In a minute." I took the stick and poked it against the wood (or whatever it was) that made up the trunk of the trembling tree.

Nothing happened.

Feeling brave, I touched my shoe to the trunk. Then my hand, making sure I was out of the reach of the nearest shaking leaf.

Still nothing.

I took the stick and plunged it into the angry leaves. They immediately drew in the stick, snatching it from my hand, and destroyed it.

Done with my experiment, I faced Lark. "The wood parts won't hurt us—they act like regular wood. It's the blackish-green parts that will mess us up."

She nodded. "Good to know. Let's *go*." Clyde was peeking out of her pocket. He was a nervous little thing. As much as I didn't want to admit it, the cowardly spider was starting to grow on me. I knew all about being anxious, and I imagined it was nice to have a big, soft pocket to hide in when the world got too scary.

We made it maybe another ten steps down the path when the creaking sound started again, but this time it filled the air all around us.

When the trees began falling, they went like giant dominoes. They crashed around us, and the sound was like drums and thunder and, well, like trees falling in a forest. I watched, frozen, as a tree directly above us began to teeter and then fall. Lark shoved me to get me going just in time. It crashed down a few yards behind us as we ran. So much for our boring walk in the woods.

We skidded to a stop as another trunk fell in front of us with a *thump* so hard, I could feel it in my bones. Tree after tree collapsed, most of them falling in the forest, but more than a few tumbling down into or across the dirt trail ahead of us.

The whole thing lasted maybe thirty seconds. When it was over, the forest was silent again except for the unnatural sound of the leaves on the fallen trees. The noise they made was a chorus of angry hornets.

"Well, this is a problem," Lark said. Her words were sarcastic, but her voice was scared.

I leaned down, hands on my thighs, and caught my breath. Ahead of us, furious trees crossed the path every few yards. My brain got busy making a choice between panic and determination. They were both totally reasonable reactions to our current predicament. I chose the second option. I took a deep breath, then another, and focused like it was my job. It's easy to choose panic, but determination takes work.

"It's not good," I agreed. But it also wasn't the end. We could get past the trees as long as we made sure to cross the trunks and avoid the leaves. Looking ahead, I could see that would be easy in some places, more complicated in others, where the wood and green were jumbled together from the fall.

The first couple of trees were no problem. Climbing over the thick trunks was tricky, but nothing we couldn't handle. As we made our way over them, the leaves still attached shook so hard, they hummed.

"These trees hate us."

"A lot," agreed Lark.

Things got more difficult as we went. The leaves of the next tree were almost unavoidable. Almost. By what was probably sheer luck, I made it over without getting attacked. Lark didn't get off as easily.

I heard her hiss, and when I turned to see what was wrong, she was holding her left forearm in her right hand. A thick, bronze-colored fog sifted between her fingers and drifted into the air.

"Are you *bleeding*?" I didn't know ghosts could bleed—in fact, I knew they *couldn't.* Not in the regular world, anyway. This new information blew my mind a little.

"Just keep going," she said between gritted teeth.

"I mean, can I help or . . . ?"

"I'm fine. It's fine. Keep going, Von Rathe."

So I did, but I didn't make it without any damage. More than once, an arm or leg was grazed by a wicked leaf. They were like razors. And every time I got cut, I found a new, more creative swear word to use.

"Quite the vocabulary," Lark said wryly after a particularly nasty cut.

"I've got more if you want to learn," I shot back.

"Oh, I'm familiar with most of those words. Just haven't heard them in a long while." That made me smile a little. I had no doubt Lark had plenty of swears she could teach me, too.

The farther we went, the more difficult it became. It didn't register at first, but the leaves and bark were getting more and more difficult to tell from one another.

Not, I realized, because their color had changed, but because there were more shadows. It was getting darker. I glanced up, and what I saw made my stomach fill with gravel.

"Lark," I said.

"Concentrating, Von Rathe," she replied from the top of a particularly leafy tree trunk.

"Look up."

She did. "Damn," she said.

Above us, the sky hadn't filled with clouds like I'd expected. It was the same clear violet as always. It was the forest around us that had changed.

The trees lining the path were no longer straight and

tall. Instead, they were leaning in toward the narrow dirt lane. Their tops were so close that some of them met in the middle, blocking out the black sun and turning the world to shades of grey.

Even as I watched, a tree reached lower. And *reached* was the right word. The trees were reaching for us the same way the branches had reached out for the rocks I'd thrown. And we'd seen what they had done to those rocks.

There was no way through or around, and nowhere lower to go. We had to get down the killer-tree-covered path and out of the forest.

"Faster," I whispered in case the trees were listening.

Lark didn't answer as she hopped off the trunk she'd been standing on. A group of leaves grabbed at her pant leg, tripping her and sending her to the ground. This time, it was my turn to reach for her. Lark took my hand and got back to her feet. It wasn't like helping a living person, but Lark was substantial in a way the ghosts in Blight Harbor weren't. She was stronger, and there was just *more* to her. I wondered if it was something special about her, or this place, or both.

We moved as quickly as we could. I tried to focus on the fallen trees ahead and the hungry trees above. But being faster and distracted meant we weren't nearly as careful. More often than not, I came away with a new scratch or six for every tree I climbed over. The lower the trees got, the darker it was and the harder it became to avoid the razor-sharp leaves.

The end of the path was in sight—cloudless purple sky and treeless black grass were visible just twenty or thirty feet away—but the ground was nearly covered in fallen trees, and the exit was closing up fast. The trees were trying to trap us. And if that happened . . .

I might have stood there, frozen, thinking, until the forest had us, if a noise hadn't snapped me out of it. Directly overhead came a whirring, buzzing sound. I looked up to see a branch full of angry leaves quaking maybe two feet directly over my head. All at once, low branches surrounded us. Leaves twitched and vibrated and filled the air with the sound of chain-saw-wielding murder bees.

"Get down!" I yelled, and Lark dropped to the ground without having to be told twice.

I crawled to her as fast as I could on my hands and skinned-up knees. "What do we do?" I asked.

"Fire?" Lark suggested.

It wasn't the worst idea. I had a box of matches, there was kindling all over the ground, and trees were made of wood. At least, I hoped they were. It might work.

Except. celest ot 12/16

Except we were literally surrounded by giant, flammable trees that were out to kill us. As soon as some caught fire, either:

> they would all go up in flames, and we'd be
>   surrounded and burned to death, or
> the trees not yet on fire would hurry up
>   and attack us, and we'd be sliced up like
>   sandwich meat, or
> both.

They were all terrible options.

"Anything else?" I asked.

"Maybe . . . ," Lark replied.

"Maybe what?" Even with us low to the ground, the leaves were getting dangerously close. Standing wasn't even an option anymore. If we were getting out of this, we were crouching to do it. Crawling, maybe.

Lark put her hand to her pocket and whispered something I couldn't hear. Clyde came out, one fuzzy little leg after the other, and stood in the palm of her hand. He didn't look all that excited to be out of the safety of his hiding place.

"Can you do it?" Lark asked. In response, Clyde jumped off her hand and skittered to the edge of the path.

"I guess not?" I said unhelpfully, even though I had no idea what it was Clyde was supposed to be doing.

"Just wait," said Lark. I swear there was a hint of a smile in her eyes.

I watched as the spider climbed up the trunk of one of the trees that lined the end of the path. The tree took no notice of Clyde and didn't send any killer branches after him. The round little spider climbed as high as he could without bumping into any murderous leaves, probably as high as I was tall, and then . . . he was gone.

"Where'd he go?" I asked.

In response, Lark pointed to the other side of the path. In a tree, directly across from the one he'd climbed, I could just make out Clyde's round grey form.

And then he was gone again.

I looked one way and then the other, trying to spot the arachnid.

"I don't . . ."

"Look," said Lark, and pointed back and forth in the air above the path between us and freedom.

I didn't see it—them—at first, but once I did, they were impossible to miss. Hundreds of fine threads were pulled tight across the path, and more were appearing by the second. They crissed and crossed over and around one another, forming a kind of mesh.

"He's . . . making a web?"

Lark nodded, and now she really was smiling.

As the first buzzing leaves touched the web, they attacked with a vengeance, but all they managed to do was shred themselves into bits and pieces against the silk barrier Clyde had produced.

This was *not* a regular spiderweb. Bird moved from shoulder to shoulder and back again, trying to keep up with it all. He was as impressed with the oversized arachnid as I was.

"Let's go," said Lark. "I don't know how long it will hold." She was right. The webbing was sagging in the middle like a net full of party balloons.

We moved as quickly as crouching and crawling would allow. There were more cuts and scrapes as we made our way over the remaining downed trees—and one particularly nasty leaf that embedded itself in my arm (I had to close my eyes to pull it out)—but it was nothing compared to what would have happened if the descending branches had managed to reach us.

With what looked a whole lot like fury, the trees did their best to cut through the web. The sounds of those sharp leaves destroying themselves against impossibly strong silk were deafening. Tiny shreds of green-black leaves rained down on us as we neared the exit. Most of them itched like that pink insulation you're never supposed to touch, and the rest just felt like tiny splinters we'd need tweezers (which we didn't have) to remove. I said a silent prayer that the web would hold. A few shards were bad enough, but if they all came pouring down at once, well, I suddenly understood the saying, "death by a thousand paper cuts."

After climbing over one last enormous tree (during which we both got cut and both said fantastic swear words), we made our way through a narrow hole at the edge of the path and, finally, out of the murderous forest.

"Let's never do that again," Lark said as she looked over her new collection of cuts and scrapes.

"Not ever," I agreed. "But we could if we had to, you know. We were pretty great back there."

That got a real smile out of Lark. "We're doing teamwork pretty well," she said.

Clyde had joined us somewhere along the way, and he perched on Lark's shoulder, looking awfully proud of himself. Without thinking, I reached over and stroked his back. He felt like dandelion fuzz in the spring. "Good work, buddy. Sorry I wanted to squash you earlier," I said.

Bird flitted from one place on my skin to another, worrying over the countless cuts and scrapes now covering my body. I patted him gently. "I'm okay, Bird. I promise."

I felt more than a little like crying. This had been our first major obstacle—second if you counted the world sliding into the Radix—and we'd gotten through it mostly okay. My arms and legs stung, but it wasn't bad enough to keep me from going on.

What did stop me was the new problem ahead of us. The path kept going, but it forked. We had a choice to make.

9

The path forked in a perfect Y. There were
two options: right or left.

I took my backpack off and sat down in the middle of
the path. I needed water and a granola bar and a chance
to sit on my butt for a minute and think. Lark sat down
next to me. The scratches covering her exposed skin were
already starting to heal.

"How come you can get hurt here?" I asked. "And
bleed? I didn't know ghosts even *had* blood."

Lark shook her head. "I don't know."

I didn't buy it.

"I don't buy it. You've been here a hundred years. I
mean, for sure you've figured some of this stuff out by
now?"

Lark took a long time to look at me, and then even
longer to answer. The look in her eyes was angry, but it
was sad, too. That look made me wish I could take my
words back, stuff them into my mouth, and swallow
them whole, even if it meant I choked.

"I'm sorry," I started.

"Me too," said Lark. "I'm sorry I don't have answers for you and I'm sorry you don't believe that. And I'm sorry I ever followed my aunt here and I'm sorry I tried to save her when she wasn't worth saving."

"Lark, I . . ." But she kept going.

"You want to know what I know? Here it is: I came here because Meredith—*that's* her name, not Portia—because Meredith was obsessed with this place. With the Radix. She started out just wanting some magic, to be special, so she made a deal to tend the Nighthouse. It was supposed to be a safe place for folks who got lost over on this side. Meredith said there are a bunch of Nighthouses all over, if you know where to look. Lighthouses warn ships *away*, but the Nighthouses are different. They're meant to guide people to safety. That was her job, to keep the lost safe.

"But after a while, magic and responsibility weren't enough, and in the end all she wanted was power. And the more she got, the more she wanted. She stole it, a little at first, and then more and more. And every time she came home to visit, she was a little less her and a little more whatever this place was making her."

Lark was crying now, streams running from both eyes.

"Lark, you don't have to . . ."

"And do you know why I came here? Why I followed her one night and tried to stop her? Because I loved her. She was my aunt, and every time she came home, we saw that even though she looked the same, she was less her and more something awful, and it was breaking my heart and Momma's heart and I just wanted her to come back to us.

"I made up my mind one Sunday. I remember borrowing my brother's clothes, because dresses are no good for this sort of thing, and feeling a little silly in pants with my hair done pretty for church." Lark touched her hair.

It was then that I noticed how even and smooth the waves were, like a lady's hair from an old-fashioned magazine. Those careful waves were proof to me that her mom had loved her, and thinking about it made my tears burn in my eyes.

Lark went on, "I followed my aunt through the door that always seemed to open for her, and I tried. I tried so hard to get her to stop, to give back all that stolen magic and just come home to us. But . . . it was too late. By the time I got there, she'd already traded her soul in exchange for all that stolen magic. She said it was a 'good, fair deal.'" Lark shook her head. "Maybe it was always too late, and all the magic really did was make some kind of awful that had always lived inside her bigger. Maybe it just grew and grew until it was all she was and showed on her outside, too. *I tried.* And when I did, she . . ."

Lark stopped and I was glad. She was crying and now I was too. She had more to tell me, but I wasn't sure I wanted to hear it. I wasn't sure I wanted to hear the story of how Lark came to this place a living girl and ended up stuck here a ghost.

"Anyway," Lark said, wiping at her eyes. "You're right, I've been here a long time. I should know the answers to your questions, about why I am the way I am. I should know everything there is to know about this place, about its tricks and traps, and how to get us to the Nighthouse and out of here. But, Evie, I *don't*." Lark's voice broke and my heart broke right along with it.

"I don't know because I've been alone. All this time, I've been alone. And Meredith—*Portia*—made it so I can't get to the Nighthouse. No matter how hard I try, how far I walk, it's been a hundred years and I've never been able to get there. And I can't get home, either. Because there's never a door. Not for me." Lark turned her whole body toward me and took my hand in both of hers.

"The path showed up for you. It won't be easy, because she made it impossible for me, but together we can get there. We have to. We can get to the Nighthouse, maybe even save Miss Dwyer, and get out of this place for good."

She had finally run out of steam. Lark sat holding my hand, and the look in her eyes threatened to tear my heart out and make me start crying all over again. Because that look was both the saddest and most hopeful thing I'd ever seen, and let me tell you, the combination gutted me.

I wrapped my arms around Lark and she sank into me, a girl lonelier and stronger than I ever would be—than I could even imagine being. For a minute it was like she was six instead of eleven, much less a hundred and eleven.

"I promise," I said. "We're going to do all those things. We're going to find Florence, and a door, and we're both getting out of here. And when we do, you never, ever have to come back." Lark nodded, her face pressed into my shoulder. I could feel Bird doing his best to stroke the top of her head and I hoped she could feel it too.

After a while, I didn't know how long, Lark pulled away and wiped at her eyes with the heels of her hands.

"Sorry—" she started, but I cut her off.

"No way," I said. "No apologies. Not to me. Not to anyone."

Lark nodded again, stood up, and turned to look at the scene ahead of us. I did the same.

The path we'd been on split in two into a Y. The path to the right was wide open. It was flat and smooth and surrounded by a little green-black grass, but mostly everything was covered in bright green leafy plants. The black sun shone high overhead, and already I could tell how nice it would be to walk with that sun on my shoulders down a scenic trail. If we took that path, it would be like taking a casual stroll on a nice spring day. But, more than any of that, the biggest selling point of that route was that it appeared to go exactly in the direction we wanted. Even Lark's weird ghost shadow shifted ahead of us, like it was anxious to head down the sunny path.

On the horizon, at what looked like the other end of the trail to the right, stood the Nighthouse. From that distance, I couldn't make out a whole lot of detail. It was tall, but how tall I couldn't say. And so dark against the violet sky that it looked like it had been cut out with a pair of scissors. It reminded me too much of the silhouette house that had almost been the end of me a few weeks before, and I shuddered a little at the memory. The dull yellow light at the top of the tower flashed, and I swear it was calling to me.

To the left, the path looked about the same as the one we'd been on. The forest we'd just escaped continued on the left side, but it was thinner and wasn't threatening to tumble down around us. The path was a little rocky and not as smooth and wide as the path on the right.

Also, it didn't seem to lead in the direction of the Nighthouse.

Also, it led steeply down and disappeared into a black tunnel maybe fifty yards ahead. Near the entrance to the tunnel, everything was dead or on its way there. The green-black grass became dried-up clumps of brown. Even the trees were brittle and colorless, and their bare branches reached into the sky like Halloween decorations. The tunnel might as well have had a flashing neon sign in front that said: KEEP OUT—HERE THERE BE MONSTERS.

"This seems obvious," Lark said, once again sounding like the brave and strong girl I knew her to be.

She was right: it did seem obvious that we should take the clear path that ended at the Nighthouse. The thing was, that felt way too easy. It felt like a trap.

"I don't know," I said, hesitating.

"You don't *know*? I don't see a question here." Lark's foul mood was threatening to come back.

"Give me a minute." It wasn't just that it was too easy—it was something about those bright green plants. I recognized them.

I closed my eyes and rifled through my brain to figure out where I'd seen them before. Then I remembered a trip I took with my parents a very long time ago. We'd gone to visit my mom's father, a man I didn't see often or know well. When he died, I'd been about six, and I remembered sadness in the grown-ups all around me, but I don't remember actually feeling much of it myself.

An image of Grandpa's house in a little town down south rose in my mind. In the memory, I could see him there, wiping sweat off his forehead, looking out over a field the very same brilliant shade of green as the one in front of me now. In fact, it wasn't just a field. There were trees as well, and some of those trees were covered up all the way to their tops by that bright green plant. Grandpa was waging a constant battle with that plant, a plant that took over everything it touched. . . .

"Kudzu," I said.

"Excuse me?"

"Kudzu. It's like the worst kind of weed you can imagine. It's all long vines, and grows superfast, and basically takes over everything around it. Trees, cars, houses. You name it, and kudzu will cover it up and suffocate it. It's pretty, but it's deadly."

"So?"

"So what if it's like the trees back there? What if it . . . eats stuff? There's no safe brown trunk to protect us— that plant is all leaves. If it comes after us like the trees did, we'll be goners."

Lark took a minute to answer as she studied one path and then the other. "So let's find out."

I was one step ahead of her. I grabbed a broken branch off the ground, walked a few yards to where the path split, and threw the branch Frisbee-style as hard as I could into the green plants on the right. The kudzu swallowed it immediately, and the plants kind of shivered as they ate the branch. That shiver seemed delighted. And hungry.

"We might be safe if we stay on the trail," Lark said. But she didn't sound so sure anymore.

I grabbed another, bigger branch and chucked it underhand into the middle of the path on the right. Almost before it landed, kudzu vines shot out toward it. They wrapped around the branch and pulled it off the path and into the green. A familiar crunching noise carried through the air. The plants shivered again, and I swear they were asking for more.

They wanted something other than leaves and branches.

They wanted us.

"It's a trick," I said, now totally sure. "It might let us get a little way down that path, but eventually the kudzu's coming for us, and there's no way we're going to outrun it. Or outsmart it. There's too much and it moves too fast. You saw it."

Lark sighed. "So we . . . ?"

"So we take the scary tunnel of doom." I wasn't happy about it. The Nighthouse was right there at the end of a sunny, straight path. But I reminded myself that was exactly how traps worked. Traps put something you wanted within reach, and then you paid for it when you took the bait. If The Clackity had taught me anything, it was that.

"Tunnel of doom it is," Lark said.

Before we headed off, I found another branch from one of the violent trees. It was smallish but had lots of those sharp, almost-but-not-quite-metal leaves.

I crouched and very carefully unzipped the empty front pocket of my backpack and put the branch in. I zipped it shut and looked up to see Lark staring at me with her head cocked to the side a little. There was a question in her eyes.

"I just . . . it's interesting. And maybe we can find out what the leaves are made of. And maybe it will come in handy." I was embarrassed and rambling because I didn't really know why I wanted one of those branches. I just did. Proof of where I'd been, maybe, when I got home. If I ever got home. I shook that idea out of my head and stood to join Lark.

"Let's do it," I said, doing my best to sound confident. "To the tunnel of doom."

It didn't take long. As we got close, a cool breeze wrapped itself around us. That breeze was coming from inside the tunnel. I couldn't help but think of the cold that had come through the black door that opened in the old schoolhouse. It felt like a lifetime ago, and I felt a million miles from home. All at once I was tired. Tired and sad and homesick.

If Lark hadn't been with me, I might have just sat my butt right there in the middle of the trail and cried for a while. But she *was* with me, and she needed me to be strong and sure, so I didn't. Instead I kept walking. That's the thing about having a friend to go through bad stuff with—it makes you stronger.

The opening to the tunnel was taller than it had looked from a distance, maybe fifteen feet high or more. It blocked out the sun, and the shade it created was so dark that my own shadow had almost disappeared, and Lark's was entirely gone.

Built into the side of a hill, the entrance was curved at the top and lined with big grey stones. The stones looked old. I know, I know, all stones are old. What I mean is they looked like they had been there for a long time. For hundreds of years. And I had a feeling in my stomach that told me the tunnel had been waiting for a long time too. Maybe for anyone desperate enough to enter it. Maybe specifically for us.

At the mouth of the tunnel—and that was what it really was, a mouth—I was shivering so hard that my teeth were clacking. Some of that was from the cold, but it was also from being scared.

Inside, the tunnel wasn't completely black. Lights flickered in the distance, but they were too far away for me to tell where they came from. Lights meant someone—or something—had been there before us. I liked that idea even less than the thought of being totally alone in there.

I started for my flashlight but decided against it. It looked like we'd have enough light to be able to see, and I wasn't anxious to draw any more attention to us than we had to, just in case whoever had been there before was still there.

Carnivorous kudzu or not, the other path was looking really good right about then.

I glanced over at Lark, who seemed to be thinking roughly the same thing I was. "I guess we go in?" I asked. I was kind of hoping she'd try to talk me out of it.

She didn't. She just nodded, a determined look almost masking the fear on her face. Clyde, who had been riding on Lark's shoulder for a while, was back in her pocket.

Smart spider.

Bird was up on my shoulder blade, helping to keep watch.

Good bird.

I didn't know what I had expected when we walked into the tunnel. Maybe for a bunch of screaming bats to come flying out at us. Maybe for it to close up behind us, trapping us underground. None of that happened. In fact, *nothing* happened.

At first.

It was really dark, but the flickering up ahead gave off just enough light for me to see that the same round stones that made up the entrance also lined the tunnel walls. I was pretty sure now that the flickering came from candles. A *drip, drip, drip* sound filled the air around us, which made sense. The tunnel was not only dark but cold and damp, too (because of course it couldn't just be dark and scary). The sound of the dripping echoed, and it was disorienting.

"Even my bones are cold," I told Lark quietly. Which, as it turned out, was kind of an ironic way to put it. We walked slowly. Quietly. It just felt like we were supposed to, like we were in the kind of place where you weren't supposed to be noisy.

As we got closer to the flickering lights, I saw that they weren't coming from candles but from old-fashioned gas lamps attached to the walls of the tunnel. There was one maybe every twenty feet. The flames were the same black as the sun outside, but they still managed to give us enough light to see by.

In the light of those black lamps, shadows danced and twisted and settled into every little hole and crevice. It made some of the stones in the walls look less like rocks and more like skulls, with deep sockets where the eyes should be and open, grinning mouths.

I reached a hand out and ran my fingertips along the wall. I didn't know why. Smooth, damp stone after smooth, damp stone passed under my fingers. That is, until I felt something different. Something both bumpy and smooth all at the same time. Kind of like when you run your fingers over the front of your teeth.

Actually, that was exactly what it felt like.

Something as big as Clyde, but not nearly as nice, felt like it was climbing up my spine.

That did it. I didn't care if we were alone or not—I wasn't worried about giving away our position. I needed to see what those walls were made of. I dropped my back-pack to the ground and fumbled around until I felt the heavy metal barrel of the flashlight. It went on with a *click*, and the light it gave was bright and white. I pointed the beam over the walls.

It didn't take long to see what they really were.

Plenty of the tunnel *was* made of those smooth grey stones. But not just stones. The flickering light hadn't been playing tricks on my eyes after all. Every so often, a skull was embedded in the wall. Sometimes just one, in other places small groups of them.

Like families, my brain said. And that got me shivering all over again.

The skulls shone in the beam of the flashlight like they'd been polished.

I sent the light ahead of us, farther down the tunnel. It was the same: skulls randomly placed where stones should be. Occasionally, other types of bones stuck out of the wall. Here, most of a skeletal hand. There, a foot. And what looked like a leg, bent at the knee.

The tunnel was a grave. The word *catacomb* came to mind. I knew a catacomb was like an underground graveyard, but I was pretty sure they didn't make the walls out of the people buried in them.

"Do you think they're real?" I said to Lark. But even as I asked it, I knew the answer. None of the skulls were exactly the same shape or size, and none had the same teeth. Some were straight and even, others crooked. One close to me had a gold front tooth, and some of them were missing teeth entirely.

"I do. And I think we should be going." Lark's voice was low and very serious. She didn't have to tell me again. I couldn't get out of there fast enough.

The walls must have been listening, because that was when they shifted. Not much, but enough that thousands of stones and skulls and bones rattled and clanked against one another. The walls were showing us they could move. That they *would* move.

"Run," Lark said for the second time that day.

"No. Walk fast, but don't run. If you run, you'll panic. Trust me." I wanted to run as badly as Lark did, but I also knew from experience that I was right.

We walked as fast as we could without actually breaking into a sprint. The tunnel wasn't a straight line. It twisted and turned and sometimes even felt like it was doubling back on itself. We took one tight turn that led us to a Y in the tunnel. I was trying to figure out which way to go when the shifting started again, but this time it didn't stop. The tunnel on the right began to close up on itself, the stones and skulls rolling in from both sides until they formed a wall. We didn't have a choice now, so we quickly took the tunnel that had once been on the left. Now it was the only choice we had.

The farther we got, the more lost we became and the more horrified I felt. There were so many bones. So many people buried around us. Fingers, and sometimes whole arms, stuck out of the wall like they were trying to grab at us. Or like they were asking for help. It was scary and so sad all at the same time.

More than once a tunnel decided to turn into a wall and we had to change course. But we were doing okay. We hadn't gotten trapped, and we hadn't gotten hurt. And, so far, I'd been able to mostly ignore the claustrophobic belt tightening around my ribs and lungs.

Around another corner, another choice to make.

This time Lark (who I suspected was beginning to panic—I knew the signs) rushed through the tunnel to the right without waiting to see if anything would happen. Sure enough, the tunnel began to close up behind her, threatening to separate us.

I screamed at her, so loud it hurt my throat, "Lark, come back!"

But by the time the words were out of my mouth, the tunnel was gone. We were separated by a wall of rocks and dead people.

I stood there for a few seconds, in shock, I guess, at how quickly and easily we'd become separated. I ran my hands over the wall, looking for weak spots. There were a few small holes between some of the newly rearranged rocks and skulls, but none of them were big enough for me to get more than a finger in.

Finally I did the thing I was afraid to do. "Lark, can you hear me?" I hoped she hadn't kept running. I hoped she hadn't gotten lost. I hoped she hadn't gotten hurt.

"Yeah, I can hear you."

Relief washed over me like warm water. She was still there. And she wasn't dead—or dead *again*, which I now thought could possibly be a thing, since I'd seen her bleed not so long ago.

I sat down hard and leaned against the rock wall. Something told me Lark was doing the same thing on her side. I ran my fingers along the cracks between the stones and skulls, no longer caring if I touched the bones or not.

"So what do we do?" I asked through the wall.

A pause and then, quietly, "You know I don't know that, Von Rathe. If I did . . ." Lark allowed her sentence to trail off unfinished.

I didn't like the hopeless note in Lark's voice. I tried again.

"What kind of place *is* this?" I didn't just mean the tunnel—I meant the whole entire messed-up world I'd found myself in.

Lark didn't answer. I didn't ask any more questions.

After a bit of silence, Lark asked a question of her own. "Von Rathe, it's too quiet. I can't stand it. Talk to me. Tell me something. How about your family? Brothers? Sisters? What're your folks like?"

I was quiet long enough for her to ask, "You're still there, right? You okay?"

"Yeah," I said. "Still here. Thinking, I guess. It's complicated."

"Your family?"

I clasped my hands tight between my legs so I wouldn't have to feel them tremble. It helped. I decided to just rip the Band-Aid off. "Yeah. I live with my aunt Des. She's amazing. You'd love her."

"Just the two of you, then?" There was something like sympathy in her voice, but none of the pity that made me grind my teeth.

"Just us. No sisters or brothers. When I was eight, there was a fire and my parents disappeared, so I moved in with Des."

"Disappeared, not died?" Lark didn't mince words.

"Disappeared, not died," I confirmed.

"You're looking for them?"

"Sort of. Yes," I said. *Always,* I thought. "I just don't know where to start. I'll figure it out someday. And when I do, they'll move in with me and Des and we'll be together like we're supposed to be."

"You'll find them," Lark said, and her voice was certain.

I didn't know what to say to that, so I just said, "Thanks."

We were quiet after that.

It was dim in the chamber of tunnels, and the dripping, echoing sound was rhythmic and weirdly soothing. The walls had gotten quiet. Bird was curled up on my collarbone, resting. I took my hoodie out of my backpack and draped it over myself.

My eyes got heavy, and at some point, I fell asleep. I probably could have slept for hours—days, even.

But when I woke up, I woke up all at once and all the way.

Because, in the dark of the tunnel, something had touched my face.

A very thin, very cold finger that felt more
like stone than flesh traced the side of my cheek.

My eyes flew open, and I was staring into the empty
sockets of a skull.

I blubbered. I mean it. I tried to make words, but
words wouldn't come out and I just made noises instead.

The skull was attached to most of a skeleton. It was
missing a few ribs, but otherwise it seemed pretty intact.
The skeleton knelt in front of me as it reached out to
touch my face again.

I let out a sharp yap of a yell.

The thing fell back in surprise, clattering to the stone
floor of the tunnel.

"You okay over there?" Lark asked through the wall.

I didn't answer. I was too busy watching the skeleton pull itself up to its full height, which was not very
tall. It held its hands out in an *I'm not here to hurt
you* sort of gesture and took a single step back as if to
prove it. It gleamed in the light thrown by the gas lamps

on the walls, looking more like opal than bone.

"What do you think?" I whispered to Bird, who was now wide awake.

I don't know. Be careful.

"Evie." Lark's voice was louder now, more concerned. "Answer me. Are you okay?"

"I don't know," I said as calmly as I could. "I have a . . . a visitor."

"What does that *mean*?" she asked.

"Just . . . just hold on."

I could hear her grumbling on the other side of the wall. Lark wasn't satisfied with my answer—and for good reason—but an idea had come to me, and no matter what happened when I tried it, it would tell me a lot.

"Hey, buddy," I said softly to Bird, "you ready to do this?"

Bird didn't have to ask what I meant, and he didn't hesitate. He made his way down my arm and into the palm of my hand. I stood and took a step toward the skeleton with my arm outstretched and palm up so it could see Bird in my hand. I knew from experience that if it drew away from Bird, tried to avoid being touched by him, then the skeleton was something to be worried about.

I took another step forward. Then another, closing the gap between me and the bone person. It didn't move away, but it did seem interested. The skeleton's head was cocked to the side a bit, and if it had had eyes, they would have been looking in Bird's direction.

Another step, and then I was just one last footfall

away from touching the thing. I stood there, and Bird stayed in my palm, both of us waiting to see what would happen next. It occurred to me then that I hadn't considered that the skeleton could react violently, that if Bird scared or angered it, it might lash out.

And it did move fast, much faster than I would have guessed it could, and grasped my sweaty hand with its cold, dry one.

I tried to pull away, but the skeleton was too strong. Panic rose from my stomach and wrapped around my throat. My breathing got shallow and my heart felt like it might explode. I'd gotten cocky and made a mistake and now I was going to pay for it. I squeezed my eyes shut and turned my head away. I didn't want to see what was coming.

What came was a gentle, bony fingertip on my palm.

Bird stayed perfectly still. I risked opening my eyes the tiniest bit to see what was happening.

The skeleton had loosened its grip on my hand without actually letting go. The fingers of its other hand were gently stroking Bird's back and his wings, then, so softly, the top of his head. Even without it having eyes or a face, I could see the skeleton was enamored with my little buddy.

Bird would have been purring if he could. It was enough for me. I trusted the skeleton.

I'd forgotten entirely about Lark, who was now full-on yelling at me from the other side of the wall. "Dang it, Von Rathe, *what's going on?*"

I thought about telling Lark the whole truth—*there's*

a skeleton here, but it's okay because Bird likes it—then thought better of it. That might've been too much for someone trapped behind a wall that hadn't been a wall not so long ago. So I went with part of the truth instead. "I'm working on getting you out of there!"

I slowly pulled my hand away from the skeleton, who was still caressing Bird. I needed to break the spell between them if either of them was going to be any help at all. To the skeleton, I said, "My friend is trapped behind that wall. Do you know any way to make it . . . move? Or come down?"

The skeleton tilted its head again, pondering. The shadows cast by the lamps on the walls danced in its eye sockets, and it was almost like I could see its thoughts. A sound like soft wind came from its mouth, but there was a pattern, a rhythm, to it. The skeleton was talking. Or trying to, anyhow.

It took my hand, with Bird still in it, and led me back to the wall of stones and bones. The skeleton placed my hand on what looked like a femur. At my touch, the long bone recoiled, trying to pull itself deeper into the wall. It didn't like my touch, or Bird, or both.

The skeleton shook its head and led me to a second set of bones, this time a hand and part of a wrist that jutted out of the wall like a demented coat hook. When I touched that hand, something remarkable happened. The hand grasped mine and I gasped in alarm, but the skeleton next to me squeezed my shoulder reassuringly.

The hand in the wall let go of me, then proceeded to grab onto the stones around it as it began to pull itself free. I backed up a few steps, unsure what was coming next.

With the skeleton came a tumble of dust and bits of rock. A tiny hole opened in the space it left behind, a hole I was certain went all the way through to the other side. To Lark.

"What is *happening* over there?" she demanded.

"I think you'll see in just a minute." Lark's response to that was an irritated huff that told me she was not at all satisfied with my answer.

The skeleton moved slowly, with a *clickity clackity* kind of sound. When it was free of the wall, it swayed a little and took a couple of shaky, unsure steps. The skeleton stumbled, awkward as a newborn deer. It made its way to us with a rambling, rickety walk.

The newly freed skeleton took my hand and touched Bird reverently before the first skeleton leaned toward where its ear would have been and whispered to it in a soft breeze of a voice. I assumed it explained to its friend what it was we were trying to do.

The new skeleton nodded and stepped aside.

The next set of bones we touched pulled away from my hand. The bones after that did the same, burying themselves deeper in the wall to avoid me or Bird— probably Bird. But the next set, a shoulder and upper arm bones, dragged itself from the wall to join us. Another hole opened up, and this time I could see Lark peeking through.

"Whatever it is you're doing is working," she said.

I just nodded, too entranced with the weird ritual we

were performing to say much of anything. Many skeletons rejected me and Bird, but enough chose to join us that when the sixth bone person pulled itself free of the wall, a loud, shuddering, rumbling noise came from directly above our heads.

"Get back," I called to Lark and to my new bone friends.

In seconds, the wall came down in a crash of stones and bones and dust, and I could see my friend again. Lark, wide-eyed and maybe a little terrified at the band of skeletons, said, "Interesting approach, Von Rathe."

"Bird likes them," I said, like that explained everything. Then I added, "I do too."

Lark nodded and crossed over the rubble to join us. As she did, an unusually long, bony hand reached out of the pile and grabbed her ankle. Lark cried out as the thing attempted to drag her down into the pile with it. She fell to her knees, and suddenly another too-long bone hand had her by the arm.

It must have been one, or some, of the skeletons that did not respond well to Bird. So I did the only thing I knew to do: I rushed to Lark and grabbed ahold of the first skeletal hand, pressing Bird firmly against it. The hand shuddered and flailed and finally pulled itself from my grasp and, in all the fighting, lost its grip on Lark. I grabbed the second hand, the one clutching Lark's arm, and that flailed and fought as well.

A skull, half-buried in rubble, turned toward me. In the flickering light of the cave, it looked as though it had only one eye socket and a smooth groove where the other should have been. And its teeth—it seemed to have too many, and those were too sharp and too broken. In that moment I was absolutely certain that The Clackity had made its way into the cave and inside that poor skeleton.

I swear to you on everything I love: that skull smiled at me.

My skin turned into a million tiny spiders, and I choked back a scream that was part terror and part white-hot rage. I gave a panic-fueled tug, and as soon as she was free, I pulled Lark off the pile and to what I thought was safety. We stood with the six skeletons who'd helped us, but I focused my attention on the first one, the shortest in the group.

"Please," I said, "can you get us out of here?" I turned back to look for the Clackity skeleton, but it was lost among all the other stones and bones (if it had ever been there at all).

The skeleton paused. It seemed to be looking at Lark. Then it nodded and gestured for us to follow.

Even as we began to move, the chaotic sound of shifting rocks filled the air. A small army of skeletons, those who had not been pleased with me and Bird, pulled themselves from the rubble and began making their way toward us. Some moved slowly, and those missing foot bones or entire legs dragged themselves along the floor of the tunnel. But others were fast, too fast, and charged us. The sight of that scene, straight out of a scary movie, might have frozen me to the spot, but I'm pretty sure I was too freaked out to panic.

We ran then, me and Lark and a small group of friendly skeletons. We followed the little one through twists and turns that would have taken me and Lark hours to figure out. Behind us, the enraged bone people screamed their skeleton screams, loud whistles and wind-filled moans coming from their grinning mouths. I blocked the noise out as best I could, because it sounded way too much like the foghorn sound of a panic attack, and I wasn't about to let that happen.

After one especially sharp turn, I saw something that made me feel a little less terrified. The tunnel straightened out, and far ahead of us was a patch of violet. It was a glimpse of that weird purple sky. We'd literally found the light at the end of the tunnel.

I took deep, even breaths and ignored the stitch in my side. We were getting close, but we still weren't out.

The light of the sky grew a little brighter with every step, the tunnel a little less black. We had maybe fifty yards to go, close enough to the end that I imagined I could taste fresh air and feel the sun, but the rattling, rabid bone people were gaining on us.

A thought crossed my mind that made it hard to keep running. *Why do you think they're going to stop at the end of the tunnel? Why don't you think they'll just keep chasing you? What if they catch you and drag you back in?*

It is always, *always*, a bad idea to look back.

I did it anyway.

What I saw was one of the Bird-loving skeletons trip and fall to the ground. Immediately, some of the

Bird-hating skeletons were on it. They were like animals. Thankfully, I couldn't tell one bone from the other well enough to see exactly what happened, but the sound of a thing dying is unmistakable. It sounded like that poor, tripped-up skeleton died a second time back there in the tunnel, and it happened because of me—*for* me. My eyes blurred with surprise tears, and my throat got hot and tight. I swore right then that I wouldn't let anyone or anything else get hurt on my way to the Nighthouse.

As I tried to pick up speed, the little skeleton fell back until it was running alongside me. It motioned at me— *Keep going!*—then fell back even farther. I glanced back again, because I was worried about the skeleton, who I was already thinking of as my new friend. It was still running forward, but it was also running from one side of the tunnel to the other. And each time it reached a wall, it tapped hard and made a low sort of bellow.

Then a new sound stopped me in my tracks. It was the sound of shifting, and then falling stones. And it was coming from somewhere between us and the angry army.

This time I didn't just look back; I turned around completely. The little skeleton caught up with me, flanking my right side while Lark ran on my left. We were almost at the end of the tunnel.

Like they had all been summoned at once—because they had been—more friendly skeletons dragged themselves out of the walls on either side of the tunnel. As they did, the walls crumbled around them. The skeletons climbed up the ruined walls to summon others higher up, and then higher than that, until they reached the ceiling. It all happened so fast, it looked choreographed, and just as the angry bone people were nearly on us, the ceiling of the tunnel collapsed on top of them, a shower of stones and bones raining down.

The attacking mob was buried completely, but so were the skeletons who'd coordinated the collapse.

Dust settled, and the tunnel, which had been full of chaotic noise, was silent. I walked back a few steps toward the rubble, instinct kicking in and telling me that I needed to help our helpers somehow. But Bird nudged me softly. *There's nothing you can do for them. They made a choice.*

I didn't know what to say. How do you thank the dead for dying again to save you? Lark didn't say anything either. I looked back at her, ready to tell her it was time to go.

But she wasn't paying attention to me. Lark walked slowly, cautiously, toward the little skeleton. I followed close behind her. Not because I didn't trust the skeleton, but because I didn't want to get separated from Lark again.

They walked toward each other, Lark and the bones. When they were just a few feet apart, the small skeleton stopped. Then it did a thing I couldn't make sense of. It bent its head down and covered its eyes with its hands. Its bony shoulders shook. If skeletons could cry, this one was doing just that.

Lark closed the gap between her and the skeleton.

Then she did the most tender thing I'd ever seen her do: she put her ghost hand on the side of its skull. The skeleton stopped shaking then and stood up straight. It put its hand over Lark's and held it there, leaned into it even.

"Do you know . . . it?" I whispered.

Lark nodded, still facing away from me and toward the bones. Then she did something that confirmed it—she wrapped her arms around the skeleton and hugged it.

I realized then that the two of them—Lark the ghost and the shining opal skeleton—were exactly the same height. Puzzle pieces started to click into place in my brain, but I couldn't make sense of the picture they were showing me.

I crept closer to the pair as they pulled apart and looked at each other.

"I'm so sorry," Lark said. Her voice was full of tears.

The skeleton reached up and touched Lark's face, and I just knew that meant, *Me too. I'm sorry too.*

I was next to Lark, looking into the face (the skull) of the skeleton, when the last puzzle piece clicked into place. It was the teeth. The skeleton had a tiny chip in one front tooth.

Just like Lark.

"It's you. She's you," I whispered.

To confirm it, Clyde crawled out of Lark's pocket and up the arm of the skeleton, perching on her shoulder just like he did with Lark.

Because this *was* Lark.

Clyde knew it too.

I closed my eyes and shook my head a little, trying to clear away what was left of my confusion and disbelief. When I opened them, the skeleton was patting Clyde with her finger bones just like Lark did.

"I'm so sorry," Lark repeated. "I didn't know where to look for you. I didn't know I *should* look for you."

The skeleton nodded like she understood.

"Are you . . . are you lonely?" Lark's voice caught on the last word. It didn't take a genius to figure out why. Lark had been alone for a very long time. She knew what lonely felt like.

The skeleton shook her head and gestured around the tunnel full of bones. *No, I have friends to keep me company.*

"I'm going to get out of here. I'm going home. And when I do, I can move on, and you can rest." I didn't know exactly what Lark meant, but her skeleton seemed to.

The bone girl sagged a little, like she was very tired, and nodded slowly. *Yes, that would be nice.*

"And we're going to finish her for good. I promise." I had no problem figuring that one out. Portia. Lark was talking about Portia.

The bone girl squared her shoulders and gave another nod, but this one was very determined. Unmistakably Lark.

Then she did something that surprised me so much, I made one of those shocked, blubbering sounds. The bone girl grabbed her left hand with her right one and snapped off her pinkie finger. Just . . . popped it off. I'll never forget that sound if I live to be a thousand.

Then she turned and held the finger out to me. *Here, take it.*

My eyes got so big, I probably looked like a cartoon drawing of a surprised person. Without moving, I glanced over at Lark. Through clenched teeth, I asked, "What do I do?"

"You take it. It's a gift."

"But why?" I asked.

"Because it will likely come in handy." And then Lark did something I'd never heard her do. She giggled. "Get it? Come in handy?"

The skeleton girl shook a little, and I'm pretty dang sure she was laughing too.

I was not.

But I also wasn't about to turn down the gift. I mean, the bone girl—Lark—had just saved my life, and then, like that wasn't enough, she'd gone ahead and pulled her finger off for me.

I held out my hand, palm up, and the skeleton dropped her finger into it. It was smooth and cold and surprisingly light.

"Thank you?" I didn't mean for it to be a question, but that was how it came out.

The skeleton nodded. *You're welcome. Don't lose it.*

I wouldn't. I placed it in the front pocket of my backpack, the one that held the killer tree branch.

The two Larks hugged one more time. As they did, Clyde crawled off the skeleton and back into Ghost Lark's pocket.

"Thank you," said Lark. "I miss you."

The skeleton squeezed Lark's shoulders with her hands, one of which was now one finger short. *I miss you, too.*

Then Bone Lark gave us a small wave and, along with the small band of helper skeletons, made her way back into the depths of the tunnel. They climbed over the pile of rubble that had buried friends and enemies alike, and then they were out of view.

Lark took a moment before she said in a shaky voice, "That was unexpected."

"Um. Yeah. You . . . you okay?" It was the kind of question I hated asking—of course she wasn't okay—but what else was I supposed to say?

"I am. I will be. Let's find some sunlight and I'll try to explain."

I was ready. Ready for sunlight, and ready for some explanations.

As I turned to the cave opening and the expanse of purple sky just beyond, movement caught my eye. I couldn't be sure what I saw, but in my heart I was certain.

Just as I turned around, something that looked very much like a long, pale limb ending in a long, pale hand slithered along the ceiling right inside the tunnel opening, then was yanked quickly out of view. Almost like someone—*something*—had begun to crawl into the tunnel and then retreated before it could be seen.

It was Portia. It had to be. She was tracking us, marking our progress.

Or Clackity, my brain added warily.

I opened my mouth to say something to Lark, but the way her eyes were wet and the way she kept glancing back toward the tunnel, toward the part of her she thought she'd never see again, I didn't have the heart to say anything.

It didn't matter anyway, right? Because I wasn't sure. I wasn't sure whether Portia or Clackity (or both) was stalking us. I wasn't sure if I was seeing things that weren't there or if I could even trust my own eyes and mind (which was an even scarier idea than being tracked).

We made our way toward the purple light and out of the tunnel. It didn't take long. As we exited, I glanced up to see if there was a sign that anyone had been there. To see if anyone still was. Nothing.

Your imagination, the foolish, brave part of my brain said.

Of course it wasn't, said the smarter part.

You'd think you could hear something as loud as a train from inside a tunnel. But not that train, and not that tunnel.

The thrum of the engine didn't start softly and grow. It was there as suddenly as a light being turned on in a dark room, and it made me jump as we crossed the threshold of the tunnel's exit, making me forget about whatever I thought I'd seen. The ground vibrated with the deep rumble of wheels on tracks. It was such an unexpected sound, such a *normal* sound, and so totally out of place.

The train was a football field away. It was an old-fashioned-looking freight train, the boxcars made of wood with big sliding doors on the sides. Some of those doors were wide open, and as the train chugged along, the cars I could see into appeared to be empty.

I looked to the right, the direction the train was coming from, and couldn't see its end. It snaked back so far, it disappeared from view. I looked to the left and couldn't see the engine. The train seemed to run right into the horizon, with no beginning or end in sight.

What I *did* see was the Nighthouse off in the distance, in the same general direction that the train was heading. Maddeningly, the Nighthouse didn't seem any closer than it had before we entered the tunnel. I could see how tall the tower was, taller than anything else in the landscape, and dark, like it ate shadows instead of casting them, but that was about it. That, and the flashing, sickly yellow light at the top. With a *light*house, a flashing light was supposed to be an alert, warning others away from danger. The Nighthouse's light felt different. It felt like a beacon, and I didn't believe it was inviting anyone to do anything good.

A thought crossed my mind, and I couldn't shake it: I was in the shadow of that awful building, and I would be no matter how far away from it I was. I *had* to go toward it, because there was no outrunning it. A weird idea, maybe, but it still made my skin break out in goose bumps.

Shuddering a little, I looked back to the train. It wasn't moving very fast. In fact, I was pretty sure I could outrun it if I tried. Not for long, maybe, but for at least a short sprint.

On the other side of the train was purple sky and black void. The tracks ran along the edge of a cliff, and beyond the precipice was the Radix, waiting to suck everything in.

Outside the tunnel, the black sun was bright and warm. I squinted, wishing I'd thought to pack sunglasses. *Next time,* I thought. But there wouldn't be a next time. If I made it home after all this, there was no way I'd even joke about coming back to the Dark Sun Side.

Through watering eyes, I watched the train pass, and even though I didn't want to acknowledge it, I knew what was next.

"I seriously do not want to get on that train."

"Are we supposed to?" Lark shaded her eyes with her hand, the bright sun shining through her edges. Most of the time I almost forgot she was a ghost, but when the sun passed through her like that, it was impossible not to remember. Her shadow flowed behind her and somehow seemed more opaque—more *there*—than she did.

"Yeah. Pretty sure." Logic told me the train hadn't shown up for no reason.

"It'll be better than walking. We can take a break while we ride the rails," Lark said.

"I'd like it better if those rails weren't so close to potentially falling into the Radix."

Lark didn't say anything to that.

I found a patch of black grass and sat down on it. The weight of the day—what we'd already been through and how far we still had to go—suddenly turned into a burden I wasn't sure I could carry. I needed a minute. Lark had a look that said she wanted to tell me to get up and get moving, but she didn't say a thing. Instead she sat down beside me, and we watched the train shuffle past us unendingly. Bird nestled into my collarbone, and Clyde was burrowed somewhere in Lark's pocket. We were all quiet—quiet and tired.

After a minute or two, Lark asked, "Aren't you worried about missing it?"

"The train? No. Look at how slow it's moving. Besides, I still can't see the back. Or the front. Like it goes on forever."

"Might be," Lark said.

"How about you tell me what just happened in there?" I didn't have to explain. She knew what I meant.

"Thought you figured it out."

"Some of it. I mean, she was you . . . *is* you. Right?"

"Mm-hmm."

I wasn't sure how to ask my next question. No matter what I said, I was pretty sure it would come out wrong. So I just said it. "I know you weren't . . . a ghost . . . before you got here. So . . . ?"

"If you're asking if I died here, the answer is yes. I was a living, breathing girl, and then I came here and then I wasn't."

"What happened?" I had to ask, needed to know. But I also really didn't *want* to know.

Lark was quiet for so long that I thought I'd made her mad, or sad, by asking. She made a throat-clearing noise before she answered. Her voice was very even, and her words sounded careful. "I wasn't totally honest before, Von Rathe. I *have* been to the Nighthouse. Once. Turned out, the Nighthouse is very high, and I wasn't always as light as I am now."

"Oh." I mean, what was I supposed to say to that? "Did—I mean—did Portia . . ."

Lark nodded, but it was so subtle that I would have missed it if my eyes hadn't been glued right to her. She said, "How about we tell stories on the train? I'm tired of the sun and I'm tired of sitting and doing nothing."

I both really wanted to hear the story of Lark's death and really, really did not. But I also knew she was right. We couldn't sit there forever, and the train was definitely the next obstacle we had to face. The problem was, I was scared. My hands were sweating. My feet, too.

I was afraid I'd try to jump onto the train and not be able to and embarrass myself.

I was afraid I'd trip and fall underneath the steel wheels and get crushed.

I was afraid of the train tumbling off the side of the cliff and plummeting into the Radix.

I was afraid of actually making it to the Nighthouse and of what we'd find there. What we'd have to do.

I was afraid of making it to the Nighthouse and *not* finding anything or anyone at all—for all of this to have been for nothing.

Lark read my mind. "It'll be okay. Like you said, it's awfully slow. And I bet you're faster than you look. Besides, what's the worst that could happen?"

Very funny, coming from a dead girl. I didn't laugh at her attempt at a joke, but I did smile a little. And her teasing pulled me out of the anxiety loop my brain had fallen into. It occurred to me that Lark was being a really good friend to me and that she'd probably been an amazing best friend to Mae. The Von Rathes were lucky to have her in our corner.

I stood and stretched my whole body. I realized then that I wasn't just tired, I was exhausted. The idea of riding in a train car for a while was sounding a little better.

"Let's do this," I told Lark. "Before I fall asleep right here." *Or lose my nerve,* I thought.

We made our way to the train in no time. In a normal place, the closer you get to a train, the louder it sounds. Not in this weird world. Even as we approached, the noise of the wheels was still just a deep, low rumble. The wooden cars were painted random colors, and there wasn't a bit of graffiti on any of them, but the flaking paint was slowly being bleached by the black sun. The reds and blues and blacks and greens were all fading toward a grim and dusty grey.

It didn't seem to matter what car we went for, as long as the door was wide open. There were plenty of those, so I just picked one at random. I jogged alongside it until I had my body in line with the open door. Lark, who had been pacing me, made the jump easily. I envied her lightness. My body and my backpack felt impossibly heavy, too heavy to make the leap.

"Toss your satchel in first!" Lark called, and I knew she meant my backpack. I didn't want to part with it, but it made sense. I took it off as I ran and tossed it into the open car, where it landed safely on the wooden floor.

Lark extended one hand. "Grab my hand, pull yourself up with the other, and jump hard!"

I was actually going to do this. I was going to hop a moving freight train.

I couldn't keep thinking about it or I would run out of nerve or steam or both. I grabbed Lark's outstretched hand and used my free hand to hoist myself onto the floor of the train.

The jump was easier than I expected, although there was a terrifying moment where I was half in and half out of the train car. My legs dangled uselessly outside, and I could see myself slipping and falling under the steel wheels. That image, which was as gross as you think it was, was enough to motivate me. Between my fear-strength and Lark's help, I got my whole self into the car in just a few seconds. Bird gave me gentle pecks with his sharp little beak, which I was pretty sure were supposed to be motivational. I could almost hear him reminding me that it was my journey, not his, so I didn't bother asking him for more help than that.

Once I was all the way in, I collapsed on the rough wooden floor of the empty train car. It smelled like sawdust and regular dust and it was warm. The steady rhythm of the wheels below us, low and constant, might as well have been a lullaby. I ached all over and was tired from my eyelids to my toes.

"Do you sleep?" I asked Lark with a yawn. "Back in Blight Harbor, ghosts don't sleep. Then again, they don't talk or have shadows, either."

"I know," said Lark. "There were ghosts in Blight Harbor when I lived there. Obviously I talk, but I certainly don't cast a shadow—some things don't change."

I almost argued with her—I'd been watching Lark's weird shadow all day—but she kept going.

"And I sort of sleep. I've learned how to close my eyes and get quiet and sort of go away for a while. Like a long catnap, maybe. I think I would have gone mad by now if I couldn't."

"Will you tell me the rest of your story?"

Lark rubbed her hands over her face and I could see that even if she couldn't sleep, she *was* tired. You can be tired in all sorts of ways, and sometimes feelings make you the most exhausted. Lark had had more than her share of feelings already that day.

"I will," she said, "but not right now. Rest first, for both of us, and then we can trade stories and family trees."

I thought about arguing with her, but I didn't have the energy. Bird was curled up and asleep on my collarbone. The tiny vibrations of his snoring confirmed it. Lark was right: rest first, talk later.

I didn't know how long I'd slept, but it was long enough for drool to dry on the side of my face. I woke up to see Lark sitting next to me, her arms wrapped around her thin knees. She was staring intently at something and didn't turn away when she said, "Von Rathe, you might want to look at this."

I sat up and rubbed my eyes. Then I rubbed them again, because what I saw didn't make any sense.

At the far end of the empty boxcar, a doorway had appeared where there hadn't been a doorway before. It was regular-sized and rounded at the top. Through a window in that door, I could see more train cars and more doors. They went on and on until I couldn't see them anymore, disappearing somewhere back at the end of that very long train. If it even had an end.

That would have been weird enough, but from what I could tell, the other cars weren't boxcars. Instead they looked suspiciously like old-fashioned passenger cars, complete with dark wood railings and padded seats and carpet along the aisle. What they did have in common with the boxcars was the fact that they were completely empty—not a soul aboard aside from me and Lark (and Bird and Clyde, of course).

"I heard it when it showed up," Lark said, meaning the door. "It made kind of a grinding sound, like an invisible saw was cutting it out. Too fast for me to see it happen, though."

"When?" I asked.

"A while now. But nothing's come out, so I figured I'd let you sleep a while longer."

"I don't like it," I said. "Doors from nowhere are never good." Bird, perched on my shoulder, seemed to agree. He wasn't red-hot with warning, but he was definitely getting warm.

"Might be," said Lark, but I could tell she wasn't as sure as I was. "Or might be interesting. At the very least, might be more comfortable over there than in this box."

She had a point—the wooden floor was not exactly first-class travel accommodations.

"I say," Lark continued, "we take a look and see what there is to see." Clyde, who had bravely made his way up to Lark's shoulder, retreated back down to her pocket.

"I don't know. It doesn't—it doesn't feel right." That was true. Between Bird warming up and the rapidly growing rock in my stomach, I had a bad feeling about the whole doorway thing.

Lark sighed. "Listen, we're on the train like you said we should be. Even if we go poke around a bit, we'll *still* be on the train. We'll *still* be going in the right direction."

I didn't know how to argue with that. I'd sound either like I was being stubborn or like I was afraid. I didn't want Lark to think either of those things. I didn't want this girl who'd been brave for a hundred years to think I was scared of an empty train (which was easily the least scary thing we'd encountered all day).

"Okay," I said. "But if things get weird, we're leaving."

"Deal," said Lark.

Stepping between the train cars was a little bit like being in that part of a carnival fun house where the floor is uneven and moves in different directions. It made my stomach lurch in a way that wasn't bad, exactly, but I wasn't sure it was fun, either.

I envisioned the train tearing apart while I was in one of those spaces between the cars—Lark told me they were called gangways—and that would be the end of me. She also told me, "Don't be a dolt," and rolled her eyes at how nervous the gangway made me.

The first passenger car was nice enough but nothing special. There was room to walk between rows of seats on either side. The seats were covered in worn emerald-green velvet that was shiny in places from all the butts that had sat on it. The walls curved up to meet at the top and were made of dark wood that looked soft with age. The air smelled of lemony wood polish and old, sweet pipe smoke—a comforting combination.

Outside the windows on the right, I could see the

Nighthouse standing in the distance. It didn't seem any closer than when we'd boarded the train, which told me that we had plenty of time to poke around. Gas lamps hung between the windows, and the flames in them were the same black as the sun. Weird black flames or not, the lamps did their jobs, and the car was well lit.

"Seems so . . . normal," I said quietly to Lark. Bird shifted a bit on my shoulder, and I could have sworn he was bored.

"Hmm," Lark said, and I couldn't tell if she was agreeing with me or not.

"A couple more cars?" I suggested.

Lark looked out the windows in the direction of the Nighthouse, which still hadn't grown any closer. "Don't see why not."

The next car and the car after that were about the same.

At the end of the third passenger car, feeling braver about the gangways, I slid open the door to step through to the next car.

I stopped cold.

Instead of another door to another train car, there was a tightly winding wooden staircase. The brass handrail glowed softly in the lamplight that managed to creep in from the car behind us. Impossibly, the staircase went down. There should have been nothing but turning steel wheels and train tracks below us, no place for the stairs to go down *to*.

My brain spun. There was an endless line of train cars ahead of us—I'd seen it myself—but I couldn't deny the fact in front of me: if we wanted to get to the next car, we'd be going down the stairs to do it.

"Do we keep going?" asked Lark.

I closed my eyes and got quiet, hoping for a sense about what to do next. Nothing. My insides were as silent as a stone at the bottom of a lake. I didn't feel anything— no pull or push, no beckoning or warning. Then, so small I almost missed it, a tiny tug at the center of my stomach. *Forward,* it said.

That tug was the best I had, so finally: "Yeah," I answered, "pretty sure."

Lark nodded.

Clyde climbed down farther into her front pocket.

Bird ruffled his feathers, wary.

I led the way down the stairs. They twisted around on themselves. *Like a coiled-up snake,* I thought. The idea of a snake ready to strike came out of nowhere, and a crawly feeling made its way up my back and into my arms, where I shivered it out. I told myself my imagination was getting the better of me, because that small but insistent tug was still there in my middle.

At the bottom of the staircase, we found ourselves in another passenger car. Same wooden walls, same green seats. It was a little darker than the others, like the gas lamps were weaker than those upstairs. The gloom made the car feel narrower, more closed in. There was another smell underneath the polish and pipe tobacco, and that smell was . . . *colder* . . . somehow, even though the temperature hadn't changed.

We made our way through the car in silence. As I

passed the gas lamps, I saw that they were actually just as bright as before, the flames just as strong. It was the shadows that were *more*, darker.

Outside the window, the Nighthouse waited. Something about it had changed. I couldn't say what, exactly, but the subtle difference was enough for my palms to break out in a pinprickly feeling. Not quite sweaty, but almost.

We reached the end of the car, and another set of stairs waited for us behind the door, leading down once again.

"Still good?" asked Lark. There was an edge to her voice.

I nodded. Bird was puffed up and unsure, and while I trusted my little buddy, I also trusted the tug in my stomach. If anything, that tug had grown stronger.

"You sure?" This time the edge to her voice was razor-sharp. Lark was nervous.

"I'm sure," I snapped, harsher than I meant to.

We descended, circling the snake of a staircase.

The next car was darker still and felt even narrower. The walls were thick with shadows now, making it hard to see out the windows. How shadows could block the windows was a mystery, but it was true. Looking back, I might have given that more thought. Might even have mentioned it to Lark. But the tug had become a steady, firm pull, and I had a hard time focusing on anything else.

Down more stairs, into darker darkness.

Now the dimness crowded the skinny train car, enveloping the seats and leaving just enough room to walk down the aisle. As focused as I was on whatever was pulling me forward, I still had enough sense to avoid touching those shadows. I glanced back long enough to see that Lark must have felt the same way, as she was sticking to the center of the aisle and sidestepping the darkness that surrounded us.

At the end of the car, I grasped the handle on the door in one motion as I pulled. If I had hesitated even a second, I would have stopped before opening it. The handle was so cold that it burned, and as my fingers touched it, Bird began pecking at my neck. A cold door handle and an anxiously pecking Bird were all the warning I should have needed. But I didn't hesitate, so none of it registered until it was too late.

The door opened, and between us and the next staircase was a figure.

It stood half again as tall as me and was made completely out of shadows. The form had a vaguely human shape, but everything about it was too long, too tapered. Its arms reached down well past where its knees should have been, if it had had any. Its hands stretched like soft wax and ended not in fingers but in knife blades made of darkness.

I had seen this thing before. Or something like it. It looked just like the shadow that had been following Lark around all day. My brain tried to make sense of it—tried to put the pieces together—but since I didn't know what the picture was supposed to look like, nothing clicked into place.

Two eyes were set deep in their sockets and glowed the dullest dried-blood shade of red.

I didn't realize the thing had a mouth until it opened.

And opened.

And opened.

Its jaw stretched down to its chest and around a gaping hole that glowed the same infected red as its eyes. A dry sort of gurgling came from deep inside the ghoul. The closest I can come to describing that sound is to say it was like the rumbling of a cavernous, starving stomach.

Immediately, I knew that whatever the thing was, it was mostly appetite and not much else.

"Wha—?" I started to ask, but was cut off before I could finish.

"GO GO GO!" Lark screamed. Her hand grasped mine and pulled hard— even harder than the pull I'd felt in my stomach. The pull that had tricked us—*me*—into heading straight to the monster on the train.

Lark and I turned to start back through the car toward the last staircase we'd come down. Before we could so much as take a step, the darkness from along the sides of the train began to spread.

Not spread, but separate.

The darkness peeled away from the walls and untangled itself. As it did, I saw countless dull red eyes open in the writhing mass. In seconds, half as many— but still far, far *too many*—gaping red mouths opened. The things separated from one another as much as they could, but there were so many of them, there was no room between each and the next.

In seconds that felt like years, we were surrounded.

Lark let out a heartrending, gut-wrenching wail as she backed into me, trying to get away from the ghouls in the train. But there were too many of them and nowhere for us to go.

I had done this. I had taken us down impossible stairs into the clutches of not one monster but a hundred. As a scream crawled up my throat, something else crawled down my right arm.

It was Bird.

He made his way past my elbow, past my wrist, and into my hand. He spread himself like black paint up to the middle of my forearm. He had become a sort-of glove, and the fingers of that glove were remarkable. Much like the creatures surrounding us, my own fingers were now elongated and thin. But instead of tapering to points, they were shaped like feathers, and those feathers were easily ten inches long and sharp as blades.

In the time I'd known him, Bird had done many things. He'd helped me avoid danger, driven out dark entities from innocent creatures, and become a mask so I could see. But he'd never turned himself into an honest-to-goodness weapon. Until now.

I could think of only one thing I might do, one thing I was *meant* to do. So I did it.

I stepped in front of Lark and lashed out at the nearest shadow creature with my bladed black hand. My fingers tore through its middle with only the slightest resistance. *Like silk,* I thought, *or a shroud.* The thing let out a rattling howl that was part pain and part fury.

The places where my fingers sliced the ghoul separated, the shadowy grey revealing more dull red light underneath. As I watched, the red light faded and the shadow-creature unraveled like ribbon, starting where I'd cut it and spreading faster than I could track, until it was nothing but a heap of shadow-colored strips on the floor of the train.

The ghouls pushed toward us and I lashed out again and again, and with each swipe, another shadow creature unraveled and fell. I swung my feather-bladed hand in the widest arcs I dared. I was trying to create a protective circle around me and Lark, who was pressed up against my back so closely, I could feel her trembling.

One creature managed to get close enough to grab my throat, but it pulled its hand away like it had been burned. The silver choker I wore felt warm against my neck, like it had been left in the sun. The warmth faded quickly from my skin, but my mind tucked that moment away as something to remember.

As they saw what was happening to their friends, the smarter creatures began to back away, retreating against the walls of the train. Huddled, they once again looked like nothing but thick shadows.

But not all the ghouls were smart. They kept coming, and I kept turning them into piles of smoky ribbon. For every step forward I took toward the other end of the car, two or three more creatures charged us. It occurred to me that I didn't know what exactly it was I was fending off, but Lark sure seemed to. She hadn't been scared when we encountered the first ghoul—she'd been terrified. I could still hear her wail echoing in my ears.

Now Lark's back was pressed against mine. For every step forward I took, she took a matching step backward, leaving no room for anything to get between us. I kept slicing the shadow creatures and she—well, I wasn't sure what she was doing except staying close.

There were fewer and fewer of the things between us and the stairs. Some I had stopped—my brain told me the right word was *killed*, but I wasn't ready to think about that just yet—and others had fled out of reach of my Bird-knife hand.

With two more creatures destroyed, the path forward was suddenly clear.

"Let's go!" I yelled, meaning for Lark to turn and follow me.

I took a lunging step forward.

The pressure of Lark against my back was gone.

Another step.

Lark was not at my side.

Another.

Silence. Except for a soft moan behind me.

I stopped and turned and almost fell to my knees. Angry, horrified tears filled my eyes, and for just a moment the scene in front of me was so blurred, I could almost pretend it wasn't happening.

But it was happening. And it was my fault.

I'd forgotten the first ghoul, the one behind the cold door. I'd been so determined to flee, to get rid of the creatures blocking our way, I'd forgotten all about the thing we were running *from*. And I'd left Lark, unprotected, to meet it on her own.

The ghoul and Lark faced one another. The thing had Lark's shoulder in one long, tapered hand. Its other hand was reaching into Lark's mouth. No, into her throat. Farther.

Lark made a moaning, gagging noise.

The thing pulled its arm out of Lark's mouth like a sword-swallower's trick, and when it did, Lark collapsed to the floor of the train.

I realized then that the thing hadn't been trying to hurt Lark as much as it had been looking for something. Because in its hand was a gleaming golden-green light. The light was so brilliant that it stung my eyes, but I could see its source. In the creature's palm was what looked like a tiny living solar system. A golden-green sun the size of a small orange was orbited by sparks and glimmers in the same bright color. The light it cast illuminated the entire train car. Shadows were crisp and black against it.

It was the most beautiful thing I'd ever seen. Both the

creature and I were frozen, staring at the small miracle it held in its hand.

Then, without warning, the ghoul's mouth opened even wider than before, and it shoved its hand, and the light, deep inside itself.

When the hand came out, it was empty.

The ghoul's mouth closed so quick and so tight that it became invisible in what passed for its face. But its eyes . . . The thing's eyes were no longer dull and red. They were the brightest crimson, with flecks and glimmers of gold. Some of those glimmers escaped, and when they did, they faded into the air like miniature fireworks.

The ghoul rushed past me, flying through the air like a horror-movie ghost, and disappeared up the winding staircase. The same one we'd been trying to reach.

Bird was Bird again, making his way back up my arm and to my shoulder. Clyde had made his way out of his hiding pocket and was running worried circles on Lark's slumped back.

Lark lifted her head then and reached back to pat Clyde. To calm him.

My heart left my chest and lodged in my throat. Lark wasn't dead—I mean, she *was* dead, but she wasn't whatever the worst thing that could happen to a ghost was. Not okay, maybe, but not *that*.

At least, that was what I thought.

I closed the two steps between us, fell to my knees, and threw my arms around her.

Lark was in trouble, and it was my fault.

She tried to push herself up off the ground, but her arms gave out and she collapsed back to the floor of the train. She looked so pale and tiny and fragile. I was reminded with a painful twist to my heart that she might've been strong and brave, but she was also just a kid who'd been all by herself for way too long.

"What can I do?" I asked her. I didn't know what to do with my hands or my words, so I sort of hovered over her—I felt completely helpless.

"Nothing," she whispered, her cheek pressed against the faded carpet.

It was the last thing I wanted to hear. I wanted her to yell at me, to swear at me, maybe even hit me. I wanted her to push up her sleeves and say we were going after the ghoul to get back whatever it was that had been taken from her. Because whatever it was, that thing was important. Anything that beautiful and blinding had to be.

"Can you get up?" It was a silly question. If Lark could stand, she would have already.

"Go," she said. "You have to go."

"Lark, come on." I didn't know what to do, but I knew I wasn't leaving her.

"It got mine. Because it's easier. But they'll take yours, too."

"Your what?" I asked, even though I didn't want to hear the answer. Because, in my heart, I already knew.

"My soul," she said.

Portia had said to me, *You can't mistake the soul light. You'll know it when you find it.* She'd been right. That glimmering golden thing taken from Lark couldn't have been anything else.

I'd been holding back a sob, and it chose then to escape. I didn't want to cry in front of Lark—she was the one who had reason to cry—but I couldn't help it. Tears streamed down my cheeks and my throat closed up, tight and red-hot.

Suddenly movement caught my attention. I whipped my head around to spot who or what was there, but it wasn't that simple. The movement was all around us. The shadows in the train were shifting and separating again, or trying to. They struggled against one another, and in seconds, the struggling became thrashing and clawing. They were . . . tangled. Somehow, in their rush to get away from me and my Bird glove, the soul-hungry ghouls had become tangled up in one another. I hoped it would buy us enough time, because I couldn't rescue Lark and use my Bird glove at the same time.

And, for better or worse, I was getting Lark out of here.

I rolled the fading ghost onto her back and slid my hands under her arms, picking her up off the floor. She didn't weigh nothing, but she didn't weigh much. Clyde crawled from Lark's back up my arm and perched on my shoulder opposite Bird. I didn't mind. I owed the little spider almost as much as I owed Lark—after all, it was his best friend I'd led into danger.

With Lark cradled in my arms, I ran.

The shadow hands that were less tangled reached out to grasp at us, but I managed to avoid them. Mostly. Long, tapered fingers tangled themselves in my hair. They caught in the elastic holding my bun, which, thankfully, broke. My hair tumbled down my back, and more hands grasped at it but none quite managed to get a hold.

Lark whimpered.

"Close your eyes," I told her. I didn't want her feeling scared, but I also didn't want her to try to help. I was determined to keep her from getting hurt again.

I got to the staircase in no time, but the ghost girl slumped against the front of me and my backpack behind me made climbing awkward. A quick glance back told me we weren't out of the woods by a long shot. The shadow things were coming, most of them still knotted and tangled together, but coming all the same. I hoped I'd be quick enough—and they'd be slow enough—that I could make it out with the three friends I now carried with me.

At the top of the twisted staircase, I risked another look back. The shadow creatures, it seemed, didn't need to climb the stairs at all. They rose up through the center, filling the stairwell with a mass of writhing, red-eyed grey. The tangled monsters rumbled as they came, the same starving, empty-stomach sound the first one had made.

I moved faster through the next car.

The shadows there, while fewer, had come alive as well. They didn't immediately reach out to us—they seemed uncertain, or even confused—but as the mass chasing us made its way into our car, the new shadow ghouls joined in the pursuit.

When the ghouls moved away from the windows, I caught another glimpse of the Nighthouse. I saw then what hadn't been clear to me before, back when I knew *something* was wrong but wasn't sure *what*. Despite our journey, the Nighthouse was still no closer than it ever had been. If anything, it was farther away.

We had to get off the train for more reasons than I had time to think about.

I walked faster, faster than I thought I could, up the stairs and to the next car. There weren't as many creatures in this one, and they were more light than shadow now, but any number was too many. Lark shifted in my arms and I pulled her in a little closer to me. The pack following us had become so large that they completely filled the car behind me from floor to ceiling. Red eyes and gaping mouths dotted what looked like one single beast that stretched from the floor of the train to the ceiling. The rumbling had become a solid sound, a growl that never wavered or stopped. Its drone filled the air completely.

Up the last flight of stairs. I knew that we had taken three down, so it would be three back up. Then a straightaway through three more passenger cars. I could pick up speed there. Then we'd cross to the first car, the boxcar we'd hopped into when we started this whole horrible thing, and then . . .

Well, I wasn't sure.

Lark was light, but thanks to the awkward angle at which I held her, my arms were trembling. I was terrified of dropping her, of losing the precious small lead that we had. My heart raced in my ribs and thumped in my temples, and I did my best to ignore the stitch that was forming in my side.

We had done ourselves a small favor by leaving the doors between each train car open when we first moved through them. If I'd had to open those, too, we would have been done for as soon as we started. I did slow as I went through each doorway, turning my body so Lark's limp form—*don't think about that, stay focused*, I heard a small voice that might have been mine, or Bird's, or both, say—wouldn't get banged against the doorframes.

In the next-to-last passenger car, a glance behind told me the things were still coming toward us, but they were having trouble with the narrow doorways. I prayed they were hopelessly tangled, that one wouldn't break away and come tearing after us.

In the last passenger car, there were no shadows at

all. The space was filled with warm daylight and soft lamplight. I'd never been afraid of the dark, but in that moment, I never wanted to see it again.

We walked through the final door, and then we were back in the boxcar, with its rough wooden floor and wide-open exit. Outside, the landscape was barren and desolate—dirt and rocks and black grass and not much else. The train still moved slowly, slowly enough for me to jump out without much of a risk, even while carrying Lark and our little friends. I had reached the boxcar door—so close to leaping that my toes hung over the edge—when a thought crossed my mind that stopped me cold.

Where had the first ghoul gone? We hadn't encountered it on our way out, and I would have picked it out easily, thanks to the golden sparks that now escaped from the holes where its eyes should have been. Somehow, it had gone out—out of the train and off to where? I had no idea. What mattered was that it had managed to get off the train at all. And if it could, so could the dozens and dozens of other shadow beasts, which would catch up to us on level ground in no time flat. I had managed to outrun them, but now I had to stop them. I had to stop them *here*, on the train, because I'd never be able to fight them all out in the open, where space wasn't an issue for their growing mass.

Carefully as I'd ever done anything, I laid Lark down in the center of the boxcar. Clyde crawled along my arm to be with her.

"Good spider," I said to him. If you'd told me a day

before that I'd be grateful for a large arachnid, I would have argued with you, but here we were.

I pulled my backpack off my shoulders and returned to the gangway door that led to the first passenger car. As I peered into the car, I couldn't make out much more than blackness, but the mass was growling louder than ever. They were still coming, and they were pissed off. And hungry.

After my first trip to the Dark Sun Side, I'd stopped making fun of Aunt Desdemona's purse full of otherworldly tools and weapons, and had made one of my own. I thought about the supplies I had in my backpack. Most of them wouldn't do us much good. Salt crossed my mind, but since I wasn't sure what the ghouls were made of, I didn't know if that would accomplish anything at all. Same problem with holy water. Thinking through my inventory, I settled on a plan and hoped with all my might that it was a good one.

From my bag, I pulled a glass bottle of oil and a box of matches. The oil, a special blend Aunt Des and Lily had made together, seemed like the best place to start. It was a complicated mixture:

tea tree for purification and protection
lavender for balance and healing
clove to ward off evil
frankincense to attract peace
rosemary to ward off nightmares and help the
    dead remember being human
eucalyptus to strip away fear

The oil smelled good—Des wore it as perfume—and when I opened it, a wave of homesickness and guilt washed over me. I had promised Des I wouldn't come back to this place, and within hours I'd broken that promise. Not on purpose, but I'd broken it nonetheless. Now I was here with gosh-knew-what chasing me through an impossible train, and I'd nearly maybe killed (again) the one friend I'd managed to make. If I kept thinking about it all, it would be too much and I'd just freeze, and then it would all be over. I had to focus.

Focus.

Focus.

Focus.

I very intentionally turned my attention back to the oil. Aside from smelling like home, it had loads of magical properties, but what made it especially helpful in my current predicament was one other important detail. Essential oils are very, very flammable.

The oil was flammable, and the train was almost entirely made out of wood. I was depending on that combination to get us out of this situation.

I knelt at the gangway to the first passenger car and knelt. The ghouls were squirming and shoving through the doorway on the opposite end of the car. I didn't have much time.

As quickly and carefully as possible with my now-shaking hands, I poured oil all along the doorway and down the sides of the doorframe as best I could. The mass of ghouls looked to be stuck in the threshold, but I knew my luck wouldn't hold.

My fingers trembled as I struck a match against its cardboard container. The flame that sparked into existence seemed impossibly small, but I knew it would be enough.

I exhaled in relief.

And that breath blew the match out.

It was such an absurd, brainless mistake that I almost laughed. Almost. As I'd feared, one of the shadow creatures had managed to break away from the tangle and was heading straight toward me.

I took another match and struck it.

It lit.

This time, I held my breath.

I touched the flame to the fragrant oil, and it immediately caught. The flames weren't as high or as impressive as I'd hoped, but it was fire. I also hoped I was right, and that fire would stop the ghouls from reaching us. If not, I was out of ideas.

The liberated shadow reached the boxcar doorway just as the flames made their way up the sides of the entryway. The creature tried to stop, but it had too much momentum and flew directly into the small but growing fire.

Turned out, oil and wood weren't the only flammable things on the train. The ghoul ignited like it was made of dry cotton and paper. In seconds, it was engulfed. It made a sound that I'd become familiar with when I dispatched dozens of its friends in the train cars below— that furious and frightened howl.

The blazing beast rushed back down the train, away

from my small fire, only to ignite more small fires of its own as embers touched velvet train seats and wooden rails. When it reached the mass of shadows stuck in the door, things got really interesting. As soon as the burning ghoul touched the others, the whole mess of them became a ball of flame.

The end of the train was an inferno, and the heat and noise of the howling creatures hit me like a living wall. My instinct was to close the door, but I couldn't tear my eyes away from what was happening. The wooden car that imprisoned the mass burned as brightly as they did. There was a tremendous creak as something in the structure of the wooden train gave way. Pieces of burning ceiling and roof collapsed in on the ghouls.

At first I thought the creatures were moving backward, deeper into the train, to escape the flaming debris. Then I saw that the train itself was pulling apart. The burning section was completely separated from the rest of the train, and without the benefit of being attached to an engine, it was falling away from the still-connected cars.

The train rounded a slight bend. The blazing, engineless car tipped dangerously to the left and was the first to tumble over on its side and off the tracks. The only place for it to go was into the black nothing of the Radix. The cars behind it, still attached, followed it one by one, and like dominoes, they plummeted into the abyss.

I stared out the door, trembling and not blinking, though my eyes watered from the smoke and perfumed oil. How many of those creatures, whatever they were, had I just killed? Were all the cars we hadn't explored full of them? Were there hundreds? *Thousands?* The weight of what I'd done fell on me, and I nearly collapsed under it.

"What did I do?" I asked the open air.

Bird stroked my back with a soft wing. *What you had to.*

The only other response was silence from the now-empty space where an entire train full of sort-of-living things had been. Silence, and then the soft moan of my friend from the boxcar floor behind me.

Lark was waking up.

I felt heavy as I rushed back to Lark's side and knelt. Heavy with what I had just done—even if it had been my only choice, it was still an ugly, violent thing—and heavy with what had happened to Lark. All of it was my fault. I was the one who'd listened to some mysterious pull rather than common sense.

I knew better.

"You have to go," Lark said, and I thought maybe, *maybe*, her voice was a little stronger than before.

"We'll get your soul back," I told her, taking her hand in mine.

"Not in time," she said.

"For what?"

"To stop me from becoming one of them. One of the soul eaters."

I gripped her hand tighter, my throat constricting around my next words. "What do you mean?"

Lark took her hand out of mine and pushed herself up on her elbows so that we were nearly eye to eye. "Living or dead, souls are what make us human. Without a soul, there's nothing good left. Just instinct and appetite and rage. That creature took my soul, probably to the Nighthouse. Those things do Portia's dirty work for her. I don't know how long I have. Not very, I think. Not out here."

Was it my imagination, or was Lark already taller than before, her hands longer? I shook my head. I was letting her spook me. There *had* to be a way to fix this.

"All those things were . . ." I didn't want to ask, because I didn't want the answer.

"People. Once. But not anymore, Evie. None of them could have been fixed. Or saved. They were too far gone. Even if we somehow found their souls, it would be like un-ringing a bell."

"You're not too far gone," I told her. But her fingers were definitely longer. She was right, there wasn't much time. My breathing was shaky and shallow as panic tightened my throat. I had to pry it off—had to focus—if I wanted to have any chance of helping my friend.

"If you had my soul right now, maybe? I don't know."

I took the deepest, steadiest breath I could. "So we get to the Nighthouse and get it back."

Lark laughed, but it was grim. "We're not any closer than we were before."

"Can we stop it? Or, like, pause it? The change, I mean."

Lark's smile was sad. "Not unless you know some witchcraft." She looked from Clyde to Bird and then to me. "If you knew a spell that could make me into a little bird or spider or something else that wasn't human, that might buy us some time." Lark was teasing me, but I was thinking.

"What if I could?"

Lark raised an eyebrow.

"I mean, it might not work, but there's one thing I want to try. Because we have to try *something*, and this is the only idea I have." I could feel tears burning my eyes, but I didn't care. I was the reason this had happened to Lark, and I had to fix it if I could.

"Are you a witch after all?" Lark's question was at least a little bit serious. And maybe, I thought, hopeful.

"No, but I know a few. First, we need to get off this train."

Getting Lark and Clyde and Bird off that train and onto solid ground was part of my motivation—I'd watched as a whole lot of train plummeted into the Radix, and it was all too easy to imagine the same thing happening to us. But there was another reason I needed solid ground, which went beyond my friends' safety. I was going to try my hand at some complicated magic— magic I had sort of done before—and no way would it work on a moving wooden floor.

Getting off the train was about as easy as I'd expected, even if I wasn't exactly graceful about it. Lark insisted she could get off the train on her own, but even though she seemed to have physically recovered a bit, I wasn't hearing it.

"I'm soulless, Von Rathe. There's nothing wrong with my legs."

"No more chances," I told her. "You're not getting hurt again."

I jumped off first, then ran alongside the train and took Lark's hand as she jumped. She was light enough that I was able to swing her away from the steel wheels and to safety. With that done, we put some distance between us and the train. Partially to get away from the sound, but mostly just to get away from *it*. We didn't have to walk too far, because now the train didn't stretch from one horizon to the other. The boxcar we'd been on had become the caboose.

Trying not to be too obvious, I scanned every direction for signs of Portia. Nothing. As close as we were to the Radix, I didn't really expect she'd risk it, but I had to be sure. I hoped I was being subtle. The last thing I wanted was to give Lark anything else to worry about, and if she knew her aunt might have been tracking us, she'd worry about *me*. I didn't think I could stand it if, after everything I'd let happen to her, Lark spent whatever energy and time she had left on me.

We kept walking, and I shuddered as a wave of icy dread washed over me. I couldn't stop hearing the howling ghouls, and I couldn't get rid of the image of the tumbling train. It was true that I'd done the only thing I could to save myself and my friends. But that didn't mean I felt good about it.

I thought it might have been one of those things that changes you a little bit forever.

I tried hard not to think about that, too.

Focus, I told myself, *focus on the next thing.* And I had to, because the next thing was really important. The next thing was saving my friend.

I had a plan (sort of). I knew what I had to do next—mostly because it was the only thing I could think of—and I needed just the right place to do it. Problem was, there wasn't much right about the Dark Sun Side, but at the very least, I wanted to put some distance between us and the cliff's edge.

Lark and I hiked up the gentle slope of a hill. It rose above the flat expanse surrounding it and had enough green-black grass to make it a good place to stop. A good place for what I was about to do. As ever, the Nighthouse stood in the distance. Lark was right—we weren't any closer to it than when we'd started. If anything, we were farther away. There was a mystery there, a riddle for me to solve. And I would. After.

Lark and I were side by side, and it was impossible to miss the fact that she was as tall as me now. And her color had changed. Where she'd been warm with golden flecks in her brown eyes, now she was . . . faded. Almost like Portia had been when I first met her. But instead of sepia, Lark was turning an undeniable shade of grey. She was changing, and we were running out of time.

At the top of the hill, I dropped my backpack and surveyed the landscape. The Radix, of course, still loomed past the edge of the cliff, and the Nighthouse still stood dark and unreachable in the distance. But if I put my back to them and looked in every other direction, it was almost nice.

We stood quietly for a while. Not long, but long enough that *someone* had to say something.

"I know we just met, but I need you to trust me," I said without looking at Lark.

"You said you have a plan?"

"I do," I told her. "It's going to be hard to explain. . . ."

"Then don't," she said.

"What?"

"Don't explain it to me. You sound worried enough, and I think if you start talking too much, you're going to talk yourself right out of it." Lark was right. I could think of loads of reasons why my idea was a bad one, and if I said any of them out loud, I might just lose my nerve.

"It might hurt," I said. She deserved to know that much.

Lark was quiet for a minute. "It can't be worse than having my soul stolen. That was . . . Well. Let's not talk about that, either."

I nodded. I wanted to say something, but tears were clouding my eyes and closing my throat. My bottom lip quivered, and I pressed my hand against it, willing it to be still.

"It might not work," I finally said.

"Then I won't be any worse off than I am now," Lark answered calmly.

My chest hitched and I let out a sob. I grabbed her shoulder and turned her so we could see one another. I had to look up a bit to meet her eyes with mine.

"Lark. I think it's going to work, but the thing I don't

know about, the thing I can't promise, is that I can undo it later."

"Will it stop me from turning into a soul eater?"

"Yeah," I said. "I'm almost sure."

"Then do it." Lark took my hand and squeezed it with her long, nearly tapered fingers. Her eyes were bigger and beginning to sink into her skull, but they were still her eyes. "Anything is better."

Bird nudged my collarbone. *It has to be now. Whatever it is. Time's almost gone.*

I nodded. "Clyde, buddy, can you come here?" If a spider could look worried, that one did. But when I rested my hand on Lark's arm, he climbed onto it and up my own arm to my shoulder. Then I put my hands on Lark's shoulders and turned her so that she wasn't facing the Radix or the Nighthouse. On the off chance that she could still see when this was over, I didn't want her stuck looking at either of them.

I took off my silver choker and handed it to Lark. "Put this on like a bracelet," I told her. "The soul eaters don't like it. I think it will help." Lark wrapped it around her wrist, and I helped her fix the clasp.

She grimaced. "It's hot."

Not on me, I thought, but I just said, "It'll be okay." I opened my backpack and dug around until I found what I was looking for: the vial of oil I'd used on the train and a small, crumpled paper bag. Inside the bag was a flower, a flower I'd taken the last time I'd been on the Dark Sun Side. It had grey petals and a pink center. Its stem and leaves were golden.

"Hold out your left hand." Lark did, and I poured a small pool of the oil into her palm. It didn't take much—the stuff was strong. "Rub your hands like you're washing them," I told her. "Then rub it all over—like your face and hair and stuff."

"It stinks."

"It does not. It's just strong. My friend Lily calls it kitchen magic—magic anyone can do. Lots of oils have powers, and these have some really good ones. When they're mixed all together like this, they make a kind of force field."

"What's a force field?"

Right, I thought. *She's been here a hundred years. She wouldn't know what a force field is.* "It's like . . . like a suit of armor. It wards off evil, pushes away fear, and helps you remember how to be human." It was that last part I was most interested in. I could tell it got Lark's attention too, because she stopped fussing and made sure she covered her hair and face really well.

"Now hold out your right hand," I said. Lark tugged at the bracelet, then did what I asked. "Clyde, do me a favor and go sit in her hand?" I took Lark's hand in mine, making a bridge for the spider.

Clyde didn't hesitate. He scurried into Lark's hand, and I released it once he was in her palm.

"Okay, this is important." I spoke directly to the spider. "Clyde, I'm going to put this flower in Lark's hand right next to you. Whatever you do, don't lose sight of it. When everything is done, I need you to mark it somehow. Like a web or something?" I hoped my words made sense, and that the little spider was as smart as I believed him to be.

I'll never be absolutely sure, but I swear the little spider nodded. I choose to believe he did, and it was the best I could ask for.

Through all of this, Lark was quiet.

"I'm coming back for you," I told her. "I'm going to rescue Florence if I can, get your soul back, find us a way out of here, and then I'm coming back for you."

"You'll need the necklace," Lark said softly.

"No," I told her. "You need it more than I do."

"Not *this* one—though it's hot as hell and I *wish* you'd take it. I mean Portia's. The ugly one she wears around her scrawny neck." I could see the necklace in my mind, a black pendant on a heavy brass chain. "It's the way out," Lark said. "It's where she keeps the doors. I'm certain of it. Get that necklace and you'll find *your* door."

A cold lump formed in my chest. "I was actually planning to avoid her if I could."

Lark shook her head. "Avoid her all you want, but then you'll never get out. You have to get that necklace. I'm trusting you to do . . . whatever this is, and you have to trust me on this."

"Yeah, okay. I'll find Florence, defeat the evil lady, steal her necklace, and come back to get you. It'll be easy."

Lark smiled a little at the sarcasm. "That's the spirit," she said. "Now do whatever it is you have to do."

"I'm sorry," I said. "This is my fault."

Lark shook her head again and looked almost angry as she held my hand in hers. "Stop it. I was going to end someday, one way or another. If this is my end, I'm glad I'm not alone for it. Thank you, Von Rathe."

All the tears I'd held back before coursed down my cheeks. I couldn't say a thing, so I took the flower, placed it in Lark's palm, and squeezed her fingers quickly as I pulled my hand away.

PART THREE

Things Lost and
Things Found

The flower acted just like I remembered, and just as quick. I'd learned from Lily that it wouldn't work for just anyone at any time: I could pick up the flower whenever I wanted, and nothing would happen. So could anyone else. The magic relied on the flower being given, like a gift, and willingly received.

As soon as I put the flower in Lark's palm, it took root and began to grow.

Lark's already-too-big eyes got even wider as she looked from the blooming thing in her hand to me and then back again. To her credit, she never once so much as whimpered. As gold, leaf-covered vines spread across her body and down her legs, where they planted themselves in the ground, I think she had some idea of what was happening. As her skin turned into golden bark and flowers blossomed out of the small branches and twigs that were once her fingers, she *had* to know.

And as the bark grew up her neck and over her jaw,

just before it covered her face, she mouthed a silent "Thank you."

I nodded and refused to cry again. The last time Lark saw me—*for a while,* I told myself, *just for a while*—I was going to be brave and strong for her. The bark twisted and toughened around Lark's legs, and she grew taller. Not as tall as the last time I'd done this, but as tall as an apple tree in an orchard.

The whole thing didn't take two minutes. When it was all but over, Lark was gone. In her place was a gorgeous golden tree covered in grey flowers with pink centers. The black sun shone through its thin edges—Lark was a ghost, so it made sense that her tree was too—and the whole thing glowed like stained glass.

All of this, though, would be for nothing if I couldn't find that first flower, the one I'd given to her, among the hundreds of others. That flower was the key to doing—and undoing—the magic.

I hoped.

"Clyde," I called. I was glad my voice sounded stronger than I felt. "Buddy, did you do it? Did you mark the special flower?" From a collection of small branches that looked a lot like an open hand, a tiny form dropped out of the tree. Clyde slid gracefully through the air, attached to the Lark Tree by an almost invisible thread.

He stopped when he was eye level with me.

"You know where it is?"

This time, I *know* he nodded.

"Good boy. I'm coming back. Soon as I can. And when

I do, I'll need you to help me find it again, okay? You have to stay with it—with her," I said, my voice catching on the last word.

The little spider nodded again and, like a magic trick of his own, scuttled back up the thread and disappeared into the leaves.

I watched from the base of the new tree as the last few reluctant buds and leaves emerged and opened themselves to the sun. You wouldn't think I'd know exactly when the entire transformation was over, but I did.

Because as one last grey petal unfurled, the whole world shook.

Earthquake, I thought as I lost my balance and fell to my knees. The ground shook, the rocks and grass and Lark Tree shook, and I shook as I lowered myself all the way to my stomach to lie flat on the ground. I'm not exactly sure why I did that. It just seemed safer somehow.

The rumbling intensified, and an impossibly loud cracking sound filled the air as three things happened:

The first thing was that the sun, which had been reliably hanging in the sky, sank like a black stone. The whole world was thrown into an abrupt evening in a matter of seconds. Enough sun peeked over the horizon that I could still see, but my eyes were still adjusting as I watched the second thing happen.

A storm rolled in, as fierce and black as any I'd ever seen. It didn't bring rain, at least not right then, but it did carry lightning in its fists. The sky was so perfectly dark that the only light I had was the unpredictable flash of that monster lightning. I've never been afraid of storms, but this one was so big and so sudden that it was impossible not to be at least awed by it.

The third thing that happened was the best and the most frightening. With every flash of lightning, the ground under me seemed to lurch forward. No, it didn't *seem* to. It did. But I couldn't tell how fast or how far, because everything around me—including the Lark Tree—moved too. In those flashes, as the ground heaved, the Nighthouse drew closer. It was still on its cliff edge overlooking the Radix, but somehow, it grew closer with every burst. I was moving, and so was it. Something was pulling us and the actual ground we were on together. It seemed impossible that a structure as big as the Nighthouse could be shifted like that without toppling over, but that didn't make it any less true. When the Nighthouse was maybe a block away from me, it stopped and stayed in place.

And then, as suddenly as it had started, the ground went still. I went from lying on my stomach to sitting on my butt, but I didn't get all the way up right away. I needed to be sure some kind of aftershock wasn't coming before I tried to get to my feet. As I sat there, Bird vibrating on my shoulder, the storm cleared as quickly as it had come in. The black sun had disappeared, and for the first time I was on the Dark Sun Side when it was fully night.

There were stars—more stars than I had ever seen—winding their way across the sky. I saw whole galaxies and constellations that had never been written about in any mythology or astronomy book. The moon, though, was what really made my heart stop in my chest. Not because that moon was scary but because it was the most incredible thing I'd ever seen. It was ten times bigger than even the biggest harvest moon, and it was a perfect crescent, like something out of a kids' story or a Halloween card. The moon glowed the palest gold, darker in some places and lighter in others, and between it and the million stars, there was more than enough light to see by. I tried to take it all in and had to blink away tears I hadn't felt coming.

I understood then what *awe* really was and what it felt like to suddenly encounter something so big and beautiful and impossible that your heart froze and swelled at the same time, and to have a new kind of tears you'd never cried before show up in your eyes. It was overwhelming, that feeling of being so, so small, while at the same time being part of something so, so . . . forever.

I sat for I didn't know how long, taking deep breaths of the night air and looking and trying to create a for-ever memory. No matter what else happened, or how scary things were going to get, I wanted this moment to be something I could always remember. I'd never really be able to describe it, but I wanted to keep it just for me.

Bird broke me out of my trance. He pecked my neck, not hard enough to hurt, but hard enough to get my attention. *We can't stay here. There are things to do.*

He was right. I didn't want to, but I shifted from look-ing at the sky to looking at the Nighthouse. I couldn't see it clearly, black against a sky that was now the dark-est shade of purple, but well enough to tell it wasn't a friendly place. Off in the distance, I hadn't been able to tell how enormous it actually was, but the Nighthouse was easily ten stories tall. The tower was made from giant stones, with cutout windows spiraling around the sides. I figured that behind those windows must have been a staircase winding right along with them. The yellow light at the top didn't shine as much as it pulsed—unsteady and decidedly unpleasant.

I was nearly there. After who knows how many hours of walking and running and fighting and riding a monster train, I was nearly at the Nighthouse. All it had taken was for me to turn my friend into a tree. Except that wasn't exactly right, and I knew it. It had nothing to do with Lark being a tree and everything to do with my being alone.

I wondered then, if I had done this alone from the beginning, would I have reached the Nighthouse in just a short while? And would Lark still be Lark, complete with her soul? The idea made me angry down to my bones. This all could have been so much easier—and safer—if I'd never met Lark in the first place. If she hadn't insisted on going with me, I might have already found Florence and been gone. And Lark would still have her smile and her golden-green soul.

My stomach ached as I remembered what had been taken from her, as I wondered how awful it must have been. And all that was mixed up with my anger at her and at myself.

My whole body was angry. I wanted to hit the tree in hopes Lark would feel it. I wanted to swear at her and tell her she'd been stupid. Most of all, I wanted her to know that I knew she'd lied to me. Or if not lied, at least misled. She had to have known, after a hundred years of trying, that she was never going to get to the Nighthouse and that I'd never get there if she was with me.

She had to have known she'd get hurt or worse.

She had to have known I couldn't keep her safe.

Bird pecked the back of my neck, harder this time. *She was lonely. She was tired. She had hope. Don't hate her for having hope.*

That knocked the wind right out of me. "I don't hate her," I whispered.

Of course I didn't hate Lark, even if I was angry at her. And the thought that she still had enough hope to try one more time after a century of failing broke my heart in a way it had never broken before. Like the fire on the train and the countless creatures I'd doomed, this heartbreak felt like something I'd never get rid of. I knew it added to my heart and shoulders a weight that would never entirely go away. If these feelings were what people collected and carried with them over a lifetime, I wasn't sure growing up and growing old were all that wonderful.

We have to go. I'd been so lost in my own head that Bird's soft words made me jump a little.

"I know," I said. I reached back and patted Bird before getting to my feet. "I know we do. It's just a lot."

Bird nuzzled my collarbone. He got it.

With a sigh that came from way down deep, I got up, put on my backpack, and went to the Lark Tree. Without thinking about it, and without even feeling silly, I wrapped my arms around its trunk.

"I'm sorry," I said. "I'm sorry, and I'll fix this. Then we're going to get you out of this place. You don't belong here." I hoped that somewhere in there, Lark could hear me.

"Take care of her," I called up to Clyde.

I was shivering. Without the black sun, the air around me had turned cool in a hurry. I found my hoodie and zipped it on, telling myself that the cold was the only reason I was trembling.

Then I started toward the Nighthouse.

16

At about the halfway mark between the Lark Tree and the Nighthouse, a dark line had formed that stretched perpendicular from the edge. I knew what it was before I could make it out clearly. I didn't want to believe it, told myself it had to be something else. But my eyes weren't lying, and my brain was working just fine.

As I drew closer, I had to admit that there was a giant crack in the ground between me and the Nighthouse. And not just a crack. It was a crevice—a chasm, really— and it was twice as wide as I was tall. There really had been an earthquake after Lark's transformation, or something like it. And one of those deafening noises I'd heard hadn't been lightning at all, but the sound of the earth breaking in half.

I got as close to the edge as I dared and looked down. A familiar swirling darkness filled the new abyss. Lark had shown me how thin the ground we walked on really was when she had me reach my hand under the cliff. Now I could see for myself how the Radix was just inches away from us all the time. The crevice itself was less than a foot deep, but right below that was nothing but black nothing.

Ten feet isn't all that far from one place to another. Unless, of course, you have no way to cross it. I looked around, hoping but not really believing that I would find a fallen tree or, I don't know, a plank of wood or a random ladder or something. Of course, there was nothing but patchy black grass and rocks, some dull and some glimmering in the starlight.

The Nighthouse was *so close*, but it had never been farther away.

Focus, I told myself.

Focus.

Focus.

And then . . .

There was a time, not that long ago, when I'd fallen into the black nothing. And I'd still be falling if Bird hadn't saved me. He'd given me wings once, and I thought maybe he could do it again.

I glanced down at the shadow sparrow. "Buddy, can you?"

Bird turned his little face away like he was avoiding having to look me in the eyes. *I can help you. Save you, sometimes. But I can't take your journey for you.*

It wasn't the first time he'd told me something like that, so I wasn't surprised, but I was suddenly and completely hopeless. For a wild moment, I considered jumping into the crevice. Then Bird would technically be able to save me. He could fly me up, and . . .

And back to where I'd started, and I wouldn't be any closer to saving Lark or Florence or myself. Because I knew that wasn't how it worked. Bird couldn't take a step of this for me. It had to be me. I was the one who had to figure this out.

I thought through what I had, which didn't take long, because it wasn't much. I had plenty of stuff in my backpack that was useful in all sorts of situations, but nothing that could get me past the crack in the earth. I paced a few yards back and forth near the edge of the crevice. As I walked, I studied the black that filled it.

Even though I thought of the Radix as a black nothing, I knew that wasn't really right. It wasn't nothing at all. It was magic and power and a tool and a weapon. And it didn't like being taken advantage of. I'd seen that when the black fog filled Lily's house to take back the bit of magic Pope had stolen from it. I'd also seen it when it tried to creep up on Portia, who, according to Lark, had been stealing from it for a century.

It occurred to me that while I'd never stolen from the black nothing, I'd never offered it anything either. Before I realized I was going to do it, I knelt down as close to the edge of the crack as I dared and started talking.

"I think you're watching me. I think you made all this happen: the ground shaking and the Nighthouse moving and this giant, stupid hole in the ground. You know why I think that? Because you're the only thing big enough and strong enough to do it."

In that moment, it seemed the only sounds in all of the Dark Sun Side were my heartbeat and my breathing. And in that long, long moment, I started to convince myself that nothing would happen, nothing would answer me. Doubt ran through my veins where blood was supposed to be.

But then . . .

The blackness directly below me seemed to rise a little, like a bubble trying to break the surface of a filmy pond.

My mouth dried up like I'd eaten sand, but I kept going. "I think you want me to get to the Nighthouse. You know why? Not because you care about me, because I don't think you care about anything but yourself. I think you want me to steal from Portia the way she's been stealing from you."

I was rambling, but all those words were doing something. The bubble rose a little higher.

"If I get Florence back, Portia will hate it. If I get Lark's soul back, she'll be *furious.*"

The bubble didn't really look much like a bubble anymore. It looked a whole lot like a head.

I kept talking before I lost my nerve and ran. "And if I can make her mad enough to come to me, I can steal that necklace from her. The one she keeps all the doors in."

Two black-as-night hands rose up and grasped the edge of the crack. I had to choke back a scream as my heartbeat filled my ears, and I scooted back just a little bit without even meaning to.

My whole body was vibrating. I took the deepest breath I could (which wasn't very deep at all) and tried to steady my voice. "And if I can get Portia's doors, she'll be stuck. And you can have her." I sure hoped I was right about that.

The thing that pulled itself out of the crack was made of the same stuff as the Radix. It stepped an inky foot up over the edge, and before I could remember to breathe, it was standing next to me on the edge of the crevice.

I jumped up, ready to run as far and as fast as I could.

Bird beat his wings once. *Wait.*

The figure was about my height, but its arms and legs were thin as bones. Black fog twisted from its fingertips and sank like heavy smoke. It didn't have eyes that I could see, but there was no doubt that it was looking at me. It tilted its head to one side, like it was trying to make a decision. In that moment, I knew it could either help me or drag me down into the endless void. Whatever I said next would either get me one step closer to saving my friends, or it would be the end of everything.

"But I can't do any of that if you don't help me."

The thing rushed at me.

The Radix-creature lost its human form and became a shapeless black fog as it wrapped itself around my face. I inhaled to feed a scream, and when I did, I breathed in giant, gulping lungsful of it. The fog filled my mouth and my chest and my stomach and all the in-between parts of me I couldn't name. It was cold and tasted like stone and I couldn't stop breathing because I had to breathe, and I couldn't stop screaming because I had to scream.

And then it was over as fast as it had started. The

black fog sank to the ground and flowed like mercury back into the crack. I fell to my knees, crying and coughing so hard, it sounded like a bark. While I gagged and tears rolled down my face, I waited for my brain to go slow and numb the way it had when Portia had breathed some of the same stuff into my face. I had inhaled so much more of it this time, and for so much longer, so with every second that passed, I expected my brain or my heart to just stop.

But that didn't happen.

Like someone had turned down a dial, my breathing began to slow and get more regular. My heart stopped pounding like a fist against a door and found a smooth, steady rhythm.

In almost no time at all, I was calm. I was so calm that I didn't freak out at all when tendrils of black rose out of the crack and slithered across the ground. Not tendrils—tentacles. More than I could count. And none of them reached for me.

Each and every one of those tentacles crept forward and searched the ground until they found a single stone. Then, like an ocean creature hoarding treasure, the limbs wrapped themselves around the stones and snatched them back into the crevice. For every tentacle that retracted into the dark, two more appeared, all intent on adding to their strange collection. For a while, there was no sound but my breathing and the clattering of rocks being pulled across the ground.

I was alert enough to recognize that my strange calm was gone, but I was too fascinated to be afraid. I didn't know what the Radix had done to me, but I was pretty sure it hadn't hurt me.

When the next thing happened, I knew I was right.

As the last tentacle grasping a rock the size of a grapefruit disappeared, there was a rumbling sound from deep in the crevice. The sound was like a thousand rocks clacking into one another.

Then it stopped, and the world was truly silent.

I opened my mouth to say something to Bird but closed it as a shape rose out of the crevice. It was as long as the crack was wide, formed a gentle arch, and was made of all the stones the tentacles had just gathered. It rose until one side just met the edge of the crack near my feet, while the other end of the arch touched the far side. It was almost pretty, with its gentle slope and sparkling stones mixed in with regular rocks. It looked like it had come straight out of a fairy tale.

The Radix had made me a bridge.

I reached back and stroked Bird. I didn't know what to say and, it seemed, neither did he.

Finally, *It's a gift.*

"No," I said. "We're making a deal. A good, fair deal. It's giving me a way to do the things I said I would."

I approached the bridge and considered it. It looked sturdy, with no gaps between the stones, and was about four feet wide. I'd crossed a much narrower and longer bridge not so long ago. Of course, I'd fallen off that one. . . .

You were pushed, Bird said. I wasn't certain he could read my mind, but sometimes it sure seemed that way.

"Don't remind me," I said. But I was actually glad he had. Falling and being pushed were two different things, and this time there was no one to push me off this wider, shorter bridge. I scrubbed my sweaty hands on my jeans and put my right foot on the bridge, testing it. It was as sure as cement. I finally, *finally* had the right path to the Nighthouse. All I had to do was take it.

Without letting myself think about it any longer, I looked straight ahead and crossed the bridge. The Radix kept its promise, and in a few quick steps I was on the other side. I half expected the bridge to crumble after I crossed it, but it didn't so much as shift.

"Thank you," I said to the Radix. "Keep it there, okay? I'll need it when I'm done."

There was no reply, but the bridge stayed put, and I figured that was the best answer I was going to get. I took a deep breath, turned away from the bridge, and looked up. The Nighthouse was just a few yards away, and so tall, I couldn't see the lantern room at the top, but the pulsing yellow glow still filled the night sky above it. The side farthest from me was, in my estimation, precariously close to the cliff above the Radix. There couldn't have been a dozen feet between it and the endless black.

The building itself wasn't ugly, exactly. The grey stones met one another neatly, and the windows spaced along what I assumed to be a spiral staircase were uniform and rounded at the top. Very high up, I could see what looked like a walkway that encircled the top of the Nighthouse. I figured that had something to do with the lantern room and provided a way for the windows to be cleaned from the outside.

No, the Nighthouse itself was fine, but it radiated something that felt a whole lot like misery. I'd always thought that buildings had personalities, and this one was no different. If the abattoir that housed The Clackity had been intimidating, the Nighthouse was foreboding. The idea of entering that place filled me with a heavy fog of dread.

"Seems nice," I said.

Bird fluttered, and I could feel his irritation with me. My buddy was clearly in no mood for jokes, even the really bad ones, which he usually appreciated.

"I know, I know," I answered him. "Sorry." He had flown to my shoulder, so I nuzzled him with my chin. "I'm worried too."

I began to make my way around the Nighthouse, looking for the door I knew had to be there somewhere. I circled the building, starting in the direction that would take me as far away from the Radix cliff as possible.

As luck would have it—*my* luck, anyway—the door was nowhere to be seen, which meant I was going to have to walk toward the Radix after all. I rounded the building, and the black expanse that emerged in front of me made me dizzy. It was disorienting, the way the violet sky and the black nothing sort of melted into each other, one never really ending and the other never really beginning. Like they were both the same, which might not have been all that far from the truth.

I began to worry there might not actually have been

a door to the Nighthouse at all. I wouldn't put it past the Dark Sun Side to have the sort of place one had to enter but had no entrance. Like a really annoying riddle.

It turned out I wasn't giving the tower enough credit, because as I kept going, the frame of a door emerged. I sighed a deep, relieved sigh and stayed as close to the Nighthouse as I could, now that I was only a few yards away from the cliff's edge.

The door was tall and arched and pointy at the top, with a peephole like a dead, blank eye. It was black, with paint flecking away in places so the wood showed through. It seemed to hang just a little crooked on its hinges, or maybe the whole thing had been built a little crooked, frame and all. In many ways, it was a whole lot like the door I'd gone through back in the old school-house.

I reached out to grasp the handle, and the winter-cold iron bit at my skin. I pulled my hand away quick. That did it. I very badly did not want to go through that door.

Bird, who had been still and watchful for a while, nudged me gently with his head. *Up to you, of course, but not really sure you have a choice.*

"I know," I said, patting him softly. "I'm just really tired of bad places and scary doors."

Let's make this the last one, then.

"Deal," I said.

If this was going to be the last time Bird and I did this, the last horrible door we ever opened—and it *would* be, I was sure of it—I was going to do it right. I wrapped my fingers around the iron handle and held them there.

The cold burned my skin and seeped into my bones so fast and deep, they ached.

I could feel the Radix watching me, waiting to see what I would do.

I did not let the handle go.

I did not open the door. Yet.

"My path, my journey," I told myself and whoever else was listening. "I'm in charge."

I took a deep breath that shook only a little.

I opened the door.

17

The door opened into a room so dark and so quiet, it might have been underground.

That's kind of an exaggeration, but the room *was* dark, except for the light from the stars and moon that crept in through the few dirty windows. Something I'd learned when The Clackity sent me into that strange neighborhood was that houses on the Dark Sun Side could have their own rules. My first clue that *this* building might not have cared about logic was the fact that the room was long and narrow rather than round like it should have been.

Before I stepped one foot through the door, I dropped my backpack and found my flashlight. There was no point in sneaking around. If anyone was in the Nighthouse, they would have seen me coming from a mile away. Besides, I was pretty sure Portia had been spying on me—us—off and on since the journey began.

The white beam of the flashlight cut through floating dust motes and cobwebs that looked like they'd been made by something much larger and less friendly than

Clyde. I stepped over the threshold softly, making as little noise and kicking up as little dust as possible. The floor was stone, so the quiet part was easy. The dust, however, was a different matter. It looked a quarter-inch thick and was the chalky grey of despair.

I trained the flashlight on the floor to find that the dust there had been disturbed by more footprints than I could count. The tracks were faint, far fainter than mine, but they were unmistakably footprints. I thought of all the ghosts gone missing from Blight Harbor—of Florence—and would have bet everything I owned that all those ghosts had ultimately made their way here.

The idea was both terrifying and reassuring.

I was in the right place.

Looking around, I saw that dust coated every surface in the room, from the two straight-backed wooden chairs in the middle of the floor to a desk in the corner that was piled with papers. In the opposite corner was an old iron woodstove. A teakettle sat on it, skirted in webs. And along that same wall was a bed on a metal frame that probably served as a couch as well. It was unmade, the blankets pushed down to the foot of the bed, like whoever last slept there either got too warm or stood up in a hurry. The bare mattress sank in the middle from use and age, and the frame was so low to the ground that sitting on it would almost put you on the floor.

The whole thing was depressing. I couldn't imagine anyone being very happy here or staying for very long. Across from me at the back of the room was a doorframe without a door. Beyond the frame, my flashlight found the beginning of a twisty set of stairs. They were made of the same stone as the building's exterior and hugged the wall. As far as I could see, there was no rail on the open side. My hands and feet got clammy at the thought of climbing to the top of the Nighthouse with nothing but empty air next to me.

It was a problem, but it wasn't my problem. Yet.

I played the flashlight around the living quarters, looking for anything that might've been interesting or useful. The room was grubby from who knew how many years of disuse, but it wasn't especially messy. Aside from the unmade bed and the cluttered desk, it was actually pretty neat—sparse, even. And no one had ever bothered to do much in the way of decorating. Even under the dust, it seemed everything was some variation of off-white or grey or old wood.

It seemed silly not to give the room a quick once-over, just in case there was something useful in it. Besides, there wasn't much to the space, so I figured it would only take a minute. I got down on my knees to look under the bed. Nothing but dust bunnies. Not really wanting to touch the thin blankets, I held my breath and shook them out. Nothing but an eye-stinging cloud of dust emerged. The oven door screeched in protest when I opened it but was empty aside from a couple of mostly burned logs and ash.

Then I turned my attention to the desk. Books and papers were stacked in precarious piles. A memory shot through my brain like a slap to the face. Clear as day, I could see my dad's desk. It had always looked just like this, right down to the stone placed on one of the piles as a makeshift paperweight.

I didn't cry then, but I thought about it. Memories were such sneaky and unpredictable things. They could come out of absolutely nowhere and had the power to make your heart fill to bursting, or make you feel like you'd been punched in the stomach. Sometimes, both.

This time, both.

I took a deep breath and got back to snooping. I didn't have time to go through all the papers, but I was hoping something might've stood out to me as important. As I slowly moved the light from one pile to the next, something did.

I almost missed it, the tiniest of purple glints that caught in the white beam of my flashlight. It poked out of a pile of old, yellowing papers that were on their way to collapsing and was the first hint of real color I'd seen in the place. I put my flashlight under my arm so I could use both hands to move the papers, lifting half of them and placing them atop a seemingly sturdier heap.

When I saw what the purple was, I did start crying.

I took the object and cradled it against my chest. My shoulders hitched as I cried from somewhere way deep inside myself, a place I hadn't cried from in a long time.

Bird stroked my back, one part worry, one part comfort, and one part confusion. *What is it?*

I couldn't answer.

I needed to sit down.

I made my way back to the sagging bed and sat, the mattress so low that my knees jutted up at an angle. I didn't even register the cloud of dust that must have erupted when I dropped hard to the mattress. Shaking, I held the purple thing in one hand and used the other to shine the flashlight over it. I inspected every inch.

Evie, what? Poor Bird, still concerned and confused, made his way to my shoulder to get a better look. I was so afraid that if I said out loud what it was I had in my hand before I was absolutely sure, I'd end up being wrong, so I didn't answer.

I looked it over again.

A third time.

I wasn't wrong.

"They're my mom's," I managed to whisper.

As impossible as it was, I was holding my mom's signature violet tortoiseshell glasses. They were intact, not even a chip in the lenses. Other than being dusty, there wasn't anything wrong with them except for the fact that my mom wasn't wearing them.

I had a thousand questions, but of one thing I was certain: these glasses had not been through a fire. The bright little spark of hope that had never quite been extinguished, no matter how sad or bad things had gotten, erupted in my chest, and thoughts as fast and bright as lightning crashed through my mind.

It was proof that my parents, or at least my mom, hadn't died in that fire.

It was proof that my parents—or someone who knew them—had been to the Dark Sun Side.

It was proof that my parents—or someone who knew them—had been here, in this room.

I closed my eyes and took a shaking breath. Then I did the only thing I could think to do.

I put on my mom's glasses.

18

The world exploded in a burst of color and light.

The change was so drastic and sudden that I slammed my eyelids shut in surprise. My eyes watered as I opened them, but this time I was prepared.

The living quarters had changed. The room was still the same long and narrow shape, the furniture in the same places, but otherwise it was an entirely different room. It was bright and clean and full of warmth. A rainbow of hand-knitted (or crocheted—I could never tell the difference) blankets were thrown over the backs of the chairs and covered the very bed I was sitting on. They looked familiar, and it took me a moment to figure out why. These blankets looked very much like the blankets from the Dark Sun Society's meeting room in the back of Irv's Clays and Glazes. The stove was clean, and the teakettle shone in the bright light that streamed through the windows. The desk was still a mess, but the papers were no longer edged with brown and yellow. And the paperweight rock was . . .

I switched off the flashlight and set it on the bed—I didn't need it anymore—and stood on shaky legs to make my way to the desk. The paperweight rock was no longer a grey chunk. It caught the light of the black sun, and all its edges and surfaces sparkled like gold. I would know this object anywhere.

It was pyrite. And not just any pyrite. It was the very same crystal my dad had received as a gift from Aunt D. The same one he'd used as a paperweight in our old house and my old life.

Seeing something of my dad's in this place almost dropped me to my knees. I stared at the pyrite, taking slow and even breaths before they had the chance to turn into quick, shallow ones. When I finally worked up the nerve to pick the crystal up, I noticed something I hadn't before. All the colors that had found their way into the room were . . . thin. The pyrite looked like Dad's in every way, but when I held it, it still felt like a roundish stone. And, as I looked closer, I could see that the jagged pyrite wasn't really there at all. It was, well, like ghosts—thin around the edges. I could still see the round shape of the grey rock just below the shining surface.

I lifted my mom's glasses up to my forehead and the room became dark, the stone in my hand just a rock.

Then I put the glasses back on and everything was warm golden magic again.

I was, to put it mildly, baffled. What was it I could see through my mom's glasses? Was it the past? That seemed possible. Was it an alternate reality? Also reasonable. I walked around the room with Mom's glasses on, searching for clues in the illusion.

Bird shifted around on my shoulder. He seemed confused. It dawned on me then that he couldn't see what I was seeing. My buddy probably thought I'd completely lost it.

"Things look . . . different . . . with Mom's glasses on," I told him. "I'm trying to sort out why."

Bird nodded. *Makes sense.* It was one of the least weird things to happen to us on the Dark Sun Side, so he probably wasn't all that surprised.

Near the desk, a small collection of unframed photographs were pasted up on the wall. They were all of my family, and mostly of me at various ages—all taken up until the time I was eight. It was like a miniature version of the collage on Maggie's bedroom wall. I reached up to take one down and my fingers slipped through it like smoke.

Right, I thought, *this isn't real.*

Except.

Except it felt real.

The blankets and pyrite and glasses and photographs all felt like things that belonged. They didn't feel staged or too perfect like the not-my-house in the strange neighborhood had felt. And the glasses *were* real, there was no way around that.

It occurred to me that someone could have brought these things here, someone other than my parents. But why the photographs? And why hang them on the wall where they'd be seen all the time?

Certainty, like a key turning in a lock, clicked in my brain. It *had* to be my parents. It was the only thing that made sense.

I went to the nearest window and looked out toward where the Radix and night sky were—where they *should* have been. Instead I saw a bright purple sky and black sun. And I saw a rolling field of tall green-black grass and wildflowers in a dozen colors. I could even smell the gasoline-and-rosewater scent that the growing things here all seemed to have. No cliff or Radix in sight.

I closed my eyes and thought. *Why show me a different landscape?*

Unless there *was* a different landscape. And a different Nighthouse. One that really did have my parents' things and photographs, and a pretty field outside it.

Because, according to Lark, there was more than one. *There are a bunch of Nighthouses all over, if you know where to look,* she'd said. And something else: *They're meant to guide people to safety.*

What if . . .

What if my parents had somehow ended up on the Dark Sun Side?

What if they'd found safety, found a Nighthouse of their own, and that was what I was seeing when I looked through my mom's glasses?

What if they'd never come home because they'd never found another door back?

My brain was spinning. All these what-ifs were just that, but I couldn't deny that it felt like I was onto something. Or heading in the right direction, at the very least.

We can't stay. Bird interrupted my thoughts, and his words almost sounded like an apology. *Whatever it is you're seeing, we still have work to do.*

"I know, buddy."

He was right. It would be too easy for me to get lost in this illusion, to settle in and not come out again until I'd solved the mystery of my parents' disappearance. But there were people depending on me right now. Lark, Florence, and who knew how many of Blight Harbor's ghosts were all in trouble, and I was the only one who could do anything about it.

"One more thing," I said as I went back over to the desk. I set the not-pyrite stone down and began to rifle through the loose papers, hoping to find anything that might tell me where my parents were. The other-place illusion was on those papers too, but it was so thin that I couldn't make out any of the writing. It was all jumbled up with the real writing on the real paper underneath.

Frustrated, I started pushing over the piles. Papers fluttered softly to the floor, making a sort of whooshing sound as they landed. I had no idea what I was looking for. I just knew I had to at least try to find some information, some clue before I moved on to the task ahead of me. I pushed over an especially tipsy pile, and when it went down, up came the whooshing sound. But there was another sound as well—a solid and satisfying *thunk*. I froze, surprised by the noise.

On the floor, almost hidden by the mess of paper, was the thin spine of a book. I reached down and freed it from the pile. Before the whole cover was exposed, my heart climbed so far up in my throat that I could barely breathe. I sat down on the floor, not trusting my legs to hold me.

It was a book. *My* book—mine and my mom's.

When I was little, I liked to be alone. I called it Lonely Time. My mom was a storyteller, and my favorite story she told me was called "The Loneliest Place." It was about a little girl who searches the world to find a place where she can really and truly be alone. My mom had made it up, but I'd loved the story so much that one day she decided to turn it into a little book just for us. She'd even drawn pictures to go with the words. It had been my favorite thing. I'd been certain it had burned up when our house did, that it was gone along with everything else.

But four years and what felt like a lifetime later, I had it in my hands again. Tears dripping off my chin, I opened it to a random page.

It looked like this:

So, she went to the star-lit desert.

It was quiet there.

But soon she heard shushing and singing
and all the sounds of the golden snakes in the
sand.

She was not alone. This was not the
loneliest place.

She asked the snakes, "Where is the loneliest place in the world?"

The snakes thought and thought and hissed among themselves.

Finally, "The winterlands," they said. All their tiny voices spoke together just loud enough to be heard.

"But there is someone at home who loves you and who will miss you if you go away. And who will fret and worry until you come back safe. Don't be gone too long. Lonely time is good. Love is better."

The girl nodded and thanked the snakes and pulled up her collar against the cool night.

I cried so hard, I thought I might vomit. In that moment, I missed my parents more than I had since I was little. I missed them in a way that reopened a gaping cavern in my chest that could never heal and never fill up. I felt like I would be empty forever, like someday I would just turn into nothing but the sadness of not having them.

Looking back, that really might have been it. That might have been the end of the whole thing. I could have stayed right there and waited for Portia, furious and denied her soul, to come looking for me.

I closed the book, put it on my knees, and rested my forehead on the cover. I tried to breathe. When that got too uncomfortable, I straightened up enough to reopen the book. I was going to read the whole thing. And then maybe read it again. And keep reading it until I either fell asleep or died of hunger and dehydration.

Inside the cover were words, an inscription that hadn't been there the last time I read the book. It was written in my mom's handwriting, and seeing it knocked the wind out of me all over again. The message was short, and I didn't know how many times I'd read it, but when I was done, something inside me had changed. The sadness was still there, but the cavern had closed. Or had been filled, anyway, with a kind of determination I'd never felt before.

I pushed Mom's glasses up with the heels of my hands and rubbed away the last of my tears. When I looked down, I saw that my hands were wet with what looked like watery grey ink.

"What the . . ."

The black nothing, Bird reminded me.

"Right." I'd completely forgotten about my encounter with the Radix-creature and how much of the stuff I must have inhaled. I cupped my hands and breathed into them. Sure enough, a small black cloud pooled there before dissipating into the air.

What will you do with it? Bird asked.

"No clue. I don't even know why the Radix gave it to me," I said.

Gifts here always have their reasons, Bird said, like I didn't already know that.

I shrugged. "I'll figure it out, I guess. Or eventually just cough it all up." I had more important things to think about than the Radix and its unwanted *gift*. Besides, as far as I could tell, aside from turning you into a power-hungry monster, it wasn't actually good for anything.

I put the book and not-pyrite rock in my backpack and slipped my mom's glasses into the pocket of my hoodie. The world was all grey and dust again. I'd be needing my flashlight. I patted Bird, who'd been pacing anxiously across my back.

"Okay, buddy," I said. "Let's go save some people."

19

I left the living quarters of the Nighthouse behind and made my way toward the room with the stairs.

This one was round, like it should have been. It stretched at least fifty feet from one side to the other. I walked to the center, looked straight up, and immediately regretted that decision. The perfect roundness and the spiraling stairs went up and up and eventually were lost in darkness. It made me dizzy. My hands and feet—even more afraid of heights than the rest of me—grew instantly sweaty.

I scrubbed my hands on my jeans and looked around, slowly swinging my flashlight around the perimeter. It didn't take long. There was nothing to see but the stairs.

With a sigh that was accompanied by a puff of black air, I made my way to the foot of the staircase. The steps were steep and maybe three feet wide, plenty wide to walk up but not wide enough to feel safe. They were made of the same dark grey stone as the rest of the Nighthouse. In fact, they looked like they'd been carved out of, rather than built into, the wall. Their edges were sharp and wicked. It was easy to imagine what would happen to a person's head if they tumbled down. And once I started imagining, I couldn't stop.

I imagined getting tired as I climbed.

I imagined getting dizzy.

I imagined falling off the side and plummeting down until I found the unforgiving floor.

Anxiety fingers crawled up my back, and my breathing got fast and sort of hitchy. I could feel the panic coming, but I didn't have time for it.

Focus, I told myself.

Focus.

Focus.

I imagined finding Florence. I imagined saving Lark and getting all of us back to Blight Harbor in one piece. There was only one way out of this situation, only one way back home. And that way was up those awful stairs.

With a deep breath, and an encouraging Bird on my shoulder, I took the first step. Then another. I tried counting them for a while, but that only made things worse, since I had no idea how high I was going to have to count. To forever, maybe.

I knew looking down was a mistake. Looking up, too. But I kept doing both. I did my best to focus on Lark and Florence and getting home to Aunt Des—all the reasons I was on those stairs—rather than on how steep and narrow they were.

At some point, I'd climbed high enough that no matter which way I looked—up or down—all I saw was a pool of shadow. There was no longer any way for me to gauge how far I had climbed or how much farther I had to go. My legs felt like lead, and each time I lifted one to climb the next stair, I was sure it would be the last time I'd manage to do it.

I walked for hours. That was how it felt, anyway. Logic told me the Nighthouse wasn't that tall, that there couldn't possibly be that many stairs inside it. But logic didn't always mean much on the Dark Sun Side, at least not any logic I understood.

I stopped looking down or up. There didn't seem to be any point. For a while I climbed with my head hung low, seeing nothing but the step I was on and the one right above it. That worked until my right knee gave out from under me.

I landed hard on the sharp edge of a step, and when I swore, it echoed for a while. My knees, already skinned up, broke open again. There wasn't a lot of blood, but it stuck to the loose threads on my shredded jeans and made a gross pulling feeling every time I moved.

A shot of panic ran through me as I thought of my mom's glasses and how they might have snapped when I fell. I found them in my hoodie pocket and was so relieved they weren't broken that I nearly cried again. I considered putting them on but didn't dare. Those glasses were full of illusions, and the last thing I needed on a flight of death stairs was not to be sure what was real and what wasn't. Gently, I put the glasses back into my pocket.

I knew I couldn't stop. If I did, I might cramp up and never be able to get started again. So I resorted to moving on all fours, my hands on the stairs in front of me, my feet below. The crawling was awkward, especially with a flashlight in one hand, but it took a little bit of strain off my legs.

As I crawled, I thought about what I'd found in the room below, the room that must have been a mile away by then. I thought about my parents and how I was sure to my bones that they'd been in this place, or someplace very much like it. I thought about Aunt Des and how she must have been apoplectic with worry. I didn't even know how long I'd been gone. Was she out looking for me right now? Asleep on Lily's couch? Waiting up in her favorite chair in case I walked through the front door?

I thought about Lark and hoped Clyde was keeping track of that flower. I thought about Florence, and all the other Blight Harbor ghosts, and wondered if I would get to them in time. I thought and thought and worried and was so caught up in it all that I nearly fell on my face when I reached for the next step only to find it wasn't there.

I'd reached not the top of the Nighthouse, but something pretty close to it. I was on a wide wooden balcony that wrapped itself all the way around the inside of the building. Above me I could see a new staircase, wooden and not built into the wall, that passed up and into what looked like the stone floor of another room.

I stood on trembling legs, slowly so I wouldn't cramp up or fall over, and took in the new space. The balcony was much wider than the stairs, six feet at least, and— wonder of wonders—it had a rail that went all the way around its edge. But it was the round wall that was the most interesting, because it wasn't blank stone. Every few feet, there was a door, and those doors went all the way around the circumference of the Nighthouse. Windows filled the spaces between the doors, enough that the landing wasn't completely dark, thanks to the giant moon and million stars.

In the regular world, those doors would have opened directly outside, leading nowhere but down. But this wasn't the regular world, and I knew those doors each went somewhere different. They were all identical to one another, regular-sized and made of what seemed like regular wood. The boards were aged but in good shape. They hung straight in their frames, and their hinges were dark brass, which glinted in my flashlight beam. The doors had matching brass handles, long and narrow, but no locks that I could see.

In the center of each door and at about eye level was a small rectangle of brass, and those were maybe four inches wide and six inches high. They weren't plates or plaques. They were more like ornate grates, the brass curlicuing into rounded shapes that looked sort of like vines and leaves. I was pretty sure that if I got close enough, I'd be able to look through those grates and see whatever was on the other side.

What do you think? asked Bird.

What I thought was that I didn't want to get too close. "I guess," I said, "I lied about not going through any more doors."

Bird sighed. *It was nice while it lasted, right?* I patted

Bird's little head and he nuzzled my collarbone. I was grateful for him, grateful not to really be alone.

I took another look around the balcony. There must have been forty doors. Fifty, maybe, and chances seemed pretty good that something awful would be hiding behind at least one of them. The one thing I knew for sure was that standing around wasn't going to get us anywhere.

"I have to go look, don't I?"

Bird shrugged. I knew what that shrug meant. *It's up to you, but of course you do.*

I sighed, and another black puff of air escaped my lungs. I loved Bird, but he could be maddening sometimes.

"Fine, I'll go look. But if long, skinny fingers poke out through the grate and stick me in the eye, I'm blaming you."

Bird didn't reply, but I was pretty sure he was shaking his little head.

I approached the nearest door slowly, and when I couldn't come up with any more excuses not to, I leaned in so my face was just a half inch away from the grate. I saw absolutely nothing. It was black as night behind that door.

"I don't . . ."

Use your light stick, Bird suggested. He meant my flashlight, and of course he was right.

"Smart bird," I said quietly. He puffed up at the compliment.

With a shaky hand (I was really managing to freak myself out), I shone the light through the grate and looked again.

This time, I could see. The room behind the door

was small, smaller than my bedroom at home, and didn't seem to have anything in it. Just a dark, empty room, which honestly was almost creepier than if there had been something—anything—in there at all.

I slowly played the light around the space as best I could.

Nothing.

I'd nearly given up when something shifted in a back corner. I didn't see the movement as much as sense it. I slowly moved the beam of light to get a better look, to see what I might have missed before.

There was a figure in the corner, covered in shadow and so curled up that it was almost invisible there on the floor. It didn't pull away from the light. It didn't react at all.

"Hello?" I called softly. "Are you okay? Are you trapped in there?"

The figure shifted then. Gradually, like it hadn't moved in a very long time, it stood. It still faced the corner, but I could see it was tall and human-shaped. It wore clothes, long pants and a long-sleeved shirt, but I couldn't make out much about the style and nothing about the color.

"Do . . . do you need help?" I asked. It was kind of a silly question.

The figure turned, but it was a slow and deliberate kind of turn, like it was thinking while it was moving. I finally caught a glimpse of its profile, but it was hard to make out any features in the shadows. Almost like it didn't have hard edges between itself and the dark.

Bird grew warm on my shoulder. He was worried.

From the figure there came a sort of guttural noise. It sounded as though it was trying to form words but had forgotten how. The sounds it made had the same animal tone as the howling ghouls on the train. I listened hard, trying to make sense of any of it. Then came one short, recognizable phrase. Except it couldn't be what I thought I'd heard. Because what I thought it had said was, "Pretty Penny." Which was what The Clackity called me.

Bird was red-hot on my skin.

By the time the figure faced me, my whole body was full-on trembling and I didn't trust what the shaking flashlight was showing me. I used one hand to steady the other and trained the flashlight beam directly on the figure's face. Or where its face would have been if it had had one. There was no sign of Clackity or of anyone else. Instead, the place where lips and a nose should have been was smooth, grey, and gently rounded. It didn't even have eyes.

At least, that was what I thought until they opened.

When the thing raised its eyelids, I screamed and backpedaled, but not fast enough to miss seeing the thing charging the door. Charging me. It had eyes, all right, and they were eyes I'd seen before. A dull, glowing red—and nothing else—filled the sockets.

The thing ran into the door at full speed, but it barely made a thump when it collided with the wood. Like it didn't weigh all that much. Bird was spinning circles on my back.

"It's a ghost, I think. But it's turning into one of those things, the things on the train. Like Lark."

A ghost you know? Bird was thinking of everyone missing from Blight Harbor.

I was too.

"I don't know. It . . . it didn't really have a face. If I had more light, maybe I'd recognize its clothes or . . ."

I stopped as a thought occurred to me. A thought so obvious, I was embarrassed I hadn't had it before that moment. I reached into my pocket and pulled out my mom's glasses. This time when I put them on, I was ready for the onslaught of color and sunshine.

There wasn't as much color this time, as there wasn't room for decorations on the balcony, but there was plenty of light. I turned off my flashlight to preserve the battery and slid it into the side pocket of my backpack. The daylight now coming in through the windows shone on the warm wood of the doors, making them appear freshly oiled. The brass hinges and grates gleamed.

I approached the door again, careful but not as afraid as I had been. The thing behind the door hadn't been able to open it. Or hadn't wanted to.

Through the grate, the room was still dim, but much brighter than it had been without Mom's glasses. Long, narrow windows were cut out near the ceiling, letting in enough black sunshine to see by.

The figure was back in the corner, huddled and, I thought, shaking. He had short-cropped dark hair and wore a white shirt rolled up at the sleeves. His pants were a dark brown, with blue suspenders holding them up. He no longer looked like the creatures from the train. He looked like a regular ghost—human. A pale orange aura surrounded him—something I'd never seen from a ghost before. It glowed and flickered like a weak bulb.

"I'm sorry I scared you," I said. "I didn't mean to."

There was no reply from the man. He didn't move.

"I'm here to help you."

The man turned his head a little. He was listening.

Bird had climbed up the side of my neck. He strained his little head to get a better view.

"I'm . . ." I thought about telling the ghost my name, but I wasn't certain it was safe. "I'm from Blight Harbor. I really am here to help."

At that, the man rose to his feet and cautiously made his way toward the door. His aura, the color of peaches, shimmered around him as he came. I found then that I did recognize him. I didn't know his name, but I knew he was the ghost from the hardware store. The same place where Des and I bought shovels and rakes and had keys made.

"I'm going to open the door now," I said, reaching for the handle.

The man stopped in his tracks and shook his head. He looked more scared than sure.

"You don't want out?" I asked.

The man shook his head again. As he did, I saw that his face was . . . thin. Like the illusions in the living quarters. Beneath it was the face of the smooth grey thing I'd first seen. A hint of dull red showed below his brown eyes. He was, I realized, both ghost and ghoul. Not entirely one or the other.

He's worried, said Bird. *Worried about what he might do. Worried he might hurt you.*

I was a little worried too.

"Did something take your soul?" It seemed like kind of an abrupt question, but I didn't know how else to ask it.

The man nodded, and I thought I saw the faintest glimmer of hope in his eyes.

"I'm going to get it back, okay?" It was a big promise. One I hoped I'd be able to keep.

The man smiled, but it was a sad smile. When he nodded, it was a small gesture. He wanted to believe me, I could tell, but he wasn't sure he could.

"I'm going to check some more rooms, okay? See who else is here."

He nodded again, but this time it was accompanied by a worried look.

"I'll be careful, I promise." Then, as an afterthought, "Hey, do you know Florence? Florence Dwyer?"

He nodded, and it came with a real smile this time.

"Have you seen her? Here, I mean?"

He shook his head.

I was disappointed but not surprised. If I was right, Florence had been the last of the Blight Harbor ghosts to be kidnapped. This ghost had probably been locked up well before then.

If he *was* locked up.

"Hey, could you get out? If you wanted to, I mean?"

The man shook his head and drew a large rectangle, roughly the shape of a door, with his hands. As he did, he shook his head harder.

"Do you mean there's no door on your side?"

He nodded.

It helped to know that. If I was going to be in the ghost-rescuing business, I'd have to be really careful not to get stuck in one of those rooms. The thought of being trapped was bad enough. The thought of being trapped with a ghost who was slowly becoming a ghoul was worse.

"I'll be back, okay? I'm going to see who else is here."

The man nodded, gave me a small wave, and went back to his corner. It made my heart sad. He was already defeated, resigned to whatever was happening to him.

I, however, was not.

I hitched up my backpack, straightened Mom's glasses, and went to the next door.

20

From the first door to the next, I stumbled.

It was one of those weird moments when you think you're putting your foot down like normal, but something goes just a tiny bit sideways and you almost end up on your butt. Fortunately, there was no one but Bird to see it happen.

I tried to play it off like I hadn't almost tripped over my own feet, but Bird didn't miss a beat. *You okay?* he asked.

"Fine," I said, blushing. "Clumsy, I guess."

And that was the end of it.

Or so I thought.

I did not recognize the next ghost, but that was mostly because I couldn't get her to even look at me. She was lying on the floor against the back wall, her grey skirt in a tangle around her knees. I knew she was still alive— or whatever it is that ghosts are—because just once she raised her hand and gestured for me to go away. Her aura was like burgundy watercolor paint.

The ghost behind the next door was a stranger as well. He was animated, angry to be locked up. His aura was crimson. Seeing the hints of a ghoul under his skin, I knew I couldn't let him—or any of them—out until I had a plan. So I didn't tell him there was a door on my side of the wall. I reassured him I was doing my best to get them all out. I asked about Florence, but he either didn't know her or didn't know where she was.

I *did* recognize the next ghost.

"Shirley?" I asked. The relief at seeing someone from home bloomed in my chest like a sunflower. Her eyes went wide and she rushed to the door. A golden-yellow aura pulsed around her.

"Shirley!" I wanted to open the door and drag her out. Shirley was one of the two ghosts who had permanent

seats in the Blight Harbor movie theater. I knew her immediately, and not just because I'd accidentally sat in her lap once when I was late getting to a movie. Everyone knew Shirley and her friend Ursula. They were always together and never missed the opening of a new film.

"Is Ursula with you?" I searched the room for her companion as I asked. There was no one else there.

Shirley shook her head, and her eyes filled with tears as she ran a worried hand through her hair.

"Did she come to this place with you?"

Shirley nodded.

"Listen, I'll look for her, and I promise I'll let you know when I find her. I'm here to get you all back home."

Shirley wiped at her eyes and mouthed the words, "Thank you. Be careful."

"I will," I said. *I'll try,* I thought.

On my way to the door after Shirley's, it happened again. I almost lost my balance. But this time, I was pretty sure it wasn't me.

"Did you feel that?"

Bird nodded as hot concern radiated from him.

"It's like the floor shifted or something."

We should probably hurry, Bird said. I didn't need him to tell me twice. I didn't like the idea that the wooden balcony, which might as well have been a million feet up in the air, was unstable.

I hurried.

Ursula was behind the very next door. With her big eyes and short, dark hair, I knew who she was immediately (even if I'd never accidentally sat in her lap). The light around her was bright, electric blue. I told Ursula that I was there to help, and that Shirley was okay and right next door. Ursula's shoulders slumped like she'd been keeping strong and didn't have to anymore. She smiled a sad sort of smile and thanked me. I asked if she'd seen Florence, but she hadn't.

When I ran back to tell Shirley who I'd found, she cried all over again. Those seemed like tears of relief, which I guess was an improvement.

I kept going, room to room, as fast as I could. Some ghosts I recognized, and at least as many I didn't. They all had auras, and no two were exactly the same.

I looked back at the first door I'd gone to, the one by the stairs, and saw that I was maybe a third of the way around the room. This was taking too long, which was partially my fault for taking the time to talk to every ghost.

I was telling myself that I'd have to work faster when the whole world moved. This time, I did fall.

The balcony turned like the dial on a combination lock. It shifted one way for what felt like an entire minute, then the other way for a few seconds. I would have held on for dear life if there had been anything to hold on to, but since there wasn't, I clung to the floor. Finally it reversed again, and when it stopped, I had to take a very deep, slow breath and force myself to open my eyes. I hadn't even realized I'd closed them.

I was trembling and breathing in shallow little gasps, but I wasn't hurt. I was also farther away from the first room—the room near the staircase—than I had been before. But that wasn't the worst thing, because I still had the staircase as a marker. I figured I'd seen into maybe a dozen rooms. It wouldn't be too hard to get back to where I had been. The Dark Sun Side was full of tricks, and this honestly wasn't the worst I'd ever dealt with. Still, I was frustrated and angry at losing more time.

"I hate this place," I said to Bird.

He fluttered in agreement.

And that was when things got more complicated.

An enormous grinding noise filled the air, wood on stone. Imagine being inside a giant pencil sharpener while someone used it. That was what it sounded like.

The wall with all the doors was moving. I sat still, helpless, as the room around me turned. Just like the balcony, the wall turned one way, then the other, then reversed itself. Throughout it all, the staircase didn't move.

I had completely and totally lost my bearings. There was no way of knowing what doors I'd already been to.

That was when I got really angry—with the situation, but mostly with myself. I'd dealt with doors before, back in the strange neighborhood. I'd learned then that if you want to keep track of where you've been, you've got to mark the doors you've already tried.

Of course, thinking about this now did me absolutely no good at all. I yelled a whole string of swears that echoed through the Nighthouse. I screamed into my hands, then slapped the floor with them both until my palms stung. After a while, I stopped and sat quietly, taking deep and ragged breaths. Tears of frustration filled my eyes.

Feel better? Bird asked, and I couldn't tell if he was

really concerned or being a little judgmental. Probably both.

I slapped lightly at him, but the truth was that I did feel a little better after my tantrum. I sat and thought as I regained my composure.

Starting again didn't make a ton of sense. There was no guarantee the world wouldn't spin again. Even if I was smart and marked the doors, it was still going to take forever. I decided to try a different approach.

"Florence," I called. "It's me. It's"—I almost used my name but thought better of it—"Maggie's friend. If you're here, can you find a way to let me know?"

I waited and tried to watch all the doors at once.

Nothing.

"Florence," I called again. "If you're saying something, I can't hear you."

I waited.

Nothing.

"Buddy, we might have to start all over again."

Bird nodded, deflating a little.

I waited.

I'd almost given up when I heard the tiniest, faintest noise. If Bird and I had been talking instead of watching and listening, I would have missed it for sure.

Clang clank.

Clang clank.

Clang clank.

It was something light tapping something metal. And I was pretty sure it was coming from the other side of the room.

"Florence, if that's you, keep making that sound."

Clang clank.

As quietly as I could, I made my way toward the sound. It continued, regular as a heartbeat.

Clang clank.

The tiniest movement caught my eye. Once I saw it, I ran as fast as I could to reach it. Something long and thin was poking through the grate, maybe ten doors away. As I got closer and saw what it was, I let out a little yelp of happiness.

It was a pencil knocking back and forth against the ornate brass. I only knew one ghost who carried a pencil all the time. She had it because it was always stuck in her bun like an oversized hairpin.

Florence.

When I got to the door, I rushed to the grate without hesitating. When I saw the ghost with big hazel eyes and a honey-colored bun, I started to cry a little.

Florence was crying too. She pressed her hand against the grate, and I did the same. Her fingers were longer than I remembered, and pointier, too. Through Mom's glasses I could see the Florence I knew and the periwinkle aura I'd never noticed before, but beneath that I could also see the beginnings of the ghoul that was threatening to take over. Like the others, her soul had already been stolen.

"I'm getting you out of there," I said.

Florence froze. Then she backed slowly away, shaking her head and holding a palm out as if to stop me.

"It's going to be okay," I said. "We're going to go find

your soul and make this right. We're going to get you home."

Sadness and something that looked a whole lot like longing filled the ghost's eyes. But she shook her head again. *No.*

"What do you think?" I asked Bird. "If I go in there, I mean. Is it going to be okay?"

Bird didn't answer right away. Finally, *I don't know. But I might be able to help you talk to her.*

I'd never considered being able to actually talk to Florence.

And, Bird added, *if things get bad, we can always . . .*

"No!" I said. I knew exactly what Bird meant. I remembered what we'd done to the ghouls on the train. "Not Florence. I couldn't."

You could. If it wasn't her any longer, you'd have to.

"I couldn't," I said again. But with maybe a little less conviction than the last time.

You can't, because if we lose her, she's never going home anyway. And if we don't stop her, neither will you.

I closed my eyes and took deep, even breaths. I didn't want Bird to be right, even though I knew he was. So I took a moment and said a silent prayer, asking that Florence be okay long enough for me to help her. It's a small thing, putting your voice out in the great wide everything like that, but sometimes it's the best you can do.

Finally, "You can help us talk?" I asked.

Yes, but you'll have to go in. She'll have to take your hand.

I could do this.

"Florence, I know you can't see it, but there's a door on my side. I'm coming in. And when I do, you have to let me hold your hand so that we can talk."

Florence's eyes widened and she shook her head, but I ignored her.

The door handle was cold and smooth, and when I pulled, the door opened without a sound. Entering that room felt like an act of faith. Because it was, I guess. I had to have faith that Florence was still mostly who I'd always known her to be and not the monster she was becoming.

The idea made me angry down to my toes, that kind and gentle Florence would have the best and most important parts of her taken away against her will. That she would have no power over who—or what—she became. It wasn't fair, and I was going to fix it.

Florence backed herself against the stone wall, trying to put as much distance as she could between the two of us. I didn't grab her hand right away. She was scared, and worried, and had every reason to want me to stay away. She'd been violated already, and I wasn't about to do it again.

"Florence, please," I said, propping the door open with my foot and holding out my left hand. "Please trust me. I'm going to do my best to get you home, because there are people who miss you. And because I love you. And because you don't deserve this."

As I spoke, Bird flew into my hand. He'd done it so many times before and for so many reasons. I hoped with my entire self that this would be one of those times he'd be a gift rather than a weapon.

Florence looked at Bird, then back up at me. With a silent sigh, she crossed the floor, reached out, and took my hand with her right one.

"Thank you," I whispered.

Even as I spoke, Bird was working a new kind of magic. He stretched and wound himself like black ribbon around my hand and Florence's. From our wrists to our fingertips, we were bound together.

I think you can hear her now, Bird said.

"Florence, say something?"

"Maggie. Does she know?" Her voice was soft and strong, just like I'd always imagined it would be.

"I can *hear* you," I said as grateful tears crept out of my eyes. "No, Maggie doesn't know you're gone. Mr. Seong made me promise not to tell her until she comes home."

"Good. That's good," said Florence. It was barely a whisper. Then, "Go home, Evie. Please." Even in this awful place with all the terrible things that were happening to her, she still sounded calm and steady.

"Not without you. I'm *here* for you."

"Listen to me. Go home. Now."

"I can't. I'm here for you, Florence, but I'm here for all the others, too. So many ghosts from Blight Harbor are here, and what happened to you happened to them, too."

Florence didn't budge. "It's not worth it, Evie. You have your whole life. It's too dangerous."

That made me mad. "And you have your whole *after-life.* And wherever you're going to next, you deserve to make that choice." It occurred to me then that I knew what might convince Florence. She might not let me fight to save her, but she'd help me fight to save a child. "Besides, there's someone else we have to save. Her name is Lark, and she's only eleven. She knows you, Florence. She loves you. She's been here a hundred years, and this is her only chance to get back home. I need you to help me help her."

That did it. Florence's shoulders sagged and she closed her eyes. When she opened them, there was a new determination there. Her periwinkle aura glowed, brighter and *more* than before.

"I know her, too," she said. There was a very long pause while Florence stared at me like she was trying to work something out, which I guess she was. Finally she nodded. "I'll help you. But you have to promise me that you'll save yourself first if you must."

I threw my free arm around Florence and hugged her as tight as I could. When she hugged me back, I knew she and I were still okay.

"If I must," I agreed. There was a lot of wiggle room in that promise.

21

We didn't waste any more time.

Hands still bound, Florence and I made our way to the wooden staircase.

"This leads up to the room below the lantern room," she said. "That's where she's keeping all the souls that aren't right."

"Right for what?"

"Her soul is in the lantern. It's that horrid yellow you see flashing from miles away. I've heard her say that she's looking for a matching soul to replace it so she can take hers back. She only ever comes here to bring someone she's tricked or to check on the souls those awful creatures steal for her. So far, nothing. I can't imagine there are many souls as sick and jaundiced as hers."

"She told you all that?" I asked. "It seems like a lot of information for Portia to give away for free."

"She's calling herself Portia?" Florence sort of smiled, but there was no humor in it. Lark had asked me almost the very same question and responded in almost the very same way.

"Yeah, why?"

"The Latin root of the word *Portia* is port, and *porta* is an entryway or a gate. Or a door. She thinks she's clever. I'm sure it isn't her real name."

Why did everyone know this but me? "It isn't," I said. "Her real name is Meredith."

I watched as Florence's eyes grew wide. "Meredith," she said. "I didn't recognize her. She's not the woman I remember anymore." There was a pause as Florence regained her composure. "And to answer your question, she *did* tell me. Some of it, anyway—she does love to ramble. And some of it will be obvious when you see."

We went up the stairs and into a round, low-ceilinged stone room. Another staircase, this one presumably leading to the lantern room, was on the opposite side. Along the walls, filling any space that wasn't already taken up by windows, were tall wooden cabinets. Each of the cabinets had two narrow doors. In the center of the room was a small workbench and stool. The setup reminded me so much of the one in John Jeffrey Pope's cellar that chills like a hundred spiders crawled up my back and arms, all coming to rest on my neck.

"What is this place?"

"A workshop, I suppose. And a laboratory. Let me show you."

Florence took me to a cabinet. She put her free hand on the knob and then paused. "I don't remember you wearing glasses. What are those for?"

"They . . . they show me things I can't see on my own. And they make things brighter." I thought about it, then added, "They're my mom's."

Florence nodded like this all made perfect sense. "If they make things brighter, you'll want to remove them for a moment."

I pushed my mom's glasses up my forehead like a headband. At first, I almost put them back on. The Florence I saw now was more ghoul than ghost. But I trusted her, so I did as she said.

It was a good choice. When Florence turned the knob, the doors swung wide. Behind them was a chaotic rainbow of colors and light. I squinted against the glare. I almost asked what I was looking at, but after a moment, I knew. Portia's words came flooding back: *You can't mistake the soul light. You'll know it when you find it. And you'll find it there, in the Nighthouse.*

Inside the cabinet were maybe two dozen glass jars— the old-fashioned kind with glass lids and little metal hinges. In each of those jars was a tiny solar system, and no two were exactly alike. The colors ranged from deepest blue to sunburst orange and everything in between. I looked for the brilliant green-gold soul that belonged to Lark but didn't see it and tried to ignore the sinking feeling in my stomach.

Florence opened another cabinet. That one too contained souls trapped in jars.

"Oh . . . ," said Florence softly. She reached out for one of the jars. I immediately saw why.

Inside the jar was a beautiful collection of sparkling

periwinkle globes, all of them orbiting the largest and most brilliant orb, like planets circling the sun. Without Mom's glasses on, I couldn't see Florence's aura, but I remembered it. The soul matched her aura perfectly.

"Florence, it's yours!"

She nodded, smiling. But there were tears in her eyes too, and something else that looked a bit like relief.

"So, how do we . . . I mean, how does it go back in you?"

Florence didn't take her eyes off her soul as she said, "It wants to come home. I think it will know how. I hope."

"I think you should be the one to open it."

"Yes, but I'll need both my hands to do it. So anything we need to discuss, let's do it now."

She was right. Also, I didn't know how much longer Bird's binding of us would last, and I didn't know if he could do it again. Holding me and Florence together had to be hard work, and his journey had been just as long and exhausting as mine.

"Can you see the auras? The colors around the other ghosts?" I asked.

"Yes. Always."

"Okay. Then I think it's simple. We match the colors and get the right souls to the right ghosts."

"It will take a while."

"We'll start with the people we know, recruit them." Then I added, "Shirley and Ursula are here. Let's start with them."

"They'll help," Florence confirmed.

There was a little more to my plan, and some of it

was still coming together, but I wasn't ready to share it all with Florence just yet.

"When we're done, everyone will need to get back to their rooms. If they're out when Portia comes—and I know she will—she'll know something's up. So we have to make them all trust us. Trust us to get them back out."

"Everyone but me," Florence said. "I'm not leaving you to fight that creature alone."

I made a noncommittal noise somewhere in the back of my throat and avoided eye contact with Florence.

"When we deliver their souls, they'll trust us," she continued.

"Good. Then—" But as I spoke, I was interrupted by a flash of red light.

A crimson soul in one of the jars was whirling out of control, its orbit falling apart before my eyes. As I watched, the tiny red sun at its center seemed to explode. Even without my mom's glasses, the light was so bright that I had to look away. There was a tiny *clink* like a pebble landing in a glass.

When I looked again, the soul was gone. All that remained was a small grey crystal at the bottom of the jar. I remembered the man the soul had belonged to. He'd been behind one of the first doors I'd checked. He'd been okay not that long ago, and now . . .

"We're too late for this one," Florence said with a sort of sad resignation. Then, "There's something you need to see."

Florence walked to the next cabinet and opened it.

Instead of jars filled with glimmering light, there were only empty jars.

Except . . .

Except they weren't entirely empty. Each of those jars had a small, smoky crystal resting at the bottom.

Florence gestured around the room. "All the rest are the same."

I knew then where all those ghouls on the train had come from. Sorrow and fury fought for room inside me. Portia had been doing this, trading countless souls for her own, for a very, very long time.

"We have to hurry," Florence said.

I wanted to reply, but tears filled my eyes and my throat burned as I tried to hold them back. The man with the crimson aura was, I was certain, now one of the ghouls with red eyes and starving stomachs. I wanted to cry because I had failed him and because I was afraid that I'd fail all the others, too.

"You first," I managed.

Florence squeezed my hand. "Whatever happens next, you are an amazing girl, Evie Von Rathe. Thank you."

My tears had broken loose and I couldn't say a word, so I just hugged Florence instead.

Without being told, Bird unwound himself from our hands, then crawled up my arm and back to my shoulder. He brushed his soft wings on my back, comforting me the best way he knew how.

I was shaking, but I wasn't the only one. Florence's hands trembled as she reached for her soul. The jar was sturdy, a little smaller than a regular canning jar, and made of thick glass that looked almost warped. As I watched the jar in Florence's quaking hands, I wasn't sure she was in any condition to open it without dropping it.

I placed one of my hands on hers. She must have been so lost in everything that was about to happen that I managed to startle her.

"You open it," I said, "but let me hold it while you do, okay?"

Florence nodded gratefully and let me take the jar from her.

I didn't know what I'd expected, but the warm vibration of the glass in my hands surprised me. I could feel it humming in my teeth and bones. If it felt like that for me, and it wasn't even *mine*, I couldn't imagine what Florence felt when she held it.

As far as I know, ghosts don't have to breathe, but Florence took a long, deep breath. She shook her hands out a little like she was releasing any remaining tremors and, without any further hesitation, unlatched the lid.

It flew open, the lid smacking back against the jar on its little metal hinges with a *clank* that echoed through the otherwise silent room. Florence's soul burst from the jar, and as it did, it grew. It grew not just in size, but its shape changed too. From the largest orb, tendrils extended, and they reminded me immediately of the black nothing as it built my stone bridge. But there was nothing dark or sinister about this: it was a beautiful and alive kind of magic.

The periwinkle wonder was on Florence in a half

second, and the twisting, somehow intelligent vines knew exactly where to go. Some curved around her throat and others wrapped around her arms and hands. As I watched, the tendrils sank into her skin and disappeared. The remaining strands braided together and pressed themselves deep into her chest like burrowing roots. While all this happened, the orb grew smaller until it faded entirely.

As the last of Florence's soul made its way back home, there was a moment when her eyes glowed a dazzling shade of fiery, pale purple-blue. The whole thing might have looked violent, like an attack, to someone who didn't know what was happening. I knew better. It was the most moving thing I'd ever seen. I was crying again (I felt like I'd been crying for days), but these were tears of awe and of hope.

I clutched the empty jar and waited for some sign from Florence, something to tell me she was okay and whole again. She pressed her hands against her chest over her heart and bowed her head low. I was pretty sure she was praying. After a time, she looked up at me, and her smile was radiant. No hint of the ghoul at all. She was wholly Florence again.

It had worked.

Bird, who'd been peeking over my shoulder, spun happy little circles.

I wanted to celebrate too, but there was no time. The memory of the crimson soul was still fresh in my mind.

"Okay," I said, "we start with Shirley and Ursula. And remember, don't close the door behind you, or you'll have to wait for someone to open it again."

I turned from Florence and started searching the cabinets until I found what I was looking for. Shirley's golden soul and Ursula's electric-blue one were right next to each other, as they should have been.

"Ursula," I said, handing the bright blue jar to Florence. I kept the gold one for myself. I felt a connection to Shirley, and maybe it was selfish, but I wanted to be the one to save her. Then I put Mom's glasses back on. I was ready.

We rushed down the stairs and searched until we found the right doors and the ghosts within. I could see Florence was talking to Ursula and listening as the other woman replied, but I had no idea what they were saying. It didn't take long before Florence opened the door and went inside. It seemed Florence, with her newly intact soul, was probably awfully convincing.

It was pretty easy with Shirley, as well. Once I showed her the jar and assured her that Ursula was being rescued at that very same moment, Shirley was in. As I had for Florence, I held the jar for Shirley. She opened it, and the process repeated itself. The orb and the tentacles and the rejoining of ghost and soul were no less magic than when I'd watched it happen to Florence.

Shirley hugged me when it was over. I didn't know what to say, so the first thing that came out of my mouth was, "Sorry about that time I sat on you in the theater."

I couldn't hear it, but I could tell Shirley was laughing. She hugged me again, which told me that I was probably forgiven.

Back in the hall, Florence and Ursula were waiting for us. When Shirley saw Ursula, she burst into tears and ran to her friend. They hugged and had a quick conversation I couldn't even begin to interpret, though the expressions on their faces were a funny combination of worry and relief.

I hated to interrupt, but we had a job to do and a ticking clock. The sound of that little crystal hitting the bottom of the jar kept playing through my head on repeat. I very much did not want to hear that sound again.

I ran through the plan with the three ghosts. It wasn't complicated, so it didn't take long. We'd have eight of us delivering jars, and then sixteen, and if my math was any good at all, it meant we'd be done in no time.

"Remember," I said, "check the grates before you go in. If you see one of the ghouls—trust me, you'll know—*do not* open the door. And don't let the doors close behind you while you're helping. Put the empty jars in the cabinet when you're done. And when everyone has their souls, everyone *has* to go back to their room and close the door. I'll—*we'll*—let everyone out as soon as we can, and then we'll go home."

I'd almost blown it, but Florence didn't seem to notice. My plan was still just mine.

The next steps went relatively smoothly. Florence was the one to find the ghoul who'd once been the ghost with the crimson aura, and I could tell it broke her heart, but she finally moved on to the next room. She'd seen what might have been her future when she looked at the creature, and that would be enough to frighten anyone.

Of course, that made me think of Lark and how brave she'd been. And that was when I realized I hadn't yet found her soul. I'd have known the green and gold of it on sight. I hoped it had been brought here, like I believed. I hoped I'd made it in time, that hers wasn't one of the many jars with nothing in them but a smoke-colored crystal. I hoped I could find it at all.

With all those thoughts going through my head, I watched as the last of the ghosts reentered their rooms and closed the doors behind them. Only Florence, Shirley, and Ursula remained.

"You two should pair up if you want," I said to Shirley and Ursula.

Holding hands, they both nodded. They chose a room, and I joined them. As I'd hoped, Florence was curious and followed us in.

"When this is over," I told them, "I may need your help. I have a friend we need to save. She's a tree right now, but I'm pretty sure I can fix that."

I was rambling, but I needed to keep talking until I had maneuvered myself as close to the door as I could.

"And when this is over," I said to Florence, "you can be as mad at me as you want to be."

Then I slipped out the door and closed it behind me, locking the three women safely inside.

22

Oh, she's going to be very *angry with you,* Bird said nervously.

"Already is, I'm sure," I said.

I was honestly glad that I couldn't hear Florence right then, because I was certain she was yelling some pretty terrible things at me.

I deserved it. I hadn't exactly promised Florence that she'd be with me until we went home, that we'd face whatever was coming together. But I hadn't tried all that hard to make her think otherwise, either. I felt bad about locking her in that room but not nearly as bad as I would have felt if something happened to her.

What if something happens to me? I thought. *If I get killed, they're all trapped. . . .*

As I climbed the staircase, I did my best to think about something else. Anything else.

In the cabinet room, I made sure all the doors were closed tight, every handle turned in the proper direction. I didn't want anyone to immediately notice that someone had been here, and I certainly didn't want Portia to see all the now-empty jars.

I stood in the center of the room and took my glasses off so that I could see what Portia would see when she came through. If she came through.

Everything looked as it should have.

What makes you think she'll come? Bird asked.

"Because she's done all this"—I gestured to the cabinets—"risked getting this close to the Radix and hurt all those people for who knows how long just to steal her soul back. She'll come."

I hoped.

The staircase leading to the lantern room was short, so I didn't have much time to think—or worry—on my way up. I'd had a picture in my head of what the top of the Nighthouse might have looked like, and I wasn't too far off.

The lantern room was made almost entirely of glass. Each glass panel was three times as tall as me, wider than I could reach with my arms stretched, and held in place by metal frames that looked a lot like iron. The panes leaned in toward the center of the room, which was capped at the top by an iron dome.

On one side, a small metal door had been built into the glass wall. It swung inward, and as I opened it, a gust of fresh night air wrapped itself around me. The door led to a narrow walkway that wrapped itself around the glass room. Just the thought of standing on that balcony, suspended over a whole lot of nothing, made my hands and feet break out in a cold sweat. I figured a proper

Nighthouse Keeper probably accessed it to clean the windows and make repairs.

Somehow, I doubted Portia did any such thing.

On the part of the rounded wall farthest from the cliff and the Radix beyond was a cabinet that looked a lot like the ones in the room below, only narrower and made of darker wood. In the center of the room was the lantern itself. I was glad I didn't have my mom's glasses on, because even without them the light in the center was bright.

The soul in the jar in the middle of the lantern was a sickly, bile-colored yellow. I wasn't a fan of yellow under the best of circumstances, but this shade was absolutely gross. The soul was bright enough, but it was multiplied over and over again by the thick, faceted glass surrounding it. That glass was arranged in more pieces than I could count, like a giant diamond. Each piece seemed to reflect the light back on itself, amplifying it again and again until it became so vivid that it was hard to look at.

The pulsing, vomit-colored light was making me feel a little nauseous myself, so I turned my attention from it to the dark cabinet. The knob turned just like those in the room below. When I swung the door open and saw what was inside, I nearly collapsed with relief. There were a half dozen jars in the cabinet, and all of them had a grey crystal at the bottom. All of them but one.

On the top shelf was a jar holding a single glimmering soul. It pulsed like a heartbeat and shone a beautiful green-gold color. I knew it at once. I'd found Lark's soul, and it still looked bright and healthy. I took the jar in my hands and lifted it off the shelf as carefully as I'd ever done anything.

"Bird, we're gonna get through this and we're going to save her."

We still must . . .

"I know, we have to get past Portia and we have to get that ugly necklace, but other than that, we've got this." I hoped I sounded confident, because I felt like throwing up.

How are we going to get her here?

That was the million-dollar question.

"If the Nighthouse light goes out, the Radix is going to know she's up to something, right? I mean, I figure that's why she's been trying to find a match to her soul— so the Radix won't know she's taken hers back.

"So if the light goes out . . ."

She'll have to fix it before the Radix comes after her.

"Yeah, I think that's right. That's the plan, anyway."

How do you snuff out a soul?

"I don't want to snuff it out!" I was horrified. "I mean, she's the literal worst, but I'm not going to kill her soul, even if I knew how. We have to hide it someplace she won't think to look."

I set Lark's jar down carefully on the floor and looked around the room. Aside from my backpack (which was the first place anyone would check), there was nowhere to hide something as bright as a soul.

I crossed my arms over my front and sighed a deep, deep sigh. When I did, a thick black fog came with it. The gift the Radix had given me wasn't proving to be all that helpful.

If I could actually capture that stuff, I thought, *maybe I could do something useful with it.*

The idea that came to me then was so simple and so ridiculous, it sort of made sense.

"Maybe," I said.

Maybe what? asked Bird.

"Just give me a sec."

I took one of the nearly empty jars out of the cabinet. The dead soul clinked around in the glass, and it made my heart hurt to hear it. I thought again of all the ghouls I'd sent into the Radix, and a wave of shame washed over me. This had to be worth it. I had to make things as right as I could by saving everyone who was left.

I took a deep breath, filling my lungs to their very bottoms, and opened the jar. When I breathed out, I did it slowly. And I breathed right into the jar. It filled with black fog, thick enough to hide the grey crystal at the bottom.

When the jar was filled to the top, I quickly closed the lid and saw that my plan had worked. The container was full of the Radix.

I set it back in the cabinet. In the shadows, the fog was less obvious. If the room was completely dark, you might not be able to tell at all.

I filled the other empty jars so they would all look exactly the same. A plan was coming together. But there was one more test, one more thing that had to work for all the pieces to fall into place. The fog had to be thick enough and dark enough to hide a sun-bright soul.

I picked Lark's jar up from the floor. "Listen," I said to the soul, "I want to get you back where you belong. And I think I can. But you have to cooperate. When I open this lid, don't you dare try to escape. You stay right there and let me do this, okay?"

I'm not sure it can hear you, Bird said warily.

"Do you have a better idea?"

Bird didn't say anything.

I took the deepest breath I could and cracked open the jar as little as possible. Lark's soul stayed put. I pursed my lips and breathed out slowly and steadily. The jar began to fill. As it did, Lark's soul looked like it was being submerged in thick black water.

The idea that the Radix fog might have been dangerous for a soul didn't cross my mind until it was too late to turn back. But, I reasoned, I had a soul, and it wasn't hurting me (as far as I knew). I remembered Lark's words from not long after we first met: *It's power. Just a whole lot of power. And it can be turned into a tool if you know how.* I just hoped I knew what I was doing.

When the jar was full, it was absolutely and completely black. The only reason I knew Lark's soul was even in there was because I'd seen it with my own eyes.

Good job, said Bird with a nudge.

This was going to work. Maybe.

I took Lark's jar back downstairs to the cabinet room. I picked the cabinet closest to the stairs and placed the jar in the bottom left corner. An easy cabinet to remember and an easy corner to remember.

Then I closed the cabinet and ran back up the stairs, taking them two at a time. One more thing to do, and if I was right, Portia would show up not long after it was done.

I squinted against the glare and searched the lantern for the door I knew had to be there—there had to be a way to get things in and out. Things like souls. I found it at the bottom of the side facing the cabinet. There was a little hatch with a tiny handle, barely visible in all the glass panes.

"You ready, buddy? I think this is gonna happen pretty fast once I'm done."

Ready, said Bird.

I almost believed him.

I opened the hatch and took out the jar that held Portia's soul.

The light in the lantern dimmed. As quickly as I could, I filled the jar with the gift the Radix had given me. Portia's soul disappeared in the mist, and the room went dark.

I took Mom's glasses off the top of my head and put them back on. The room filled with daylight. I'd be able to see what Portia couldn't.

I ran to the cabinet and put Portia's soul, now hidden by the Radix, on the top shelf where Lark's had been. As an afterthought, I opened the front pouch of my backpack. Careful not to lose the tiny finger bone that rested at the bottom, I took out the branch covered in killer leaves. It was the closest thing I had to a weapon.

I lifted Mom's glasses from my eyes long enough to make sure the room was as dark and shadow-filled as I thought it was. Then I waited.

I didn't wait long.

The door showed up almost immediately.

It was as ugly and bent and black as all of Portia's doors seemed to be.

The door stood between me and the staircase. I backed away from it as far as I could, until my back was pressed against one of the tall windows.

When it opened, there was nothing but shadows on the other side. Wherever Portia was coming from, it was dark there. One very long, very pale arm came through first. The arm ended in something that was less hand and more claw, tipped in thick black nails that were broken at the ends, turning them into jagged razors. The fingers tapped the floor with those claws like they were making sure it was solid.

A second arm followed and pulled the rest of Portia— or what used to be Portia—along with it. She had grown so tall, she had to duck to get through.

What emerged was a monster.

Portia's limbs were distorted and elongated—her

knees and elbows jutted out at odd angles from her torso, which had become almost skeletal. She walked on all fours. It seemed impossible that those legs could support her on their own anymore.

Portia's face bulged at the top and narrowed down to a pointed jaw. Her eyes had moved to the sides of her head and were so black and round that there was nothing human left in them. She had no nose at all, and her mouth was so full of pointed yellow teeth that it didn't close properly and leaked grey drool.

What was left of her dress hung on her mangled frame in tatters and shreds. Her long dark hair had mostly fallen out, and what remained writhed and crawled over her scalp like centipedes. The ugly black pendant still hung from her neck, the only thing unchanged.

I had no idea how I was going to get that necklace and not die in the process.

For a totally irrational moment, I thought about making my way to the door in the window of the lantern room and out to the walkway, where I would take my chances. Anything had to be better than sharing a space with this creature.

A quick glance out the window behind me told me that was no longer an option.

The Radix must have sensed Portia, because it was coming. The same helpful tendrils that had built my stone bridge were now clawing at the walkway, tearing it apart piece by piece. Going outside now meant going straight down. Forever.

"Where is it?" Portia's voice was gravel being run

through a steel shaft. It rumbled and shrieked, and the sound found its way into me like drinking a glass full of metal shavings. I clutched the branch, which felt like a toy compared to the creature I was facing.

"WHERE IS IT?" This time she screamed, and the windows shook.

I glanced behind me again. The walkway was completely gone now. The Radix had risen to lap at the bottom of the floor I was standing on. It was as if it was waiting to see what I would do and how the next few minutes would play out.

This was it. It was time for me to either finish this myself or have the Radix finish it for me. And if the Radix was calling the shots, there was no guarantee I'd be able to get that pendant. Which meant no way home.

"I don't have it," I told her.

"Lies," she snarled.

"I didn't say I don't know where it is. I said I don't have it."

Portia stared at me from across the room, the empty lantern between us. "What will it take," she said, and as she did, she began to slowly make her way around the lantern toward me, claws clicking with every step, "for you to tell me where. It. Is?"

"Your pendant," I said. "And a promise that I can go home."

As she moved closer, I moved farther away. Round rooms with a barrier in the middle were useful like that.

Portia laughed—it was a cruel and mocking sound. "And you'd leave your friend behind?"

"She's gone," I said. "One of your ghouls got to her." It was technically true.

"Good," said Portia. "She was a nuisance. Forever in my way, forever between me and what I wanted. What I deserved."

That made me angry. "Lark told me what you did, Aunt *Meredith*. She told me how she tried to help you, and you threw her out of the Nighthouse. How you killed your own niece."

Portia didn't so much as flinch when I used her real name. She really wasn't Meredith anymore at all, then. Lark had been right: she was a monster all the way through. Still, it had been worth a try.

She must have known what I was thinking. "That name has meant nothing to me for a very long time. I stopped being Meredith long before I got rid of that child. She was just too stupid to see it."

That was it. "You're so tough, killing a child, but you're too worthless to do your job and take care of the Nighthouse. And you're too greedy to stop stealing souls and magic and whatever else you want. And you're so scared of the Radix that you sent a kid to get your soul back for you." I took a deep breath, and it shook with all the rage I felt for Lark and everyone else Portia had hurt. "You're pathetic."

The last word was barely out of my mouth before Portia had me by the throat. She'd moved so quickly, I hadn't had time to react.

Stronger than she looked, she lifted me into the air and pulled me close, so our faces were inches apart. Her ragged claws dug into my skin. I could smell her, something like rotten meat and mold, and I saw that it wasn't just her hair crawling on her scalp. Small, scuttling things with too many legs squirmed over her skull as well.

"You will tell me where it is now, or you will die, and I'll find it myself."

I couldn't breathe.

I thrashed my arms and kicked my legs but didn't connect with anything but air.

I couldn't breathe.

I remembered the tree branch in my hand and lashed out at her with it. The razor leaves cut into her, drawing bile-colored blood, but she either couldn't feel it or didn't care.

I couldn't breathe.

Wildly, I swung the branch at the window behind me. I don't know what I was thinking—I guess I was hoping to make a noise loud enough to scare her, or at the very least distract her. What happened was much more dramatic.

Maybe it was the sharp almost-but-not-exactly-metal of the leaves, or maybe I struck at just the right angle, but when the branch connected with the window, it exploded. A million shards of glass came crashing down. Some of them fell to the floor; others fell into the Radix.

As afraid of the hungry darkness as ever, Portia dropped me. I landed mostly on my feet. My left hand hit the floor and I felt the sharp bite of glass in my palm. Portia scuttled back to the side of the room nearest the cabinet, putting as much distance between herself and the now-open window as she could.

"It will take you, too," she screeched.

"It won't," I said, standing up on quaking legs. My voice was creaky and hoarse. "The Radix and I have a deal. A good, fair deal. I traded you for safe passage." I did my best to make my words sound confident, even though I had no idea if the shadow being would keep its end of our bargain or not.

"You *lie*," she spat. But her voice didn't sound as sure as her words. I had no idea what her black eyes said. They were unreadable.

"I don't," I said. "How else do you think I got across that crack in the ground? The Radix helped me. In exchange for you." Every breath and every word burned.

"TAKE IT BACK," Portia screamed. As she did, she yanked open the cabinet door, snatched a jar off the bottom shelf, and hurled it toward me. It missed and sailed out the already broken window. She grabbed the next jar and threw it as well, and that one hit the ground at my feet and shattered. If the black fog that leaked out was visible in the dark-to-her room, she didn't notice it.

"Tell the Radix your deal is off, and I'll let you live." Even as she bargained with me, she threw the next jar. I had to duck as it sailed over my head.

"No."

"You wretched . . ." She threw the fourth jar. Her aim was off, and it went wide, cracking a window next to the broken one.

". . . horrible . . ." The fifth jar finished the job of breaking the next window. It didn't explode, but the bottom half of the pane cascaded like a glass waterfall.

"...child." She had the sixth and final jar in her hands. The jar that held her soul. It was my last bargaining chip, and without it I wasn't sure what I would do.

"Portia," I said as calmly as I could. But even as I spoke, she threw it at me. The jar smashed against the iron frame of the broken window, and when it did, the

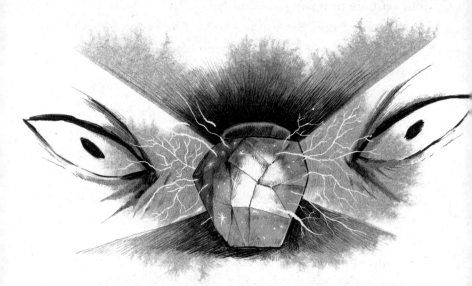

fog dissipated, revealing her infected-looking soul.

Portia and I both froze. The soul hovered for a moment, then rushed toward Portia, ready to be reunited with its owner.

Portia's face split into a triumphant sneer. "I told you you wouldn't—" But her words broke off before she could finish.

The soul was fast, but the Radix was faster.

Just before the diseased, yellowed thing reached Portia, black tendrils shot into the room from one of the broken windows. They grabbed Portia's soul, and I didn't have time to take a breath before they dragged it out the window and the Radix swallowed it whole.

Time stopped and I forgot how to blink. I looked from Portia to where her soul had just disappeared and back again, waiting to see what she would do. I figured she would go ahead and kill me.

But the noise that came from Portia was nearly the same as the noise Pope had made when I trapped him in his salt cage, after everything was over in the strange neighborhood that The Clackity had sent me to. It was an inhuman wail that was made of fear and anger and something even darker that I didn't have a word for.

Portia leapt over the lantern, and I thought she was coming for me, but she made straight for the broken window. She must have thought the walkway outside was still there.

I knew better.

If she went over and into the Radix, so would my way home.

As Portia passed me, I grabbed for her, trying desperately to stop her from falling.

I missed, catching nothing but cold, stringy black hair. It tore from her, and as she fell past where she'd expected the walkway to be, she screamed.

I leaned out the broken window, unable to keep myself from watching.

She kept screaming as she fell. I could hear her even

after she was swallowed by the Radix. I heard those screams until she fell so far that I couldn't hear them anymore. I knew that just because I couldn't hear her didn't mean she wasn't still screaming.

Forever is a long way to fall.

Portia was gone, but somehow I'd still lost. My heart shattered like the broken windows. There'd be no way out and no way home.

Still looking out the open pane, I let go of the twist of hair I held in my hand.

I shouldn't have heard it land on the floor. But I did. The sound of something solid hitting flat stone broke my spell.

I looked down. The pendant and the now-broken chain lay at my feet.

I hadn't caught her by the hair after all.

I picked up the pendant.

I was shaking so hard that the chain rattled. I found a mostly glass-shard-free spot on the floor and sat, leaning against the now-dark lantern. I knew Portia wasn't returning, but I didn't want to turn my back to the window and the Radix just yet.

Bird spun happy circles on my shoulders, but I was too tired and felt too empty to celebrate right then. I patted him and let him have his celebration.

"It's over," I said, and hoped the Radix was listening. "If you ever want this place lit up again, find someone better. Find someone who cares about the people they're supposed to be guiding. Maybe someone who won't use souls for this oversized flashlight. Electricity is a thing, you know."

I didn't expect a response. I didn't get one.

After a few minutes of quiet, I put the pendant in the pocket of my jeans and said, "I guess we should go, buddy. There are a bunch of people downstairs waiting for us."

And Lark, said Bird.

"And Lark," I agreed. I still wasn't absolutely sure I could undo what I'd done to her, and worry gnawed little holes into my stomach. "And I need to figure out how this magic necklace works."

I stood slowly. All the adrenaline had exited my body. I was left with sore, scabbed knees and a bleeding palm and scratches on my throat and shaking limbs and a deep and desperate need to get home to Aunt Des and have her yell at me and hug me and make me some tea.

I took one more look around the lantern room. I didn't think this was the last Nighthouse I'd ever see, but I hoped the next one would be a whole lot different.

Then I went downstairs and straight to the cabinet where I'd hidden Lark's soul. I picked up the jar and shook it just a little. My heart froze and I didn't breathe as I listened for the sound of a little grey rock at the bottom. When I didn't hear anything at all, I cracked the lid just enough to let the black fog seep out.

The green-gold solar system was as bright as ever.

I made a half laugh, half sob sort of noise. "We're gonna get you home soon," I said. I hoped I was right, that the spell I'd used could be reversed as easily as I thought. But that was a problem for future Evie. First I had to get down one more flight of stairs and release all the ghosts who were waiting behind doors they couldn't see. I tucked the jar into my backpack, making sure it was sealed tight and safe before zipping it in.

"Florence is going to be so mad at me," I said.

So mad, agreed Bird unhelpfully.

I slapped at him a little, but not very hard and mostly on principle.

I walked down the next flight of stairs. When I reached the bottom, I called out, "I'm back." If the ghosts responded, I couldn't hear them. So I went to the room that held Florence, Shirley, and Ursula.

As predicted, Florence was furious. When I opened the door, she flew out and gave me the tightest, angriest hug anyone had ever given me. I didn't know ghosts could squeeze so hard. After a bit, she pulled away and put her hands on my shoulders. I had no choice but to look her in the eyes—they were stern and soft at the same time and mostly filled with relief. I'd seen the same expression on Aunt Des, and it made me miss her and home so badly that my insides cramped.

"I'm sorry," I said. "And I didn't lie to you. Not exactly. But I needed to be sure you were safe. The whole reason I came here was to bring you home. Things just got a lot more complicated than I expected."

Florence shook her head. The anger had left her eyes and been replaced with something that looked more like love. She placed her hands on the sides of my face, her fingers brushing the sides of my mom's glasses, and stared at me for a beat. When she hugged me again, it felt a lot better than the first one.

Once we started opening doors, it didn't take any time at all. When it was all said and done, every ghost but the man with the crimson aura would be going home.

It took a while to get us all down the almost endless stairs, but not nearly as long as it had taken to go up them. Shirley and Ursula took the lead, and I was at the end. The Nighthouse seemed to be respecting physics, for now anyway, and we descended maybe ten stories rather than a hundred or more. Then we made our way through the living quarters and out the front door.

Before I left, I went back to the photo collage that wasn't really there. I touched each picture and looked at the faces of my parents. "I'll find you," I promised. "I love you." I took my mom's glasses off, wrapped them in the extra socks I'd packed, and placed them carefully in my backpack. I'd need them again, but not right then.

Outside, it was still dark, the sky still full of that glorious moon and ocean of stars. And thankfully, the stone bridge was still there. The Radix had held up its end of our bargain.

"Everyone cross here and head to that tree." I pointed to the Lark Tree, which was sort of unnecessary, as it was the only tree nearby. "I'll meet you there in a minute."

The bridge was as steady and sure as it had been when the Radix first built it for me. Once we were all safely across, Florence hung back as the rest of the group went on. She looked at me with a question in her eyes.

"I promise I'll be there in a minute," I said. "There's something I have to do first."

Florence nodded, but the concerned look was still there as she turned and joined the others.

I sat by the edge of the crevice, not far from the bridge. The black nothing near my feet was as calm as a placid lake. It was hard to believe it was the same stuff that had just snatched Portia's soul and dragged her to her doom.

"Thank you," I said. "Thank you for holding up your end of our deal. And thank you for what you did up there. We're all out now, and the Nighthouse is empty." I thought of the crimson-souled man and what he'd become. I was pretty sure I'd carry the clinking sound of that little grey stone around with me for a long time. Maybe forever. "Mostly empty. If you look for another Keeper, maybe be more careful next time? Or, I don't know, just tear this place down and start over."

As if in response, the stone bridge collapsed. It was there and then gone in a second. That bridge had been as sturdy as any bridge anywhere, and watching it disappear so suddenly reminded me how powerful the Radix was and how easily it could have let me fall if it had wanted to.

"Didn't mean to offend you," I said. "I really am grateful. But you're . . . a lot. And even good people have bad stuff inside them. Next time, try to find someone who's mostly good and has the bad under control, okay?"

I was about to stand when two familiar hands reached over the edge of the crack. This time, when the silhouette pulled itself out of the crevice and sat next to me, I wasn't afraid.

"Thank you," I said again. Then, "I might still have some of your magic left, but I'm not sure. If you want it back, you can have it. It came in handy."

The figure placed its hand over mine, and I very clearly heard a new voice in my head, one that didn't belong to me or to Bird. *YOU DON'T THINK YOU USED IT ALL, DO YOU? THAT WAS A SMALL BUT*

IMPORTANT THING YOU DID. YOU HAVE PLENTY LEFT.

If I had been sitting in a chair, I would have fallen out of it. I hadn't thought there was much left that even *could* surprise me, but I'd been wrong. The voice of the Radix was low and not loud, but it still managed to come from everywhere at once. Even from inside me.

I took a deep, only slightly shaky breath. Now that I could talk to the Radix, and it could talk back, I wasn't sure what to say. "Do you want it back? What's left, I mean?"

KEEP IT. YOU USED IT WELL. BESIDES, WE HAVE MORE THAN ENOUGH.

I swear there was a smile in that voice. I was pretty sure I was being given a gift, but I also knew what that same stuff had done to Portia. Or what wanting more of it had made her do. I'd have to be careful to figure out what strings might have been attached to this present.

"Can I ask you something?"

OF COURSE. THERE IS MUCH WE KNOW, SO WE LIKELY HAVE AN ANSWER.

I took a deep breath. "The pendant, the one Portia wore? I know it's how she called the doors. And I know she got all her magic from you. So can you tell me how to use it? *Can* I use it? I want to get home. They need to go home too." I nodded toward the Lark Tree and the ghosts waiting beneath it.

CONSIDER IT A PARTING GIFT. THOUGH WE EXPECT WE WILL SEE YOU AGAIN. AS FOR THE PENDANT, JUST ASK IT. POLITELY. AND BE VERY CLEAR ABOUT WHERE IT IS YOU WANT TO GO.

"Thank you." I didn't know what else to say (because what else *can* you say to an infinite, endlessly powerful being?).

YOU ARE VERY WELCOME, EVELYN VON RATHE.

The figure released my hand and slipped back into the dark crevice below.

I had never told the Radix my name, but it wasn't terribly surprising that it knew it anyway. It seemed to know a lot.

Then another question occurred to me. An important one.

"Have you seen my parents?" I called.

There was no response. I waited a short while just in case, but an answer never came.

At the Lark Tree, the ghosts waited patiently. Some stood in pairs or trios, talking softly among themselves. Others stood off a bit from the group, like they weren't quite done processing all that had happened to them and needed some personal space.

Florence gave me another concerned look as I approached them.

"I'm really okay," I said. "And I know how to get us home. I just have one thing left to do." I actually wasn't very okay. In truth, I was as terrified as I'd been when I'd found the tiny Aunt Des doll in that awful cellar and realized I was the only one who could fix her.

I went to the base of the small golden tree and called, "Clyde? Buddy? Are you still there?" I fought to make my voice smooth for the sake of my ghost audience.

I felt dozens of otherworldly eyes on me, curious to see what I was up to. Quick as a wink, the fuzzy grey ghost spider climbed down a thread that was invisible in the starlight. I offered him my palm and he climbed onto it.

I stroked his back with one fingertip. "Good job, Clyde. Good spider."

Clyde purred. I swear he did.

"Can you show me where the flower is?"

Clyde nodded.

Your mother's glasses might be useful, Bird suggested. It was a good point.

I put the violet glasses on, and when I did, the night didn't go away. Instead it became . . . more. More stars in the sky and more colors in the stars. The moon glowed, and so did the Lark Tree. A green-gold aura surrounded the whole thing.

Tears sprang to my eyes. Lark was still in there. She was still okay, still Lark.

I watched as Clyde made his way back up the thread and over to the flower. But the truth was, I didn't need him to find it. The flower I'd placed in Lark's palm glittered and gleamed in the night. Magic radiated from it. A good kind of magic.

I stood on my toes as tall as I could, grabbed ahold of the branch it was on, and gently pulled the flower toward me. When I had my fingers on it, I said, "I take it back," and plucked the flower from the tree.

The effect was immediate and spectacular. I hadn't realized how close Shirley and Ursula had drawn to me until Shirley reached out and grasped my arm. I turned to her in surprise and found a look of wonder on her face. I couldn't blame her. It was pretty incredible.

The flowers and leaves released themselves from the tree and rained down on me and the ghosts. I felt them brush my skin and catch in my hair. The bark peeled away and became nothing more than papier-mâché. First the smallest branches, then the larger rolled up and fell to the ground. Finally the trunk unraveled, and when it did, my friend was standing right where I'd left her.

"Lark!" I threw my arms around the blinking and somewhat dazed-looking ghost. My heart swelled against my rib cage, and I blinked away the tears that tickled my eyes.

"Back already?" she asked, like no time at all had passed for her (and maybe it hadn't). "And did you—"

"Yeah," I interrupted. "It's done."

Lark looked around at the crowd of ghosts watching us. I wondered if she'd lived in Blight Harbor at the same time as any of them (other than Florence, of course). Or if any of them were already ghosts when she was alive. I wondered how many she knew or at least recognized. And I wondered if she felt overwhelmed. It was more people than she'd seen in a very long time.

"I have something for you," I said, reaching into my backpack. Her soul glowed bright as ever and it spun around inside the jar faster than usual, like it was excited to be going home. A number of the ghosts came closer. They knew what was coming (it had happened to them only a little while earlier) and probably wanted to see the sort-of miracle for themselves. One especially serious-seeming man in overalls wore a smile so big, it made him look like an excited kid.

"Oh," was all Lark said. But there was so much relief and gratitude in that word, it made me want to cry.

"Open it," I said. "It should be with you."

I held the jar, and then it was in Lark's hands, which shook as she opened it. The soul sprang out and went straight for my friend. This time, the magic looked more like an embrace than anything else.

When it was over, Lark nearly tackled me. She hugged me almost as hard as Florence had, but minus the anger.

"How did you do it? And is she . . ." Lark unwrapped my silver chain from her wrist and handed it to me as she spoke.

"Gone," I confirmed, putting the necklace back on. It felt good to have it back around my neck. "Portia is gone. And I'll tell you all about it when we get home. But first, there's someone I want you to see."

I took Lark by the hand and led her to Florence.

"Lark, you remember Miss Dwyer. And Florence, I doubt you could forget Lark."

Florence took Lark's face in her hands and stared at it. They were both crying when Florence wrapped her arms around my friend and kissed her on the top of the head.

I gave them a minute, but not much longer. "It's time for us to go home," I said. I pulled the pendant out of my jeans pocket and held it tight, praying the magic was as simple as the Radix had made it sound.

I closed my eyes. If this one last thing didn't work, if I couldn't get us all home, everything leading up to this moment might have been for nothing at all.

"We need a door, please," I said. Then I remembered to be specific. "We need a door that will take us to the Old School in Blight Harbor. A regular-sized door would be nice. Thank you."

Lark gasped, and I opened my eyes. A door stood no more than five feet away. It was a soft, honeyed brown color, with silver hinges and an ornate silver handle. When I touched the door, warmth like spring sunshine radiated from the wood.

I opened the door and saw a familiar classroom.

"Let's go," I said. "I'm last."

I was the last one through. After I stepped into the classroom, I turned to the door and said, "Thank you. We're all here."

It disappeared like it had never been there at all.

The old classroom was just as I'd left it, and I wondered how much time had really passed. Yellow sun streamed through the windows, and the distant sounds of cars passing and children playing filled the air. The ghosts were already making their way out of the building and into the yard beyond. Before joining them, there was one thing I had to do.

I turned to the chalkboard, intending to scrub it clean of Florence's capital R, the warning that she never got to finish. It wasn't needed anymore. The building was perfectly safe. I knew, because I had the door in my pocket.

But the R was already gone. In its place was something else. Something worse:

We Made a Good, Fair Deal Pretty Penny

I hadn't imagined any of it—the photo, the skeleton— it was all real. I thought about the lucky penny I'd found when I first entered the school. It was still in my jeans pocket, but I didn't want to touch it—not even to take it out and throw it away—because now I knew where it had come from.

The Clackity was back.

I grabbed the eraser and attacked the words until they were nothing but dust. As I did, I pictured Clackity skulking through Blight Harbor under the cover of night, through quiet neighborhoods and finally into the Old School, gibbering to itself all the while. I wanted to cry and scream and throw things, but I couldn't, because outside the school, under a blue sky and yellow sun, the ghosts were all waiting. And so were two other people: my aunt Desdemona and a man in a bright orange cap I sort of recognized.

When I saw Des, I burst into giant, ugly tears as the weight of all the responsibility I'd been carrying fell away, while the burden of what I'd just learned came crashing down on me. "I'm sorry," I said as I half stumbled through the schoolhouse door. "I didn't mean to."

Des was there in a flash, her arms wrapped around me. I felt her tears where her face pressed against mine. Or maybe those were my tears. Both, probably.

"Baby, I've been so worried. You never made it to Lily's, and I thought . . . I knew something must have happened." She released our hug but kept her hands on my shoulders. Her eyes were red and wet, and she looked like she hadn't slept in a month.

"A lot," I said. "A lot happened. But I didn't mean to.

I'm so glad I did, because—" I broke away and waved my hand toward the crowd of ghosts watching us. "But I didn't mean to."

"I know, sweet girl. I believe you. We need to get you home. You too, little guy," Des petted Bird softly, and he fluffed up under her touch. "You can tell me all about it when you're ready."

"How did you know I was here?" I asked.

"Irv," she said, pointing to the vaguely familiar man in the bright orange cap. "He found your bike. We put the pieces together and figured you must have ended up going through a door." Des didn't bother wiping away the tears running down her face, but she did reach up and wipe away mine.

"I got tricked," I said, still trying to defend myself, even though it seemed I didn't need to.

"I believe you. But we've all been so worried. Lily's beside herself. And I"—D's voice was hoarse—"I didn't know if I'd get to see you again."

This time, *I* was the one who hugged *her*.

"How long this time?" I asked.

"Three days." Des's voice cracked on the last word. I hugged her harder.

When I let Des go, I saw that all the ghosts were still there, waiting for something. Waiting, I realized, for me.

I gestured to them but looked at my aunt. "This is why—"

"I know, baby," she interrupted, smiling through her tears. She turned to them. "It's good to have you back, friends."

Most of the ghosts responded with a nod or a wave or a smile of their own.

Then, one by one, they approached me. Each shook my hand or touched my face or gave me some other little gesture of thanks before leaving. Some just nodded, but I understood.

At the end, only four ghosts remained.

Shirley and Ursula came up to me together. Shirley bear-hugged me, and Ursula squeezed my shoulder.

"See you at the movies?" I asked.

They both smiled and nodded, Shirley crying just a little.

Then it was just Florence and Lark.

"Hey, Von Rathe. Can you still hear me?" Lark's words were playful, but her tone was heavy with hope.

"I can!" I smiled as best I could and hugged my friend. And she *was* my friend. With Clackity back, she would be one more person to lean on, but also, one more person to protect. "Thank goodness you're a strange ghost."

"The strangest," she agreed.

I took Lark's hand and half dragged her to meet Desdemona. "Aunt Des, this is Lark McCreary. We need to take her home. Florence, too. Then us, okay?"

Des looked at Lark carefully. "Lark McCreary? Oh honey, there are some people who are going to be so very glad to meet you."

Florence joined us on the walk to Lark's family's house. The two ghosts held hands and talked the whole way, though I could only hear Lark's side of the conversation.

When we got to the McCreary house, I was nominated to ring the doorbell. Lark stood behind me, as nervous as I'd ever seen her.

"What if they don't like me?" she asked in a small voice.

"They'll love you," I said.

"But, Evie, what if they don't?" I could hear real worry in her tone.

"They will. But if I'm wrong, you can move in with me and Des. Either way, you've got a family, okay?"

Lark nodded.

I rang the doorbell. Chief Mary answered. She was in leggings and a sweater. It was definitely not a workday for her.

"Evie!" she yelled, grabbing my shoulders with strong hands as she held me at arm's length to look me up and down. "We've looked everywhere. Did anyone hurt you? Are you okay?"

I was honest. "Yes and yes, but I'm all right. That's not why I'm here. There's someone you need to meet." I stepped aside so that Chief Mary could see Lark, who was still tucked behind me like a shadow. Clyde peeked out of her pocket, and I hoped the McCreary family didn't mind spiders. Even if they did, Clyde would grow on them in no time.

Chief Mary stared at Lark for a long time. I could see the wheels spinning behind her eyes.

"Auntie Loretta?" Chief Mary said in a whisper.

"Lark, please. And, yeah. I guess so."

Chief Mary didn't just hug Lark; she picked her up so her feet dangled a foot off the ground. "We've been looking for you for a long, long time."

Lark didn't answer. I could see her shoulders shaking, and I knew she was crying. When the older woman set Lark back down, they were both wiping at their eyes.

"I don't know why I can hear you, or how you got home, but I want to hear every word. There are folks for you to meet and some others we'll have to call. Everyone, I mean *everyone*, will be so very happy to have you back."

"So I can stay?" asked Lark. I could tell it took a lot for her to ask the question.

"Can you stay? Of course you can stay! You have to. You're family."

Lark turned to me and grabbed my hand. "Thank you, Evie. Truly. You and Mae . . . you're a whole lot alike. I'll see you soon?" she asked.

"Very," I said, and squeezed her hand before letting go.

"Evelyn, whatever it was you did, you likely should not have done it." Chief Mary was using her official voice now. Then it softened. "But I'm so *very* glad you did. Thank you."

I thought about the tiny finger bone I had in my backpack and how, if Lark ever decided to move on, we'd be able to give her a proper burial. I was willing to bet that that time—if it ever came—was a long way off. Besides, it didn't seem to be the right moment to think about good-byes.

Chief Mary waved at Des and Irv—who I'd forgotten about again—and walked Lark into her new home. The door closed softly behind them.

I turned to Florence. "You next."

When Mr. Seong opened the door to find Florence

there, his kind eyes filled with tears. "Florence, I'm so glad you're home," he said simply. He held the door open for her.

Before she entered, Florence gave me a hug. She put her hand on the side of my face and looked into my eyes for a long moment.

"You're welcome," I said. "I'll see you soon."

Irv walked with us when we went back to the school to get Des's car. When Aunt Des got behind the wheel to turn on the air conditioner, Irv pulled me aside.

"What you did," he said, "was very brave. There are some of us in this world, not many, who are willing to risk everything to help others. We sacrifice what we love, sometimes even who we are, because it's the right thing to do. If you are one of those people, and I think you are, then you need to trust yourself to know what is worth sacrificing for and how much you're willing to give. No one else gets to decide that for you. Does that make sense?"

It did. Sort of. But it was also kind of weird that this man I hardly knew felt like this was the right time to give me that particular speech. I tried to look him in the eyes when I responded, but the way his face wouldn't stay put in my mind was giving me a headache. So I looked down when I said, "Yeah. I think so."

"Good. It's important." Then he waved and tipped his cap to Des and was gone, strolling away from the school toward who knew where.

Suddenly I remembered something. "Irv," I called.

He paused and turned to face me.

"Lily gave me your pin. Do you want it back?"

He shook his head. "You earned it. Hang on to it—it might come in handy."

"Uh, thanks," I called. *Weird,* I thought. Which was when I realized that Irv had already replaced the shiny black circle pin Lily'd given me with a copy that was now firmly attached to his orange cap.

"There aren't many of us," he said before turning away, "who've seen that black sun and returned to tell about it."

I stared after him as he went, wondering how many others there were in our weird little club of people who'd come back. It was a question for another time, and I hoped I'd recognize Irv soon so I could ask him.

I climbed into the car, and Des leaned over to hug me again.

"Baby, let's go home. Lily has been panic baking for three days straight, and there's more shortbread in our kitchen than we can possibly eat. How about a cookie and some iced tea, and you can tell me all about everything? And we'll call Lily to let her know. She'll be furious if we don't."

That all sounded perfect, and I told Des so. What I didn't tell her was that I wanted her home and safe.

"And sweet girl, one more thing. This is where you promise me you'll never go through another door by yourself again if you can help it."

I nodded because I was supposed to, but I wasn't so sure anymore that my aunt could protect me from everything, no matter how hard she tried or how badly she wanted to.

"I need to hear you say it," Des pressed.

I didn't think my aunt noticed, but I hesitated. "I promise."

Des nodded, content. We never lied to each other, me and Des.

Except . . .

Except that was the first time I ever made a promise to my aunt that I fully intended to break.

We drove home. Des talked a mile a minute about how glad she was to have me back, how much she had missed me, and just how many baked goods there really were stacked up in our kitchen. Apparently, there were a lot.

I half listened, but mostly I thought. I thought about breaking promises and the odd speech what's-his-name had just given me and what The Clackity could possibly have been up to and how soon I could go back to the Dark Sun Side so I could finally find my parents.

Mostly, I thought about the inscription my mom had left in my book. The inscription meant only for me.

Beautiful girl,
if you've found this, you can find us.
Love you forever.
Mom

ACKNOWLEDGMENTS

To my young readers—I'm going to thank a bunch of people over the next couple pages, but it's *you* I appreciate the most. I cannot imagine a bigger honor than sharing my stories with you. All the love you've given to me and my words since *The Clackity* came out has truly been the highlight of this whole author thing—I save every picture and note and letter I get. Adults are (mostly) great and all, but I wrote *The Nighthouse Keeper* with you in mind. Evie and Lark and Bird and Clyde are for you, and I can't wait to tell you what happens next.

To my incredible editor, Julia McCarthy—I didn't have to tell you there was more to Evie's story. You already knew. I will forever appreciate you for advocating for our scared-but-brave girl and her strange world, for helping her continue her journey and find her readers. The words in these books are endlessly better because you gave your wonderful brain and huge, huge heart to them. Thank you, always.

To my fabulous agent, Ali Herring—I never lost faith in Evie or Blight Harbor, but I did lose faith in myself. You helped me find it again. When I doubted my words, you told me, "You've done it. Just finish it." This book would still just be a nearly finished manuscript collecting proverbial dust if you hadn't given me the confidence to complete it. I cannot imagine a better partner to be with on this path (even if it is sometimes surrounded by carnivorous trees). Thank you, my friend.

To the kind and brilliant Alfredo Cáceres—somehow, you've done it again. This book is every bit as beautiful as the last one, and that's because of you. I cannot imagine anyone else bringing Evie and her friends (and foes) to life. Blight Harbor is as much yours as it is mine, and I'm so honored to share it with you.

To the amazing team at Atheneum/Simon & Schuster—stories don't become books without a lot of help and hard work from talented and tireless (not really—we're all exhausted) humans. All my gratitude to Karyn Lee, Anum Shafqat, Nicole Valdez, Thad Whittier, Jeannie Ng, Valerie Shea, Elizabeth Blake-Linn, Irene Metaxatos, Amanda Brenner, Erin Toller, Reka Simonsen, and Justin Chanda for helping the Blight Harbor books find their way into the world.

To the librarians and teachers and booksellers and parents and grown-ups who put books into children's hands—what is there to say but thank you? You ensure kids have access to the stories they want and need in a world that doesn't always make it simple or easy to do so. You have all my admiration and appreciation.

To my early readers—Darlene Shinskie, Anna Gamble, Georgia Oswald, Paula Gleeson, Kellie McQueen, and Jessica Conoley—thank you for holding my hand and reading my words when they were still messy and raw and probably misspelled. I love you a lot.

To all my readers—you could be reading anything, and you chose to give your time and attention to this story. You have all my gratitude always for reading and sharing and talking about the Blight Harbor books. I am the most fortunate person in publishing to be able to write these books and have you read them. I appreciate you so very much.

To my parents, Tom and Darlene Shinskie—knowing you're reading these books means more to me than I can ever possibly say. You told eight-year-old me I could do this. Thank you for believing in her (and me). I love you.

To my family—Martin, Miriam, and Pete—this all means so much more because I have the three of you to share it with. I write *for* my readers, but I do it *because* of you. Thank you for being my people. I love you forever.